HARVEST OF SCORN

F.G. Cottam is the award-winning novelist responsible for eleven paranormally themed thrillers including *The House of Lost Souls*, *The Lazarus Prophecy* and *The Waiting Room*.

His stories are atmospheric, coloured by an encyclopaedic knowledge of history and folkloric myth and propelled by relentless action. His books have been translated into 16 languages and his most recently completed project is his *Colony* trilogy, inspired by the present-day repercussions of an occult curse inflicted in revenge by a dying sorcerer.

F.G. Cottam was born and brought up in Southport in Lancashire, attending the University of Kent at Canterbury where he took a degree in history before embarking on a career in journalism in London. He now lives in Kingston upon Thames and his fiction is thought up over daily runs along the towpath between Kingston and Hampton Court Bridges.

If you'd like to hear more from F.G. Cottam, follow him on Twitter, @fgcottam, connect with him on Facebook or check out his Goodreads page.

ALSO BY F.G. COTTAM

Dark Resurrection: A Colony Novel
The Going and the Rise
An Absence of Natural Light
The Lazarus Prophecy
The Summoning
The Memory of Trees
The Colony
Brodmaw Bay
The Waiting Room
The Magdalena Curse
Dark Echo
The House of Lost Souls

HARVEST OF SCORN

F.G. COTTAM

ipso books

This edition published in 2016 by Ipso Books

Ipso Books is a division of Peters Fraser + Dunlop Ltd

Drury House, 34–43 Russell Street, London WC2B 5HA

Copyright © F.G. Cottam, 2016

All rights reserved

You may not copy, distribute, transmit, reproduce or otherwise make available this publication (or any part of it) in any form, or by any means (including without limitation electronic, digital, optical, mechanical, photocopying, printing, recording or otherwise), without the prior written permission of the publisher. Any person who does any unauthorised act in relation to this publication may be liable to criminal prosecution and civil claims for damages.

Contents

Chapter One	1
Chapter Two	19
Chapter Three	35
Chapter Four	53
Chapter Five	70
Chapter Six	86
Chapter Seven	102
Chapter Eight	117
Chapter Nine	134
Chapter Ten	147
Chapter Eleven	165
Chapter Twelve	178
Chapter Thirteen	193
Chapter Fourteen	212
Chapter Fifteen	227
Chapter Sixteen	238
Chapter Seventeen	249
Chapter Eighteen	261

Chapter One

In his rare episodes of what he'd have dismissed as navel-gazing, Greg Cody thought of himself as an unimaginative man, hardly ever given to flights of fancy. He was clear-headed and pragmatic, orderly and precise. He was one of those men who didn't so much submit to routine as impose it whenever disorder confronted him. His work was shore-bound, but in one of the clichés he was fondest of, he ran a tight ship. He thought this probably as often said of him as he said it of himself. It was the trait to which he owed his livelihood and the one that would shortly play a decisive part in killing him.

The project he was working on was less straightforward than really suited Greg. It was nowhere near as mundane as he would have liked it to be. It was something routinely described as visionary. To its investors, both public and private, it had been sold as a new age sanctuary, cultural hub and white-knuckle adventure park rolled into one. 'Disneyland with a good university degree', someone had apparently called it at one of the board's meetings, and the story was that the more macho of the suits present had hammered their fists on the table they sat around in excited appreciation of the pitch.

Cody tended to see only the challenges. There was the physical isolation of the island. There was the unpredictability of the volatile weather in the Outer Hebrides. There was the fact that the old colony settlement at the island's rough heart had recently been declared a World Heritage Site. That meant going there without official sanction was not only trespassing but potentially an act of vandalism. It was one more concern to factor in when they opened up and the paying guests finally began to arrive in their substantial numbers.

Right now, he thought that date, five full months hence on their schedule, almost impossibly remote. Most of the infrastructure was already in place. But January wasn't June and the island had about it a persistent, desolate bleakness Cody thought of almost as a tangible affliction, especially during its long and sometimes pitch-black nights. New Hope was not welcoming in this hostile season. It was the last place anyone would consider hospitable. Its name in his mind had degenerated from misnomer to bad joke. Degree or no degree, Disneyland in its winter mood, it very definitely wasn't.

Cody wasn't someone generally given either to nervousness or to speculative thought but had discovered New Hope to be a place that provoked both in him. He felt alone there, which he was most of the time, but also constantly observed. This was an unhappy contradiction. Worse than unhappy, it was actually quite weird. It pulled and teased at the senses, sort of fraying them, making the island's sights and sounds seem somehow threatening. It had compelled him after enduring it for a while to research the history of the place during a week's home leave and doing that hadn't provided him with any comfort at all.

The truth was that despite the natural obstacles of his character and will, the island had really got to him. It had done so to the point where he was now counting the days until the boat came to take him off. He was looking forward to the banter of the pub, to the cheery bustle of a pizza house, to the solid, unambiguous comforts of the suburban home he shared with his wife. A growing part of him craved double-glazing and double-locks, central heating and a burglar alarm, the security light bought one Saturday from Homebase that he'd positioned above their porch and most of all, the intimate touch of his wife's sleeping body spooned against his own in the night.

At least, Cody was looking forward to those things when he had the time for reflection. He didn't have that now, though. He'd awoken to a noise he'd heard in his sleep and couldn't consciously remember, with a feeling only of empty dread and the suspicion that something or someone lurked and prowled beyond the canvas and steel compound he was quartered in. It was an interloper, he feared, a presence unwelcome there and surely up to no good. Bird watchers and nature-trailers didn't steal ashore in the small hours. He came-to suddenly, gloomily sure an innocent intrusion hadn't awoken him.

They were at the island's southern extremity. They were sited on the slope above where New Hope's only recent habitation stood. That was a crofter's cottage, deserted now and though structurally sound, empty and therefore derelict.

No one else in the compound stirred.

He wasn't its only resident. Somewhere on the island, three members of their six-strong security team would be patrolling. The other three, their day-shift, were asleep. Like the four-man maintenance crew, they were right now bunked cozily down in their huts. So he had seven other men onsite for company. But when he looked at his watch it was just after three in the morning. With no switching on of lights or rising hum of human voices, the complete lack of commotion told Cody he was the only person there at that moment awake and aware.

Oh, and of course if he was doing a proper New Hope inventory, there was Helena Davenport. She was their distinguished architect from the Glasgow-based practice of Davenport Associates. But she was comfy and secure in the residential complex they'd constructed at the other end of the island. She was domiciled in one of the suites they'd been too tastefully shrewd to describe as their first-class accommodation, though that's what it most emphatically was. She was over there right now, her mission to make sure everything was going to run like clockwork for their most privileged guests when they opened up. At 3am though, five months pre-season, she'd be soundly asleep on the plush mattress of her suite's king-size bed.

Greg Cody could yawn and scratch and bury his head under his pillow. Except that he couldn't really do that, because he was where the buck stopped. He was site manager, a fact reflected in his pay grade. He could bollock the security blokes when the time came for their negligence, but ultimately site integrity was his responsibility. And he was too unnerved anyway to try to go back to sleep. He knew he wouldn't be able to do that.

He got out of his camp bed and went over to his single window. The sky was cloudy and the light very limited in his view of the velvet sea and inky sky spread endlessly above it. As his eyes adjusted, he could just make out the white-washed shape of the cottage, dirty and indistinct looking 500 metres away in the darkness. And as he looked he thought he saw movement outside it, something or someone stumbling or scurrying, just an indeterminate shape but animate, moving, uninvited there. A trespasser.

Greg didn't know quite how to react. The feeling of dread he'd awoken with changed in him, morphing into indignation at the suspicion that someone was squatting on the island, maybe hoping to pilfer their supplies or steal plant or take materials to sell on as scrap metal. He didn't know whether fishermen were particularly light-fingered, but he knew that the fishing quotas made their living harder these days than it had ever been for their fathers and grandfathers. And he knew that on a calm night, this part of New Hope's coastline was easily approached clandestinely by boat. There were no reefs. There was no heavy surf.

He quickly got dressed. He had a big Maglite torch of the sort that was used by the police where Maglites were made, in America, and often doubled as a club. He hefted it and took it with him, but he didn't switch it on because he didn't want its powerful beam to give his intruder sufficient warning to be able to bolt. He thought he knew the island's topography well enough to catch anyone blundering away from him blindly and he kept pretty fit. But he didn't want to work any harder on his own time than he needed to.

He was confident of his physicality, his fighting prowess, should any confrontation now occur. Tasty, had been the word used about him in his younger, single, more tempestuous days. He'd had then what the jargon now defined as anger issues. He'd always been a big lad for his age and he'd needed to let off steam and he'd done it at the dojo; grappling and punching and kicking his way through years of judo and jujitsu and full-contact karate. Mixed martial-arts, they called it nowadays. The terminology didn't matter much and he wasn't itching for a scrap. Still, he thought, it was nice to have all that stuff in the tank. Push might yet come to shove. And it was reassuring to heft the weight of the Maglite he'd armed himself with.

There was no sound coming from his destination and the cottage as he got nearer to it was not only silent, but entirely still. His own footsteps were quiet, he was sure of the ground, but it was impossible to be completely noiseless on loose shale and then the scatters of shingle flung there by the waves of the island's frequent violent winter storms.

The entrance to the cottage, its single door, faced the sea. He shivered. The wind was a stinging, briny assault this close to the water. It pricked at the naked skin of his face. He thought about the man who'd rebuilt the cottage, if the story was true a senior Metropolitan Police officer on some sort of sabbatical. Apparently he'd stuck it out there for six months.

Cody reckoned that was one copper with steel nerves, iron balls and even less imagination than he claimed to possess. The story ran that the Met Commander had been recovering from the grief inflicted by his wife's death. She must have been a very special woman, Cody thought, not for the first time. The cottage grew larger and more detailed with his approach, though no less still or silent, his vigilant eyes and ears alert to any sound at all beyond the expected.

He stopped. He could hear something unexpected, suddenly. He could hear something curious. It was a coarse and rhythmic sound and it rattled like the bellows-wheeze of laboured breathing. Because he'd stopped, the sound of his approach had stopped and then the breathing noise stopped too, as if in response to his own halted progress. Greg Cody didn't like that. It suggested a degree of cunning and it hinted at a trap. He listened, strained listening, concentrated, fully alert now and unsurprisingly tense. He raised the torch in his right hand and felt it tremble slightly, slick in a palm sweating despite the cold as he switched it on.

The beam was powerful and it washed the cottage door and doorframe in a white circle of light and Cody thought he heard a scuttling sound from within, as though startled and cowering. This emboldened him. Whatever skulked hiding inside that one-room shelter was more scared than scary, this new sound told him. His rigid muscles relaxed and he moved forward. He was at the cottage entrance in four or five determined strides and booted open its wooden door with a juddering crash. He played the torch on the building's interior. The blackness before him resolved into something crouched stilly against the far wall and he dropped the torch with a metallic clatter onto the stone-flagged floor and screamed.

The scream was loud but swiftly stifled. In spite of its size, the thing confronting Greg Cody was inhumanly quick to pounce.

Felix Baxter gathered himself before punching the number into his phone. You didn't cold-call a Metropolitan Police Commander without due consideration. It was 9am on Saturday, six hours since his people on New Hope had been awoken by a scream and discovered that their site-manager had disappeared.

Or so they said.

It was a worry. Five months before its official opening, his New Hope Experience didn't need any bad publicity or damaging speculation or raking up of a history that could be picaresque and intriguing or brutal and terrifying, depending entirely on one's perspective concerning the place.

The man to whom he was about to speak was arguably the world authority on New Hope Island. Commander Patrick Lassiter had been on the expedition seven years ago to try to discover what had happened to the island's original colony, the 140 settlers who vanished without trace from there in the first half of the 19th century. Then 18 months or so ago, for reasons that were still obscure, he'd apparently felt obliged to go back there. That episode had been followed by an island sabbatical of six months. Lassiter had spent a season of grief restoring the cottage ruin built there in the 1930s by the celebrated bohemian and sometimes crofter, David Shanks.

He'd departed the island before the ground had been broken on the complex site at the heart of Baxter's New Hope Experience. He hadn't witnessed a minute of their inspired industry since. But if anyone had a handle on the history and mystery of the place, it was Lassiter.

'Sorry to call you so early and at the weekend, Commander,' Baxter said, after introducing himself. 'I'm –'

'I know who and what you are, Mr. Baxter. And I know too about your lost man. Western Islands Area Command called me an hour ago to inform me of Greg Cody's disappearance and to discuss generally the island's inherent hazards.'

'A disorientating sea fret, the wash from a supertanker?'

'That kind of thing.'

'I'm speculating on foul play,' Baxter said. 'He didn't know it, but Greg Cody's nickname among the crew was Captain Sensible. Pardon my French, but to a man they thought him a pompous prick.'

'You didn't think to replace someone so unpopular?'

'It's a balancing act, morale versus efficiencies. He's always been well organized and conscientious. He's always been too good to lose.'

'You seem to have lost him now.'

'Unless he's not been lost but actually deliberately dispensed with.'

'The mood can turn mutinous among men working in close confinement in an isolated place,' Lassiter said. 'The odd fistfight wouldn't be a surprise. Anyone can snap. But those Scottish coppers are shrewd and thorough and violent crime is messy. I'm told Cody was a tough bloke on his own account and none of his crew has a notable criminal profile or so much as an incriminating bruise.'

'Using the past tense about him sounds a bit ominous.'

'It sounds pragmatic to me.'

'The other alternatives are an accident or suicide.'

'You're entirely free to speculate, Mr. Baxter.'

'What does that mean?'

'The island's got form.'

'You think it suspicious?'

'The weather was benign, Mr. Baxter. It must have been for the radio transmitter to function when your people there called it in and for Area Command to get men on the island so quickly afterwards. I don't think Captain Sensible was swept out to sea in a storm when there wasn't a storm to do the sweeping.'

So Cody's disappearance was a mystery. Felix Baxter didn't mind historical mysteries. They helped endow a place with character and atmosphere. They were a positive because they hinted at cultural pedigree and thus could actually become a selling point. Properly manipulated they drew the punters. But this was a mystery intruding rudely into the present and Baxter wasn't at all partial to those.

He asked Lassiter outright, 'Do you think the island dangerous?'

Lassiter hesitated before replying. Then he said, 'It's an inherently dangerous place. But I was left alone there.'

I was left alone there.

'You haven't asked me how I got your private number, Commander.'

'You're the engine driving the New Hope Experience. The Experience plans to bring a lot of money and prestige to the Hebrides. Consequently you're the blue-eyed boy among some serious Scots politicians unscrupulous enough to lean on the police there to get that kind of information.'

'I don't have a Scots politician in my pocket.'

'No, Mr. Baxter, your suits are far too well cut to accommodate the bulge.'

'You don't think we'll find Cody?'

'No.'

'The thing is, I really don't like loose ends.'

'Which is why you'd like foul play and an arrest and prosecution. You'd settle fort suicide, which is a bit sombre but neatly emphatic. A fatal accident suggests the place might be prone to them, which isn't ideal. But even that's better than the enigma you've got.'

'Thanks for your time, Commander. It's genuinely appreciated.'

'I'm sure.'

Thanks for nothing, Baxter thought.

Ruthie Gillespie and Phil Fortescue very rarely talked about New Hope. He didn't dwell on the subject, she supposed, because he didn't want grief to become the defining characteristic of his ongoing existence. She didn't mention it partly through sensitivity to that but mostly because she was quite a modest person. The idea of being a decisive woman of action, which she'd had to be when she'd gone to the island, seemed 18 months on absurd to her. And she didn't want to be Phil's saviour, she wanted to be his equal and partner in the ongoing romance they were sharing.

But the island was so much in the news, it was becoming hard to ignore. And there were persistent hazards there, or there were according to Patrick Lassiter, a man who'd spent a season of despair and recuperation from his own loss on New Hope and had come away from the place genuinely afraid for anyone who might follow in his bereft and lonely footsteps. Patsy had been vague about the nature of those hazards. At least, he had whenever he'd mentioned the place to Ruthie since his return from there.

Now Patsy Lassiter had called Phil. He'd done so that morning, quite early for a Saturday. And Phil was refusing to disclose any detail about the call. This was uncharacteristic in so open a man and was provoking some tension between them. They only had their weekends together and Ruthie thought any part of the weekend spent unhappy a waste of their valuable shared time.

'You'll tell me eventually,' she said.

'Curiosity killed the cat,' he said.

'They had their big hit when I was four, so they don't actually mean much to me.'

He smiled. He said, 'I was fourteen. I thought they were very cool. I wanted a beret like their singer wore but it would have been suicide in my part of Liverpool back in 1987.'

Ruthie smiled back, despite herself. They were at her cottage in Ventnor and it was chilly and raining. She thought that to a man with a flat in London, Wight must seem a bleak place in the cold and damp so far out of season. That said, Wight held a lot more allure than New Hope ever had. She'd lit her wood burner. It was a recent, extravagant acquisition. She'd told herself the money she'd save quitting smoking would pay for it. That was still, sadly, a theoretical bit of economic reasoning.

'Patsy Lassiter calls you on a Saturday morning. He doesn't do that to ask for help with a crossword clue, or for fashion advice or to share a recipe. Whatever he says, it has you hopping off into the garden to carry on the conversation.'

'I don't hop.'

'Despite the cold and the rain, for privacy, so the woman whose guest you are, whose bed you're sharing, can't eavesdrop. That's charming, Phil.'

'Sarcasm doesn't suit you.'

'Stop provoking it then. Tell me what Patsy wanted.'

Fortescue took a breath. He stared at the flames flickering orange through the glass of the wood burner. Ruthie generally thought the dimensions of her home well proportioned. Conflict though made it feel suddenly cramped. She thought that perhaps she wouldn't persist with this. She was naturally curious, but people were entitled to a bit of confidentiality, even when you were intimate with them. It was an aspect of the trust you shared. Or at least it was supposed to be.

Fortescue said, 'Patsy took a call from Felix Baxter early this morning.'

'The New Age mastermind who dreamed up the New Hope Island Experience?'

'I think he's more entrepreneur than visionary, Ruthie. The language around the project is pretty airy-fairy, but the motive is profit, pure and simple.'

'Why'd he call Patsy?'

'One of his people has gone missing there.'

'Patsy Lassiter's hardly in the frame for that. He's been back living in Maida Vale for months.'

'The missing man's the site manager,' Fortescue said. 'There's only a skeleton crew on the island because most of the infrastructure's ready, apparently. They open on May 1 and they're fully booked for the entire season until the end of September.'

'Shame we won't be going,' Ruthie said.

'Sarcasm really doesn't suit you.'

She wanted a cigarette. She wanted a drink. She looked at her watch. It was much too early, with Phil there, even for white wine. Phil discriminated against white wine on the grounds that it contained alcohol. You had to tolerate peoples' eccentricities, if you loved them, so Ruthie did, but not always happily.

'There were seven other people present at their compound when a bloke named Greg Cody vanished. In the small hours, they were awoken by a scream. They found Cody's camp bed empty and a Maglite torch inside the crofter's cottage. Their compound's at the southern apex of the island, so close to the cottage. Cody's bed was still warm but there was no trace of him.'

'I don't understand what this has to do with Patsy,' Ruthie said.

Fortescue said, 'Patsy was still on the island until a fortnight before the Baxter project began. Of anyone living, he's the authority on the place. Western Isles Area Police Command were told about the disappearance straight away and so were the coastguard. Baxter wanted to know, based on his experience of New Hope, whether Patsy could float any theories.'

'Did he?'

Fortescue bit his lip. He said, 'Look, Ruthie, I wouldn't normally dream of saying this, because it's only eleven o'clock, and you've lit that fire and all, but I think we should take this to the pub.'

'Only if you absolutely insist,' she said.

. They weren't the only people in the Spyglass Inn, which meant that they weren't the first there either. This could have worked on Ruthie as an argument for making up for lost time. She thought that the civilized world would have been a good fit for her inclinations drink-wise in the golden period between the mid-1960s, when women were first lured respectably into pubs, up to the wine-bar boom of the early 1980s, after which matters started becoming generally a bit more health-conscious. Those carefree days and their breezy values weren't returning anytime soon. And they'd played out before her birth. She sipped demurely at a small glass of house white slightly nostalgic for a time she'd never known.

'Why did Patsy call you?'

Phil didn't answer her directly. He said, 'Most people who think about the mystery at all still think the New Hope Island vanishing the world's most spectacular incident of alien abduction. They think the colony founded by Seamus Ballantyne in the 1820s whisked off into space a decade later.'

'But the expedition you and Patsy were part of disproved that.'

'The chronology wasn't quite that clear cut. Neither were the personnel. I wasn't even part of the original expedition. I've been reluctant to discuss it since in any detail, even with you. What's significant is that when Ballantyne was still master of the slave ship Andromeda, well before his epiphany and religious calling, he was doubly cursed.'

'By a witch doctor manacled in his slave hold,' Ruthie said, 'a powerful sorcerer who said Ballantyne's dead daughter would come back to haunt him and a monster would eventually devour him. And all of this was written up in a journal describing the voyage. The ship's physician Thomas Horan wrote it in secret and you rediscovered it and you went to the island and destroyed the monster there.'

'Did I?'

'You thought you had. Seven years ago.'

'Getting on for eight.'

'And now you're not so sure?'

'It's all so bloody vague. You'd think you'd remember something that horrific in better detail.'

Ruthie thought just the opposite true. She thought what had happened to Phil's memory of that event no more than a defence mechanism for a mind seeking escape from something too horrific to dwell upon. 'I'll get us another drink,' she said.

There was no queue at the bar. The other people in the pub were pensioners, people with their lives pretty much behind them. Or at least with the active part of it, their ambitions and achievements, firmly anchored in their past. Their futures were a plodding and predictable matter of routine.

Thinking this made her think of the funding campaign with which Felix Baxter had swamped the internet trying to sell the New Hope Experience to the world when it was still at the concept stage. *Failure of nerve is a dream's greatest obstacle to becoming reality. Achievement is just an ambition in three dimensions. Fulfilment is only ever a dare away from your grasp;* plus many other meaningless platitudes and bits and pieces of pun and motto and alliterative nonsense. It had worked, though. It had done the trick in spectacular style. He'd raised his investment capital and steamed ahead with his project.

She sat back down at their table.

'Cheers,' Phil said, raising his fresh pint of Guinness. He'd made short and thirsty work of his first, which was uncharacteristic. It was out of character for him to drink at all in the daytime.

Ruthie said, 'So here's our scenario. You didn't destroy that thing that devoured people on New Hope. You just discouraged it for a few years. It's licked its wounds and regained its appetite and it's back with a vengeance.'

'I'm not relishing this idea for a sequel,' Phil said. 'It consumes a couple more unfortunate night-watchmen or maintenance staff, maybe a plumber or an electrician and the Western Isles police close the whole thing down. They declare the island too hazardous for human habitation and quarantine the whole God-forsaken rock and Baxter's investors take a hit on what was always a reckless gamble.'

'Why always reckless?'

'Take your pick,' Ruthie said. 'There's the unpredictable weather, the island's remoteness, its sinister reputation, its alarming mortality rate and the fact that there's a demonic spirit there in the guise of a dead child. Is that list not long enough to make the New Hope Experience just a tiny bit foolhardy?'

'There might be a relatively innocent explanation for Cody's disappearance,' Fortescue said.

'And you might be clutching at straws in saying so,' Ruthie said. 'You think that thing is back, that it never really went away. It's why you're halfway through your second pint at 12.30 in the afternoon.'

'It's the weekend,' he said, with a wink.

'You're really worried, aren't you?'

He was silent, staring at his glass. Then he raised his eyes to meet hers. He said, 'That creature wasn't just malevolent and hungry. It was intelligent and sly. Above all, Ruthie, it was real. It took the lives of half the people who went on the expedition. Patsy Lassiter will back me up on that.'

'Did he see it?'

'He was there when the expedition's priest went into the colony settlement's windowless church to confront it. He was there when Monseigneur Degrelle screamed and when I went in after him. He was there when I came back out again afterwards.'

'But he didn't actually see it.'

'I think it might wait. Imagine four or five hundred people on the island in June or July and one of those storms you get there setting in. Imagine them, just families, the island isolated by weather for four or five days, or a week.'

'You think this is really possible.'

'Patsy only settled on New Hope to recover from losing his wife. He told me this morning that he became aware of being watched there.'

'By Rachel Ballantyne,' Ruthie said, 'by Seamus Ballantyne's daughter who died at 10 of diphtheria. That crofter, David Shanks, caught her on cine film in the 1930s. Patsy Lassiter sourced the film in the run up to the expedition. And 18 months ago, you saw her in the flesh.'

'It didn't much resemble flesh. Anyway Patsy didn't think it was Rachel doing the watching when he was rebuilding the Shanks cottage. His watcher wasn't just curious. It was intrigued, hostile and there was something else.'

'What was the something else?'

'He felt as though he was being studied. He thought he was being learned from. He came away from there with the conviction that he was only tolerated because of that. It was the only reason he was left alive.'

'I suppose from Patsy's perspective, being watched is better than being devoured.'

'No argument there.'

'It's a long lifespan, though, almost 200 years.'

'I don't blame you for being skeptical.'

'I've been to New Hope, Phil. You know I have. You were there. So you know I'm not *that* skeptical. What are you going to do?'

'When I first read Horan's journal, my instinct was to find a professor of comparative religions or an anthropologist familiar with the pagan belief system of the slave-sorcerer's tribe. There wasn't time for that then. But I'd like to know what it actually is and the claims made for it mythologically. I'd like to see a picture of one, if such a thing has ever been drawn or painted.'

'More likely carved,' Ruthie said, 'if it's African and tribal. You told me he gave it a name, that Horan wrote it down.'

'He did. He called it, The Being that Hungers in the Darkness.'

Ruthie shivered. She sipped wine. She said, 'Felix Baxter always peddles the theory that aliens abducted Seamus Ballantyne's community.'

'Well he would, wouldn't he,' Fortescue said.

Chapter Two

The money had come from a rich assortment of sources because the New Hope Experience appealed on so many different and rewarding levels. Tourism Scotland had provided funding. The Scottish Arts Council had given a generous grant. There'd been EU development money and lottery cash. Both the Scottish and British Governments had provided funding, not only promising tax breaks but giving the sort of generous official backing to the scheme that naturally encouraged private sector personal and hedge fund investment.

Such had been the level of financial support that the project was still cash-rich after recruiting the executive personnel and building most of the infra-structure, ahead of schedule, right on budget and without any serious setbacks. The weather had been factored into their timetable and there was already talk of the complex building – designed by a Scottish practice, of course – winning architectural awards.

Felix Baxter wasn't going to let all that go down the pan because someone had been careless or inconsiderate enough to disappear. Damage limitation was one of his skills. He hadn't needed it yet on a project thus far blessed by good fortune; but it was there when it needed to be called upon.

Their architect was on the island. She was Helena Davenport, 38 years old, internationally renowned, the chic, multi-lingual darling of her profession and a standard-bearing Scot of whom Scotland was rightfully proud. If she'd been the one to vanish...well, that didn't really bear thinking about. It was a perspective from which Baxter felt quite grateful their fatal casualty had been uncharismatic workhorse nobody Captain Sensible and not his glamorous trophy creative.

The glamour hadn't really been a factor in Helena's selection from his short-list. She'd been as talented as any of the other names there, but her gender had swung it for him. It did a developer no harm to champion feminism in so male-dominated a profession as architecture. It earned positive headlines above sympathetic stories in the liberal press titles. But Helena was voluptuously photogenic in her stylish designer outfits and the glamour, for Baxter, was the icing on the cake.

At noon on Saturday, he put a personal phone call in to Greg Cody's wife. Officially, since no body had been discovered, the man's status was still listed as missing rather than deceased. But if he wasn't on the island, he was in the water. And he definitely wasn't on the island. In the water, at this time of the year, the temperature of the North Atlantic meant that a fit man fully immersed in it had about ten minutes of life left to him. Greg Cody had been fit, but this statistic meant he was emphatically dead. So Baxter to his own mind was actually putting in a call to Captain Sensible's widow.

'May I call you Janet?'

'Yes of course, Mr. Baxter.'

'Felix, please.'

'It's good of you to call yourself, Felix.'

'I wanted to offer you my deepest condolences. They're sincerely meant, so of course I had to offer them myself.'

Her breath hitched. She said, 'You don't think there's any possibility he's alive? He's only been gone nine hours.'

Cody had lived in Epsom in Surrey. There was no reason for his Surrey widow to be an authority on hypothermia. There was no hope on New Hope, but wishful thinking was human nature, another of Baxter's areas of expertise.

He said, 'I've authorized an interim payment. It might sound callous to mention compensation at so early a stage as this, but I want money to be one consideration you know is well taken care of. You've enough anxiety and stress to cope with in your grief.'

There was that hitch in her breathing again; she said, 'Thank you.'

'I know you shared a bank account with your husband. A hundred thousand pounds will be paid into that account this morning. There'll be further sums to follow, of course.'

'You're very kind.'

He knew he could afford to be. Ultimately the bill would be met by his company's insurers.

'I'd ask one favour of you, Janet. And it's for your own sake, to save you unnecessary heartache. It's that you don't speak to the press. They look for the lurid in tragic circumstances such as these. I had a reporter cold-call me first-thing asking was Greg depressed and a possible candidate for suicide. I told him in no uncertain terms that the suspicion was deeply offensive.'

There were two lies in this statement. Baxter hadn't spoken to a reporter. And the protocols he insisted upon anyway made cold-calling him impossible.

His words had the desired effect, however. Janet Cody was sobbing freely on the other end of the line, now. She said, 'Greg has never been depressed for one moment in his entire life. Little things make him happy, DIY, barbecues in the garden.'

It irked Baxter slightly, this stubborn use of the present tense talking about the deceased Captain Sensible. But it was understandable.

'I'll speak to no one, Felix. I swear that.' There was a pause. She said, 'His memory's too precious to have his character dragged through the mud.'

This woman was living proof to Baxter that there was someone for everyone, however lumpen and unlovable. 'Those are my sentiments entirely, my dear,' he said.

'I'm not giving up hope, Felix,' she said. 'He's only been gone nine hours.'

'That's your privilege, Janet,' he said.

Baxter concluded the call, after saying a few more comforting words, quite satisfied. Since the actual details of Cody's death had been successfully fudged, his publicity people could still insinuate suicide if that yet proved to be contingent. At the moment, a tragic accident seemed the interpretation thought least likely to bring unnecessary attention. One death was acceptable in so ambitious a project and they'd planned for a fatality because statistically, on so substantial a build at so challenging a site, it had actually been quite likely.

They couldn't, though, afford another as mysterious as this first had been. It was one thing dealing with the police and coastguard. Fending off inquisitive reporters was much trickier. And the internet meant rumour spread at the speed of light. So far there had been nothing but goodwill in response to their regular announcements, their bulletins and updates on the progress towards the opening of the New Hope Island Experience.

That might change if one of the men it had awoken mentioned his departing scream as the last of Greg Cody. It had roused and no doubt spooked all of them there. But they'd all signed binding confidentiality agreements and he'd only worry about this gruesome detail when he'd have to, if it leaked.

In terms of negative publicity, the death of their site manager wasn't quite a lunatic running amok with an assault rifle at Thorpe Park. But New Hope could be a sombre, daunting location and bad things had happened there before and they'd done so inexplicably. Baxter had rehabilitated the island with great success and wanted desperately for that success to be sustained and built upon. He believed in the dream and wanted it fully realized. He'd do all he could, to see that it was.

He wondered, in the immediate term, whether getting Helena Davenport off New Hope might be a pragmatic move. But she was only scheduled to be there until Monday, for just two more nights.

What's the worst that can happen? He thought.

Edie Chambers had lunch that Saturday with Patsy Lassiter. To her, he was family. She loved Phil Fortescue, her wicked stepfather, and she liked Ruthie Gillespie both as a person and for the happiness their relationship had brought him. She had a special bond too with Patsy. They were the New Hope survivors. There weren't many of them left. She'd suffered a lot of bereavement for someone only 20, not yet graduated from university.

At the age of 14 she'd encountered a ghost. Much of what had happened subsequently had happened as a consequence of that. Her ghost in life had been Jacob Parr, a second-mate aboard Seamus Ballantyne's slave vessel *Andromeda*. Parr had provided the clues that led eventually to her stepfather finding Thomas Horan's journal in a closed shaft at the long abandoned Elsinore Pit in Barnsley.

He hadn't been her stepfather then; he'd just been a kind maritime academic, a stranger prepared to answer an adolescent girl's desperate plea for help.

Now, to Patsy Lassiter, she said, 'I've got the chance to interview Felix Baxter.' Her degree course was journalism, which she was studying at London's City University.

'That's quite a coup,' he said.

'Tell me what you really think.'

'It poses a question, Edie. Does this mean going back to New Hope?'

'You went back. You stayed for six months.'

'My wife died there. I needed the time and the space to reconcile myself. And the privacy, I needed that too.'

'What I mean is you survived the experience. You were left alone.'

'The very phrase I used when I took a call from Felix Baxter this morning. One of his people on the island vanished in the early hours. At 3 o'clock this morning a site foreman named Greg Cody was heard to scream, though Baxter omitted that detail from his account. Cody had vanished. I don't think they'll find him any time soon. I don't think they'll find him at all.'

'So New Hope's dangerous again?'

'It's inherently dangerous and innately hostile and always will be.'

'Yet you rebuilt the crofter's cottage there and stayed for half a year.'

'An experience that answered a need in me,' he said. He looked her in the eye, 'If I'd returned to work in the weeks after Alice's death I'd have started drinking again. I'm certain of that. New Hope was a suitable place for exile, a necessity for me just then. That said, I wouldn't recommend it to anyone of a nervous disposition.'

'I'm not of a nervous disposition, Patsy.'

'It's foolhardy at best for you to go there.'

'Baxter's New Hope Experience brochure makes it look absolutely beautiful,' Edith said.

'Beauty and danger aren't mutually exclusive.' He smiled. 'Often the contrary is true.'

Edie nodded. She knew this. Her feelings about the island were ambivalent. Had her mother not gone on the expedition seven years earlier, she'd never have met the clever detective she was sharing a table with, who had also gone. She'd never have met the stepfather who'd given her mother the happiest years of her too short romantic life. It was sometimes terrifying when the other-worldly intruded into your own life, but it made living a much deeper experience.

How had her mum put it? She'd said it was swapping a small room for a huge hall of mirrors. All the certainties disappeared, but they were replaced by possibilities that were so vast they were endless. She'd thought it an ordeal all those years ago when Jacob Parr had come in the night and shown her the wheals in the flesh of his back from the flogging he'd been given for drunkenness aboard the *Andromeda*. In retrospect though, she thought she'd actually been privileged to be singled out for her haunting.

Lassiter said, 'When's your interview set for?'

'He's only agreed in principle. We haven't nailed it down yet and he might change his mind, after this disappearance.'

'He won't,' Lassiter said.

'I'm only a student.'

'Egos like his don't discriminate when it comes to attention. Anyway you're a bright and amenable student. Assuming he does grant the interview, have you found anywhere you might place the piece?'

'I've had a couple of big magazines say they're interested. They have three month lead times and want something substantial to coincide with the grand opening. The June editions actually appear at the end of April. Publication depends on the strength of the article, but I'm pretty confident that if I write it, it will run somewhere.'

'You'll write it to the best of your ability, which definitely means going back to the island. You'll have to tour the complex they've built there. He'll probably take you himself aboard his helicopter. It has a facsimile of his signature coach-painted onto its doors.'

'He's not at all your sort of person, is he, Patsy.'

'Not many people are, Edie.'

'I don't seem to ruffle your feathers.'

'You're the exception that proves the rule. How're Phil and Ruthie, by the way. Still getting on?'

'Like a house on fire.'

'That's a horrible cliché for an aspiring journalist.'

'It's true, though. They're mad about one another.'

'Good to hear,' Lassiter said.

Edith sipped from her glass and put it down carefully onto the table. She folded her arms across her chest. 'Do you think there'll be more disappearances from New Hope?'

'It's impossible to say without going there and investigating what happened to Baxter's man.'

'And it's very early days. Actually less than a day.'

'He's not there Edie, which means he's gone, irrespective of the time-frame.'

'What happened to him?'

'As far as I know, the Western Isles police have no leads and the fellow who vanished usually had both feet firmly on the ground.'

'So Greg Cody didn't walk into the sea.'

'If he did, he didn't leave a note.'

'What did Felix Baxter want from you?'

'Something I couldn't provide him with,' Lassiter said. 'He wanted a clean bill of health for the island. He was after reassurance and I couldn't give him that. I could only tell him truthfully that I was left alone there.'

'Have you discussed this with Phil?'

'Yes, this morning.'

'And you didn't think to ask about him and Ruthie?'

'Since I knew we were having lunch together, much easier to wait and ask you, Edie.'

'Jesus,' she said. 'Men.'

'Can't fault you there, Jesus was by all reliable accounts a man.'

'I'll bet you've told Phil more about your New Hope Island exile than you shared with Baxter,' Edith said. She was smiling now.

'Then you wouldn't lose your money. I told him I was watched there and that the observation was hostile.'

'The spirit of poor dead Rachel Ballantyne,' Edie said, with a shiver.

'No,' Lassiter said, 'I had the feeling this was even worse.'

'What could be worse?'

'Rachel Ballantyne was human, once.'

'Are we talking monsters?'

He didn't answer straight away. Then he said, 'Monster, singular. But it was really just an intuition.'

'I'd love to know how you managed on New Hope for six months, what you did, what you actually found there. You're a curious man, Patsy, in both senses. You uncovered secrets there, didn't you?'

He smiled at her. He placed his knife and fork on the table to either side of his plate and leaned against the back of his chair. He said, 'How much time do you have?'

'I'm a student. It's the weekend. You're the one with the schedule to keep.'

'Not on a Saturday in London, Edie. Not since Alice's death, at least. I've all afternoon and no good reason to keep anything secret from you.'

He was glad of the company, she thought, with a sorrowful blossoming of sympathy in her chest. She wondered how hard it was for him not to drink just to fill his empty evenings. He looked well enough. She hadn't been to their house in Maida Vale since before Alice's death. She would go there this afternoon, though, she decided. She'd invite herself.

'We'll go back to your place, Patsy,' she said. 'If the story's any good, I might cook you dinner tonight.'

'It's a deal,' he said.

Of course the story was good, Edie Chambers thought. Finding things out was what Patsy Lassiter did. More than that, it was largely what he was for. He was a much nicer man than he mostly pretended to be to most people. But it was her abiding belief he'd been born to solve mysteries.

'Do you think your monster took Greg Cody?'

He frowned and gestured to a waitress for their bill. He said, 'If it's there, it's the island's monster. But Cody didn't disappear voluntarily.'

Helena Davenport was bored. She'd done all her coke the previous night and couldn't now get through to her boyfriend. Since he was her boyfriend of only seven weeks and a decade younger than she was, she was quite naturally concerned to keep him corralled. This wasn't possible in the Atlantic Hebridean wilderness of New Hope Island, because phones didn't work there. She wasn't used to failure and it was pissing her off.

They had some solar power at the visitor complex she'd designed, largely out of the need for the design to push all the relevant buttons when it came to political correctness. It hadn't cost anything, subsidies had paid for it, but she reckoned its actual contribution to providing light or heating water would be negligible until at least June.

They had wind turbines too. These were more contentious than solar panels because some significant environmentalists considered them a blight on the landscape. The eminent mountaineer Sir Chris Bonnington had successfully opposed their spread in the English Lake District. The Scottish Government liked them, though, which had been the deal-clincher. Helena didn't think them a particular eyesore, but they were noisy, the power they generated couldn't be stored and wind-strength could never be accurately predicted. So they weren't trustworthy. None of this really mattered, since a subsidy paid too for their construction and when they were brought into play, their maintenance.

The water for the long hot bath she was contemplating having would be heated by the same power-source that kept the lights burning in the ceiling above her and chilled the walk-in fridge in the suite's spacious kitchen. And that was an old-fashioned oil-burning generator about as far from renewables as it was possible to get. It was big, powerful, dirty, thirsty, costly and dependable and they actually had a pair of them, just in the unlikely event the one they were depending upon ever failed.

Hypocrisy and pragmatism were close bed-fellows in Helena's line of work and the fictitious claims made in parts of Felix Baxter's glossy New Hope Experience brochure gave her no sleepless nights as a consequence. Architects were required to be quite adept politically if they were going to be involved with substantial projects at environmentally sensitive locations. It was just the modern way.

The generators were kind of a dirty secret, hidden away forty feet below surface-level in bunkers hewn from the rock before construction above them had ever begun. In everything naked to the eye, by contrast, Helena had gone for the vernacular. The public areas of the complex were built from deliberately rough-hewn granite blocks. The stone hadn't been quarried on the island, that would have been an environmental crime; but it was exactly the same in character as the indigenous stuff present there.

The timber fascias of the suites and lodges and guest apartments had been treated so they'd bleach and weather to look more and more in character over the years like driftwood. The wood hadn't come from the island's tide-lines, but it had come from a sustainable source and the way she'd used it, its accents and details, gave the complex a hand-fashioned, human dimension where it might otherwise have looked monumental.

The windows were important. From the outside they were tinted so that sunlight didn't reflect off them in a way Helena Davenport always thought of as flashily corporate. They had the low, wide dimensions of cinemascope movie screens so that from the inside, they made the most of their spectacular Atlantic vistas. The glass was immensely tough, bullet-proof to stand up to the withering strength of the onshore winds in the winter storm-season. They'd been the most expensive element of the entire build, but Baxter had only glanced at her budget proposal and smiled and nodded. By that point, the project was awash with investment cash. And though her client had his numerous flaws, scrimping wasn't one of them.

The flaw with the complex, she thought exasperatedly, was communication. Baxter had characteristically presented this as a positive, saying the island's isolation from email and text and phone and internet access generally made it a happy sanctuary from the energy sapping preoccupations of the day-to-day world. A sojourn on New Hope was an opportunity to restore and replenish your creative energies without distraction. Contemplate in peace, he said; give your ideas and inspirations the virgin birth they deserve, he challenged.

It was all bullshit. Helena wanted to challenge young Jacques to find out whether he was contemplating any mischief and to put a stop to it if he was. To do that she'd have to use the big analogue transmitter at the workers' base at the opposite end of the island and she'd have to do so with a radio operator helping her and listening in because the rig was complex and required technical know-how to use. And Jacques, at the other end, would have to be a radio ham to pick up the transmission and she didn't think her new boyfriend that.

She decided she'd have a walk before taking her bath, not far, just down to the cobbled quay Ballantyne's colonists had built 200 years ago. She could see that through the picture window of her suite sitting room, below her, a quarter of a mile away, weak sunlight glazing the stones and making a tranquil sea shimmer beyond.

She laced on her hiking boots and filled a flask with coffee, stuffing a cagoul with the flask into her small rucksack aware that the weather could change very quickly and without warning in this part of the world. When she got outside, the air felt mild against her exposed skin and the sunlight had coaxed just a hint of honey from the heather and scrub in the thin soil on the rocks descending to the sea.

That changed as she approached the cobbles of the dock, salt filling her nostrils with its sharp tang, the world utterly silent beyond the ambient sounds of breaking wavelets and seagull cries.

She thought briefly about the missing man. She'd only been told about Cody's disappearance that same morning by one of the security guys, literally cap in hand, calling on her to break the news formally about the apparently fatal casualty the island had claimed. She was sorry. She had liked Cody for his equable temperament facing challenges she tended to escalate into crises without someone phlegmatic around. He'd been quietly and stolidly dependable and to her mind an improbable candidate for suicide. Despite that though, he'd never struck her either as at all careless or accident-prone. It was a mystery.

There was a wife, of whom Cody had spoken adoringly when she'd shared a beer with him on nights back when the Experience complex had been little more than a blueprint and a set of foundations. It was a paradoxical characteristic of all of the men on the island. They doted on partners and children they all missed terribly in their willing isolation from their families. They were providing financial security in the only way they could.

When she reached the quay and the water's edge she turned to look at her handiwork, rising backed by the crags behind it. She knew something of New Hope's enigmatic history and unlucky reputation. She thought her design might have been influenced subconsciously by that knowledge. There was just the slight suggestion of a fortress or redoubt about the complex from this distance. It looked built to defend itself and not just from elemental assault.

She sat and drank her coffee. In her isolation there, she reflected on who and where she was in her life. And she thought that there were areas of her existence she really needed to improve upon. The coke habit was only manageable because she told herself it was. It was undignified at her age and she really ought to quit the stuff for good. And her romantic life was an oxymoron. What was she doing with a callow narcissist possessed of a combination of good looks and immaturity that would make his cheating on her simply inevitable?

She smiled to herself. Maybe there was something to what Felix Baxter said about being incommunicado here and it clarifying your thinking. She was in the mood suddenly for resolutions. The time to put them into practice was straight away. Life was too short for anything else, as Greg Cody had just demonstrated in the saddest way possible. She thought that the more she pondered on it more likely an accident than suicide, proof that none of us knew how long we had and a sober lesson in the folly of prevarication. 'The time is now,' she said to the sea, the breeze, to the briny air.

The ascent on the way back, even in the pallid sunlight, made her perspire and look forward to her bath. She adjusted the water temperature running the single fashionable tap into the slate coloured tub and returned to the sitting room, stripping off her clothes to her underwear and letting the garments trail her on the waxed-wood floor, putting some music on, cranking up the volume through the concealed speakers in the walls and ceiling, listening to the Elbow anthem *My Sad Captains*, enjoying Guy Garvey's lugubriously beautiful voice, humming along, unclipping her bra and shrugging down and stepping out of her panties, naked with her back to the window.

When the room abruptly went dark, and over the music, she heard something thump against the glass behind her, heard the pane shudder. She turned sharply, as light slipped across the room again, aware of nothing substantially different. She went into the bathroom and turned off the tap. Then she went back and switched off the music. She walked to the window. A vertical crack now ran the length of the pane. She knew this was impossible. She knew the hardness coefficient of the glass. She ran a finger along the crack. The interior surface felt smooth under her fingertip. The crack wasn't the depth of the full thickness of the pane. It would still need to be replaced, though; visibly flawed now, its integrity fatally compromised.

Helena saw that something had snagged at about head height in the fissure in the pane's exterior. At first she thought, incredulously, that it was a scrap of seaweed. But it wasn't. Nor was it the feather from an eagle or an albatross, which would have made at least a modicum of sense. Instead it was a single hair, coarse and thick and as black as pitch.

Chapter Three

It was almost three in the afternoon when Ruthie Gillespie and Phil Fortescue got back from the pub. The fire in her wood burner had gone out and her sitting room had become chilly as a consequence. He glanced around for newspaper to screw up under kindling re-lighting it, but she shifted her head to one side and gave him the sort of frank look that said they'd not only be warmer but happier too upstairs in bed.

She was right about that, they were both warm and happy and then afterwards they dozed off, waking ravenous just after 6pm, by which time it had long gone dark.

'A day goes nowhere,' Fortescue said, pulling on his jeans.

'I don't fancy cooking,' Ruthie said.

'Then it's back to the Spyglass,' he said.

'We've totally gone to the dogs.'

'I've led you astray, Ruthie,' he said, leaning across the bed to where she was dressing on its other side, kissing her bare shoulder.

'I was headed in that direction anyway,' she said. 'It's my default route.'

'How many words did you write in the week?'

'I'm averaging 2,000 a day.'

'So you did 10,000 words.'

'Just over, actually.'

'At the length you write, that's a third of a book. I'd hardly call that kind of industry going to the dogs.'

'You're right, Phil. It's you, corrupting me. I was fine till you came along. Are you going to do anything do you think, about New Hope?'

'I'll tell you over dinner,' he said. 'I'm too hungry to think, let alone speak.'

They found two chairs in an alcove at the pub with a barrel between them serving as a table. They ordered from the bar menu. There were nautical charts in narrow brass frames mounted on the alcove's walls and an oil painting of a clipper canting alarmingly as storm waves broke over its bow, threatening to engulf the vessel. Their yellowy light came from a ship's lantern hung above them and they didn't really speak until their food arrived and they'd eaten a few fortifying mouthfuls each.

'Sometimes,' Fortescue said, 'fish and chips is exactly what the doctor ordered.'

'On the subject of doctors,' Ruthie said, 'where's Thomas Horan's journal now?'

'It's in the archive at the museum in Liverpool. Since his bloodline dried up at the battle of the Somme in 1916, there was no family member to claim it. It's my property unless someone else tries to establish a claim and no one would because there's no intrinsic value to it. History had forgotten him.'

'You only lent it to the museum?'

'More a case of storage, I doubt anyone's touched it since me. The museum's concerned with maritime history, not the occult. I could have them send it to me, but think I'll go and pick it up personally on Monday morning after leaving here.'

'And then what?'

'Tomorrow I'm going to do some internet research into academics who'll likely know something about occult and folkloric beliefs in West Africa in the early 19th century. I'll try and make an appointment to see someone with some expertise on that early next week. So it's Liverpool and then probably Oxford or Cambridge, depending.'

Ruthie was quiet for a moment. Then she said, 'Is this a case of trying to determine exactly what it is you're up against? Have you discussed this strategy with Patsy?'

'I'm not up against anything, Ruthie. And I'll tell Patsy what I'm looking into but there is no strategy. Cody's disappearance is a mystery that's made me curious about the island again. It goes no further or deeper than that.'

'Not yet, it doesn't.'

'And it very likely won't,' he said.

'What did Horan say about the sorcerer?'

'That tribally he was Albacheian. Horan called him the Lizard Man. His skin was tattooed to resemble scales and his teeth were filed to points and he was very thin. His name was Shaddeh and he claimed to be a healer, though he could do other much less wholesome things than heal. Said he'd been born to it. Spoke English, learned from a missionary he said had been intent on martyrdom.'

'Was that a joke?'

'More the truth spoken in jest, I think. Shaddeh had a rather dry sense of humour.'

They had finished eating and were huddled against the cold outside the pub so that Ruthie could smoke when she said, 'You could probably find out what you need to know on my laptop on the internet tomorrow.'

Fortescue shook his head. He said, 'Anyone can say anything without substantiating their claims on the internet.

People discuss this stuff without ever citing sources. On any forum discussing matters magical or paranormal, 90 per cent of those contributing are speculative cranks. I need someone objective and authoritative who can give me a proper perspective.'

'I sometimes forget you were an academic yourself.'

'I still am.'

'You don't look like one.'

He grinned. 'Is that a come-on?'

'Absolutely,' she said.

He thought it remarkable, what a decent meal could do for a person's libido, thinking maybe it should actually be thought of as an indecent meal.

'We'll have a nightcap, Professor,' she said, reading his mind. 'Then I'm afraid it's back to bed.'

Alice Lang had been a distinguished psychiatrist. She'd also been a genuine and gifted psychic. It was how Patrick Lassiter had met his wife, heading up investigations on the murder squad at New Scotland Yard she'd felt compelled to assist with after seeing things to which most other people were happily blind.

Their romance had begun just before the New Hope expedition seven years ago. She'd gone as their psychic, so he'd felt obliged to go to take care of her there. He considered in taking him on, she'd saved his life and he was in her debt. Also, by then he was deeply in love with her.

She'd been among those to die on New Hope when circumstances had compelled them to go back there 18 months ago. Eight of them had gone to the island then in the end. And only four had lived to return from it. The four were Lassiter, Ruthie Gillespie, Phil Fortescue and Edith Chambers. Lassiter was alone at the wave-swamped ruin of the crofter's cottage out of which Alice had been dragged by the sea and drowned. He had a full whisky bottle raised at his lips, already grateful for the oblivion the drink had not yet brought him when he smelled his wife's perfume and felt the flutter of her hair, wind-blown, on his face. And he heard two words spoken in her familiar voice.

Those words were, *Patrick, please.*

He left the island a little over 24 hours after hearing those words, but already bent on returning. He requested and was granted his leave of absence from the Cold Case team at the Met assigned to murder investigations. He went back to New Hope to rebuild the ruined cottage. It was a tangible challenge that could occupy his mind and body and he could mourn fittingly in solitude. Of course he hoped to feel his wife's presence again and thought that likeliest in the place where she'd died. But that was a secret so closed he kept it almost from himself.

He told Edie this in the conservatory of the house he'd shared with Alice during six blissfully happy years of life together. Nowhere near enough, but better than nothing and more than he would have conceivably imagined when she'd first invited him into her life.

'You sell yourself short, Patsy. I expect you always have.'

He shook his head. He said, 'I was a sour drunk back then, patronizing and surly. That's how I was towards him when I first met your stepfather, before the New Hope expedition. Can you believe that, when Phil Fortescue's one of the finest men I've ever met?'

'That wasn't you, it was the booze.'

'It was me drinking the booze, Edie.'

'What was your frame of mind when you went back?'

'Haunted,' he said. 'I kept wondering whether Alice had seen her own death in the moments leading up to it.'

'We've never know,' Edie said.

'I think I know,' Lassiter said. 'I think we both do.'

'How did you manage? I mean with no shelter and no food.'

Someone had tipped off the Southern Isles Area Police Command. Lassiter never found out who that was. But it was summer and the sea was often calm enough for the crossing and some of the officers based at Stornoway took to making it, bringing supplies for their very own Ben Gunn, the Scotland Yard Met Police Commander taking an island sabbatical.

'Never, ever believe the bad things people say about the Scots,' Lassiter said to Edie. 'A builder came to advise on the cottage reconstruction and ended up staying a fortnight in a frame tent he'd brought. A trawler dropped anchor and they paddled in an old wooden rowing boat with a pair of oars for me. A couple of young lads came and taught me the basics of sea angling and donated me a rod.'

'Fishermen steer well clear of New Hope, don't they?'

'Generally they do, they're a superstitious breed. They can just about tolerate the island's southern apex, away from the surf and the reefs. And they were curious about me.'

And all the while, Rachel Ballantyne left you in peace?'

'Yes,' he said, nodding. 'I'd brought a stock of tinned and powdered food and thought to live on that, when suddenly on July evenings I was barbecuing fresh fish on the beach and the cottage was almost complete and I was learning to accommodate grief without being in a constant state of despair. We'd had the time we'd had and I had that comfort to cling to.'

Edie said, 'In a sense, this was your island honeymoon.'

Lassiter sipped tea. He'd made them a mug each. It was quite warm in the conservatory, despite the chill outside. It was fully dark, now. He said, 'You're going to be a brilliant journalist, Edie.'

'You're biased.'

'You are, though.'

'You had your New Hope honeymoon. The hostility only began when the secrets started revealing themselves.'

'See?'

'Tell me that part, Patsy.'

They both knew the island harboured secret places. One of these had been revealed to them there 18 months earlier. It was the cellar store where Ballantyne's colonists had kept the whisky they'd distilled before selling it to merchants from the mainland. It was a substantial space hewn out of the stone ground close to the colonists' quay.

One of the experts on the original expedition, the forensic archeologist Jesse Kale, had believed there to be a large communal storm shelter on New Hope. He thought a run of severe Atlantic winters somewhere so exposed would oblige them to build one and it would be in the nature of their community to face their elemental enemy collectively.

The virologist Jane Chambers had thought there a plague pit on the island, a mass burial site which would explain the original vanishing. She'd been wrong about the cause of that, but New Hope thrived for a dozen years before the catastrophe. Some among its men, women and children would have perished from natural causes during that period. Yet there were no individual graves on the island. That pointed to the excavation of a catacomb or sepulchre to house their dead in the period of the colony's prosperity and contentment.

'I thought that both those places probably existed,' Lassiter said to Edie. 'The colony settlement is surrounded by a wall, but it's not far from the island's heights and in bad weather would have been mercilessly exposed. So the storm shelter idea made sense.

'But the catacomb theory was even more compelling. Child mortality ran at 50 per cent back in those days. Cholera and diphtheria routinely killed their victims. They got lead poisoning from the paint they used and died of tetanus when dirt got into their cuts. No one survived appendicitis.'

'The good old days,' Edie said.

'Unless the subjects of Seamus Ballantyne's Kingdom of Belief buried their dead at sea, there was a mass tomb.'

'And you found it.'

'I found both those places eventually. And it was after I did that the mood of the island began to shift towards me.'

'Have you got much in?'

'What do you mean?'

'For the dinner I'm cooking you.'

Lassiter smiled. Edie could make him smile and was grateful for the fact. His face was composed of the hard planes of someone who'd seen too much life. He was lean and tough looking and burdened by sorrow. His smile was a gift. His gaze moved away, travelled back the Hebrides, and he resumed his story.

It was a fair bet at least some of the colonists would have been coal or maybe tin miners in their former lives. And some of them would have been the men who dug the canals in the early years of Britain's Industrial Revolution. They would have had the instinct, the know-how and the wherewithal to dig. Excavation would have been second nature to them.

The logical place for their storm shelter was close to the colony settlement. Not under it, because if a bad storm leveled its buildings, that could trap them underground and they'd likely die of suffocation before being able to dig their way out. Lassiter discovered it, finally, looking between the settlement's perimeter wall and the island's heights, a small aperture concealed by a stunted stand of thick-trunked bushes that he crawled into holding a torch. After a couple of feet it became a passage it was possible to stand erect in that opened out after forty feet into a large gallery.

'It was a natural geological feature they'd discovered and then expanded,' he said. 'They'd flattened out the floor using chisels and hammers. The marks are still visible. And they'd gouged and drilled at the rock, excavating further, until the space was sufficiently sized to shelter their entire population.'

'Bloody hell,' Edith said. 'How did you find their mass tomb?'

'That was about a fortnight later,' Lassiter said, 'no detection involved. It was the singing led me to that.'

Helena Davenport was spooked. She tried for an hour after dark to tell herself it was cocaine withdrawal that was itching at her scalp and making her heart take those fluttering lurches but she was hard to fool and even harder to fool when she was the one attempting to do the fooling. She tried to listen to music, but that strategy didn't work. She loved Elbow and she liked Ed Sheeran and in bombastic moods Kasabian and she could even tolerate a bit of Coldplay. But she was too alert to the possibility of someone sneaking up on her to willfully drown out noises she sensed she needed now to be alert to.

It was about 8pm. She was sipping wine from a large glass she'd filled from a very good bottle of Merlot. She was watching the movie *300*, trying to concentrate on what elsewhere would have been her enjoyable appreciation of Gerard Butler's six pack, when she heard a ponderous, rhythmic beating at the main door downstairs.

They planned a live-in concierge for whom Baxter's people were still thinking up a hipper, less stuffy job-title. But that person had not yet been hired. None of the lower-rank staff had been recruited. There was no one down there to let whoever was doing the hammering in. More pertinently, there was no one to protect her should the person at the door grow impatient and force an intrusion.

That's if it was a person. Waiting for the banging at the main door to resume, she remembered the manner in which the sitting room of her suite had grown dark and the whump of impact and the thorny bristle still wedged in the crack in her supposedly unbreakable picture window.

She switched off the movie she'd been trying to watch. She looked around her, absently inventorying the high-end fixtures and fittings among which she stood. Just for a moment Helena felt a bit like that screaming woman must have felt in her deserted hotel in a TV movie she'd seen once, years ago, entitled *The Shining*. Helena wasn't one of nature's screamers. But that hammering on the main door had just started again and was doing everything possible to push her in the direction of flapping, screeching, bug-eyed hysteria.

She had no means of calling for help. She had nothing resembling a weapon. She thought about this. She thought about the island's baleful reputation, about its reputed ghosts. Maybe that was Seamus Ballantyne himself down there, ragged and frayed and indignant about the space surrounding her she'd stolen from his little kingdom's sky. Or perhaps it was someone more recent, Greg Cody cold and clammy having stumbled dead from the chilly depths.

She went to the bathroom and her disobedient fingers pushed everything on the shelf above it crashing into the sink. The hammering continued. By now she was badly shaken. She retrieved a deodorant aerosol and shook it. She did so deliberately, though her hand was shaking anyway. If she smoked she'd have a lighter and the means to improvise a flame-thrower from the aerosol can, just by igniting the spray jet at the nozzle. But she'd never smoked. What she had instead was a piss-poor alternative to pepper spray or Mace. It wouldn't deter Ballantyne, if he'd dragged himself from hell to confront her. It wouldn't disarm whatever had collided with the window and eclipsed the light.

She heard a voice, then, faint but clear. It was shouting her name and the tone of it sounded familiar. She knew it, she realized. She closed her eyes and relief bathed her like some buttery lotion applied expensively to the skin. Only then did she notice that her skin had been covered in raised goose-bumps that were fading now. It was Derek Johnson's voice. Johnson was the head of the island's small security team, charged with maintaining the island's integrity and guarding the plant and other equipment there. She'd seen him only that morning, when he'd come from their base at the island's western extremity to tell her about poor Greg Cody.

She went down and let him in. He was large and burly looking in his fur-lined Davy Crockett hat and heavy gloves and ski parka. She could hear the tick of the engine cooling in the night chill on the quad bike behind him he'd ridden there. She had recovered her composure to the point where she could just about resist hugging him in joyful relief.

'You look pale, Ms. Davenport,' he said. 'Hope I didn't startle you.'

'Come in,' she said.

She made him coffee. He took off his jacket. His sleeves were rolled to above the elbow and his thick arms were heavily inked in Maori-type designs. He had dense dark hair and his brow was an Easter Island ridge. His eyes were warm and friendly but he looked a handful, which he probably was. The other five members of the security crew were built to similar dimensions. She was reminded for the second time that day that Felix Baxter didn't scrimp.

'Why have you come here, Derek?'

'Fluke, really, Ms. Davenport,' he said.

'Helena, please,' she said.

'Most of the time, that big analogue transmitter we've got is just an ornament. There's something strange about atmospheric conditions on the island.'

You can say that again, Helena thought.

'All we get out of it most of the time is this banshee wail. It sounds like something not human, singing. Must be static or interference, I suppose. Very intermittently, though, it functions. It functioned an hour ago when the chief came on and ordered me over here to come and check on you.'

'This was Baxter himself?'

'He's the only chief I answer to.'

'Sounds like a premonition.'

'Maybe it was,' Johnson said. 'He actually instructed me to stay the night, here at the complex, both nights, till you're scheduled to leave, if you've no objection?'

'I've no objection whatsoever,' Helena said.

'I think Cody is the reason he sent me,' Johnson said. 'Cody isn't really adding up.'

'Does the island ever strike you as kind of spooky?'

Johnson didn't answer for a moment. He held her gaze. He said, 'The mood's shifted since Greg disappeared. It sounds a bit callous now but to us all, behind his back, he's always been Captain Sensible. Not rash in the slightest, if you get my drift. Not a fanciful sort. Not accident prone, without some provocation. And I felt watched, riding over here tonight. I didn't see anyone, but it wasn't a comfortable feeling.'

'What's the official line on Cody?'

Johnson shrugged. 'There isn't one. The chief says it's unhelpful to speculate. He's severely allergic to bad publicity. I'm sure you know that.'

'Off the record?'

'He screamed, Helena. Every single one of us heard it. It woke us. Do people scream, walking into the sea?'

Helena swallowed. It was time to change the subject. 'I'd just started watching a movie, before you started banging on the door,' she said, '*300*.'

Johnson grinned. 'Gerard Butler in a jockstrap,' he said. 'Lena Headey in not very much at all.'

'So you've seen it already. Could you bear to watch it again?'

'Absolutely,' he said.

'There's beer in the fridge if you'd prefer that to coffee,' Helena said. 'There are tortilla chips in the kitchen.'

His grin broadened. He said, 'Shame we can't send out for pizza.'

She smiled at that. The joke was a bit limp, but she couldn't honestly remember feeling more delighted in her adult life, just at the sight and sound of another human being. She'd been properly spooked. And if her reaction was out of proportion to what had actually occurred, it didn't feel at all that way to Helena.

'I was in the settlement when I heard the singing,' Lassiter told Edie. 'It was this forlorn, papery sound. The song was, *The Recruited Collier*. You remember when we were leaving 18 months ago, you told me to bone-up on my folk music if I was coming back to the island?'

'You said you listened to a bit of Laura Marling and I said that wouldn't do it.'

'I'd taken your advice by the time I returned. Eliza Carthy, Cara Dillon, The Fishermen's Friends, even a bit of Bellowhead. And Kate Rusby, so I was familiar with the song I was hearing.'

'Next you'll tell me you were there in the dark.'

'I was. After Alice died I was invulnerable in the sense that I didn't fear anything because nothing could be worse than that. I'd been terrified of losing her because I was so scared of being left alone and that had gone and happened to me, the thing I was most afraid of.'

'Sometimes love is selfish.'

'Yes, Edie, sometimes it is.'

'What were you doing there?'

'Looking for what it was I found.'

He followed the source of the singing. It drifted out of a metal grill over an aperture between two settlement buildings, the gap between their stone flanks narrow enough to conceal the entrance unless you knew it was there. In moonlight, Lassiter could see a set of descending steps roughly cut into stone. The grill was iron and rusted in flakes that the metal shed when he tried to shift it and though it moved heavily, it wasn't secured. Hinges moaned in stiff protest after two centuries of disuse. Cold iron death-rattled in his grip. The singer he was listening to hadn't apparently required the space he did to get down there.

There was a torch in his pocket he didn't take out or switch on. The beam of bright light would have been intrusive. Darkness was relative that far north in June and there was enough dusky illumination for him to see by as he descended the steps and his eyes adjusted.

The remains of the colony's dead, those that had been fortunate to die naturally, were laid out in cavities cut into the rock. They were skeletal under the tattered remnants of their clothing and shoes and they were still. Some of them were elderly. About half of them were children. He'd found their sepulchre. More accurately, he'd been led to it. Or was it truer to say he'd been lured there?

Rachel Ballantyne was not quite still. She was clothed in a fusty, ragged nightgown and her hair was a straw halo of neglected curls. She had her back to him and sang with her hands at her back, clasped demurely at the base of her spine. It didn't do to examine the flesh of her fingers too closely. After all this time, their resemblance to claws was too close for comfort.

After a moment, Lassiter saw that her torso was entirely motionless because of course little Rachel had not been mortal for an age. She sang without breathing. She had no requirement of breath. This was unnerving. More unnerving was his observation that she performed her song with her feet, petite and filthy, trailing the ground down there by as much as a metre. The song, with its sad lyrics and melancholy refrain, eventually concluded.

'You're a curious man, Mr. Lazziter,' Rachel said, into the thick, subterranean silence.

Her speaking voice was somewhere between a whisper and a moan. Her accent was the spoken English of two centuries ago. He didn't think it safe just then to answer her.

'Fierce curious,' she said, 'even with your heart cleaved. I'm sorry for your loss.'

'And I for yours,' he said. His voice, to his own ears, sounded level and calm. It was not a reflection of how he felt. Her torment was awful, almost contagious this close.

The scent of human decay came off her in a sweetish, nauseous assault. He dreaded her turning around, just drifting unmoored through the dim space down there and thereby showing him her time-dimpled vestige of a face. She might touch him. He could not imagine anything more dreadful than her cold and lonely caress.

'Did you like my singing?'

'It was beautiful, Rachel.'

'Beautiful, as I once was. At least, my father said I was.'

'By all accounts, he was not a man inclined to lie.'

The thing that had once been Rachel Ballantyne hung there silently for a while. Lassiter thought this might be his cue to leave, but didn't wish to miscalculate that. And when she spoke again, he realized he'd been mistaken. She said, 'I'd beg one favour of you, Mr. Lazziter.'

'I'll do anything I can,' he said.

'I've never asked a favour once of anyone till now.'

'Then I'd say after all this time you've earned the right.'

'Tis grievous troublesome a task, Commander.'

'I'll do anything I can for you,' he said again.

'End this for me,' she said. She held out her arms to either side of her in a pose just for a glimpse in the prevailing gloom ragged and angelic. Whatever she was, whatever wretched thing she'd become in death, her dimensions remained those of the petite child she'd been alive. 'I'm tired and broken and piteous,' she said. 'I'm so sorely desirous of rest.'

'If I can find a way to bring you peace, I will,' he said. 'I promise you that, Rachel.'

'Find a way,' she said. 'Help me die.'

And so Patrick Lassiter completed the story of his stay residing in the cottage on New Hope Island. Edie knew there was more, but he'd stuck to the facts. The rest concerned his suspicion that something hostile and malicious observed him there and that its hostility grew until the balance between his wish to grieve privately and his need to escape its growing threat had shifted far enough to force his hand.

Edie said, 'My stepfather is a man who always keeps his word. In that regard, I expect you're exactly like him. It means you'll be going back there. You'll have to. You'll do all you can to keep your pledge to Rachel Ballantyne.'

Lassiter seemed to ponder this. He cleared his throat with a cough before speaking. He said, 'I've never been a father. And she isn't a child, really and hasn't been for a very long time. But her torment's a terrible thing to witness. I'm sorrier for her than I can say. She deserves an end to her suffering. That encounter haunts me, Edie.'

'It would haunt anyone. But you're not just anyone. She chose you and it sounds as though she chose wisely.'

'Your stepfather is going to find out everything he can about the magic practiced by the sorcerer described in Thomas Horan's journal. The island is a malevolent place again and in a few months Felix Baxter plans to have it packed with affluent New Age tourists.'

'Folkloric myths from 200 years ago aren't going to give Baxter a moment's pause for thought. He'd think my stepdad a crank. He'd laugh out loud at him.'

'Laughter can sometimes make a very hollow sound,' Lassiter said

'Things changed for you there after you found those secret places,' Edie said. 'Someone or something wasn't happy about you finding them. You were tolerated before that. After that, you were trespassing.'

'You're very astute.'

'I've had some good teachers,' she said. 'When are you going back there?'

'It has to be before Baxter's experience opens up. And it can't come soon enough for Rachel.'

'Despite the monster?'

'Like Phil, I keep my promises.'

'I'd guessed that.'

'But I don't think I can keep this one without help.'

Chapter Four

Ruthie Gillespie was an early riser. She woke every morning with a twin craving for caffeine and nicotine she liked to answer at the table in her garden, regardless of the weather, with a cafetière of coffee and two or three cigarettes, getting these needs out of the way before brushing her teeth vigorously and greeting her guest and lover with what she hoped was an innocent smile.

She was up at 6am on this particular Sunday morning and didn't wait for Phil to stir naturally. They'd had a pretty early night and he'd had enough sleep to her mind by 7am and she had a proposal to put to him that was best served by an early start.

'Is there a fire?' he said, when she'd shaken him awake, 'Did somebody die?'

'Do you think you can research your voodoo academic on the move?'

'Depends,' he said, after a pause. 'I can't do it at the wheel of a car.'

'But you can do it in the passenger seat.'

'Theoretically,' he said. 'But why would I have the need?'

'Because we're going north today,' she said. 'We can spend the night at that nice hotel that footballer owns in Southport. We can be there by mid-afternoon. We can take a stroll along Lord Street and visit the arcade at the end of the pier.'

'Why on earth would you want to visit a seaside town, when you live in one?'

'Because it's romantic,' she said, 'because it's spontaneous, because Ventnor doesn't have a pier. And because it means you'll only have to drive 18 miles tomorrow morning to pick up the Horan journal from your old museum.'

'Steven Gerard doesn't own the Vincent. He's just a shareholder.'

'Splitting hairs because you've woken up grumpy,' she said, reaching for a pillow and clubbing his head with it.

'Ouch.'

'It'll be exciting for me,' she said, 'driving your car.'

'Exciting is one way of putting it.'

Fortescue's car was a 21 year-old Pininfarina-designed Fiat Coupe Turbo his brother had sold him claiming it was a babe-magnet. This had not proven to be the case. Not on a single occasion, it hadn't. The car was fast and powerful and nice to drive if you didn't mind positioning your backside six inches above the tarmac but he felt ambivalent about it and very ambivalent about someone so inexperienced as Ruthie was, driving it the 300 mile route north to Merseyside.

'I know you've got mixed feelings about your car,' she said. 'Basically you were conned into buying it. But that doesn't matter now because I'm in your life.'

'And you're totally indifferent to cars.'

'Picky about my men, though,' she said.

'Less of the plural, please,' he said.

'Are we going north today or not?'

'Yes,' he said.

'Then get your arse in gear, Professor,' she said. 'We've no time to lose.'

⚜ ⚜ ⚜

Edie Chambers had arrived home on Saturday night in a taxi Patsy Lassiter had ordered and insisted on paying for. She'd been troubled by a bad dream in which Rachel Ballantyne had turned floating in space to face her and had possessed the features of her flogged ghost Jacob Parr, lewd and rum-ravaged and scarily revolting above her waifish body and framed by her lustreless blonde curls.

Despite the dream, she woke up on Sunday morning feeling refreshed and energized. He kept booze for guests, but she'd been sufficiently diplomatic at Patsy's house to drink nothing stronger than Diet Coke. She was clear-headed and decided to do some research into Felix Baxter, the property magnate and entrepreneur behind the New Hope Experience.

She hoped to finalise a date for their interview over the coming week and knew that thorough research saved time later face to face for the really important stuff. Questions asked from a position of obvious ignorance understandably annoyed interview subjects. Asking them was amateurish and insulting and she'd make sure she was well informed enough about him to avoid doing that.

He was 39 years old and single, though there was a love child he'd fathered in an early relationship with a regional beauty queen from his home city of Newcastle. His son was named Danny and he was 18 and enjoying a gap-year travelling before going to Goldsmith's College at the University of London to study film production. Judging from the number of pictures of them together at premiers and concerts and the biggest fixtures on the football calendar, the two were close.

Higher education had not figured in Felix Baxter's life. Like most young men eager to make their fortune he'd lacked the patience for that. He'd gone instead the Richard Branson route and started a business when he was the same age as his son was now. His background had been solidly working class – dad a foreman at an engineering works and mum a nurse – so there'd been no capital to back his first enterprise.

He'd started off selling second-hand motorbikes and graduated to second-hand cars. When he'd made enough money doing that he'd bought the first of the run-down properties he'd do up. He got into this at the right time, in the mid-1990s when the property collapse of the early part of the decade meant that there was still precious little confidence in the market. By the boom of the late 90s he had a large enough portfolio to make a killing, which he did. He sold off his auto dealership and moved from domestic property into clubs, pubs, leisure centres and gyms.

He had his finger nowadays in lots of pies. He ran the biggest public venue door-security firm in the north east of England. He put on boxing shows and promoted rock concerts. His real and consistent talent though seemed to be for finding a theme that made the specific location he was marketing attractive to the punters.

His flagship restaurant and bar in his home city were patronised by top-flight footballers and reality TV and soap stars. He'd created a golf course on the Northumberland coast prestigious enough to stage world-ranking tournaments. He'd opened half a dozen upmarket caravan parks – all at obsolete RAF airfields – on spectacular coastal sites in Cumbria and Wales.

Felix Baxter hadn't quite done it all, though. He hadn't yet made the Sunday Times Rich List. The New Hope Experience easily ranked as his most ambitious project to date and therefore as his biggest career gamble. The inspiration for it seemed to come partly from the Center Parcs model and partly from what Peter de Savary had tried to do at Land's End in Cornwall. The rest of it, he must have dreamed up personally.

The New Hope Experience was going to be somewhere you could either become immersed in Celtic mysticism or ride the longest, fastest zip-wire in Europe. You could jet ski or sea kayak there; or you could just enjoy the solitude. You could study the abundant wildlife, at one with the wilderness. Or you could rock climb on some of the most demanding pitches in the British Isles.

The environmental credentials of the residential complex he'd had built there were impeccable. Cost alone would deter the riff-raff, it was subtly implied. The rates were eye-wateringly high. But guests would anyway be discretely vetted, before being invited to apply for their fortnight's residence as members of the New Hope Community.

Edie thought she got what it was all about; it was a place to which rich people would go to indulge themselves while feeling creative and worthwhile. You could live it up there and have your sins against nature absolved while doing it because of what you'd paid and where you'd had the taste and sensitivity to come. On New Hope, by some subtle osmosis, the soulless would be endowed with spirituality and the trivial gain gravitas. And the sheep given to following the fashion flock's shepherd would, well; they'd *flock* there, wouldn't they?

The New Hope Experience was a very modern concept. It created a demand because it answered in them what those wealthy enough to go there fooled themselves into believing was a need. And on forward bookings it was already a sell-out success.

Edie looked at pictures of the man. Felix Baxter had a ready smile but she couldn't source a single shot in which the humour reached his eyes. He was prematurely grey and slender and quite tall and had an obvious weakness for well-cut Savile Row suits. He favoured wristwatches with clunky cases and faces busy with sub-dials.

He lacked any distinctive features or characteristics other than that air of detachment, which actually had the effect of making his appearance quite vague. She thought his would be a difficult face to draw or describe or pick out with any certainty in an identity parade. Perhaps that was why he wasn't a man to Patsy Lassiter's taste. But she thought there likely other reasons, just as good, for that.

Felix Baxter had travelled to the Maritime Museum in Liverpool where he sat waiting in an area to which the general public never normally enjoyed access. It was Sunday morning and he was there to meet a museum staffer who would ordinarily have had the weekend off. She held the influential position of Keeper of Maritime Artefacts. His interest was in something left to the museum not long after its foundation in the early 19th century. He wasn't generally engaged by history except where he believed it could be exploited for profit. But this morning's mission was specific. He'd heard an intriguing story, a rumour, an urban myth about one particular artefact and was there only to discover for himself whether it was true.

A sea chest full of nautical belongings had been donated back then. They'd been the property of Seamus Ballantyne and the donator had been Ballantyne's ex-wife. Divorce had been unusual in the period and generally frowned upon by polite society, but hers had been seen as fully justified. She'd been scandalized when her husband abandoned the respected office of slave-ship master to become a hellfire preacher. As he attempted to gather converts, bellowing out sermons atop a fruit crate on the harbour cobbles, Liverpool's gentry sided unanimously with her.

Baxter wasn't really interested in the woman he waited to meet. He was, however, greatly interested in her immediate predecessor in her role. That was Professor Phil Fortescue, a man with a strong link to New Hope, someone Baxter suspected had been party to some of the island's most stubborn secrets.

Fortescue intrigued Baxter. He was a man of whom Baxter was instinctively wary, and he tended to trust his instincts. He was the reason Baxter had said yes when Fortescue's stepdaughter Edie Chambers had approached him for an interview. Or he was the clincher, since Baxter might have said yes to Edie anyway. She'd been to New Hope too and might be holding onto insights of her own about the island.

The Keeper wasn't late. Baxter was waiting because he'd been a quarter of an hour early. Generally he was tardy concerning appointments, which was deliberate and a habit dictated by status. But he was intrigued and a bit excited about what he was about to discover and experience and had paid a generous endowment to the museum, simply to engineer.

'It's a substantial sum, Mr. Baxter.'

'It's a goodwill offering,' he'd said.

'Can we do anything for you in return?' They'd said.

'Actually –' he'd replied.

And after some bureaucratic fuddling, they'd agreed.

Now he wiled away the few minutes before his appointment thinking contentedly about the names he'd given the various locations on New Hope Island and just how richly atmospheric they sounded. There was Ballantyne Cove, Shanks's Reach and the Gulf of Andromeda. There was Kingdom Heights, the Black Lagoon and Gibbet Hill.

He was still undecided about the early 19th century sailor's tavern he'd dreamed up for the Cove. It might be slightly over the top, a bit contrived. They could always add it later. Grog and ship's biscuits, ale and sea shanties; they'd call it *The Hope and Glory,* pack it to its oak rafters with antique nauticalia. Film companies using it for location shooting would make his pirate pub a lucrative earner in the off-season.

The Keeper arrived. She was short and plump and nondescript in a fawn suit and brass framed spectacles. After the niceties of introduction she said, 'Are you sure you want to do this?'

'Why wouldn't I be?'

'Generosity of the sort you've shown to the museum should be rewarded rather than punished, Mr. Baxter.'

'What on earth does that mean?'

The lenses of her glasses reflected the bright ceiling lights above them. It meant that he couldn't see her eyes to read her expression properly.

She said, 'Ballantyne's sea chest has always been burdened by reputation. None of the objects within it are ever exhibited here. The story is that collectively, they inflict bad luck.'

'Do you believe that?'

'Superstition and the sea have been linked probably since our ancestors first pushed off aboard dug-out canoes and coracles. I keep an open mind. I'm suggesting pause for thought.'

'Are you warning me?'

She blushed slightly. She said, 'I'm merely informing you, as a courtesy. It's something our Director said I should do before giving you the key to the chest.'

He took the key from her. He followed her precise directions. He located the chest where she said he would, in a basement room that felt a bit small and more confining than was entirely comfortable. The room was windowless and the overheads feeble and the warmth of an antique radiator gave the gloomy space a slightly fetid air. The chest was of brass-bound wood and had Ballantyne's initials inlaid in mother of pearl in its lid. It was the first thing personal to the New Hope colony's founder he had ever encountered and a thrill of wonder ran through him at the thought that this elusive man had really lived and breathed, dressed and eaten, spoken and drank.

And suffered a mysterious fate, he thought.

He sank to his haunches and put the key in the lock and turned and opened the trunk lid. He saw rolled navigation charts secured by ribbons and a boat cloak and leather boots and a dress sword with scrolling on its elaborate scabbard. The object he'd come there to see lay in a depression its solid weight had made in the black woven fabric of the boat cloak.

It was a silver pocket watch. It was a Breguet. It had an immaculate enamel face and blued steel hands. It was so collectible it was probably priceless and it was ticking audibly now the chest lid was open and when Baxter looked at his own wristwatch to check, he confirmed that it was showing the correct time.

He picked up Ballantyne's Breguet. He could feel the mechanism pulsing strongly through the smooth precious metal of the case against his palm and the tips of his fingers. Handling the watch forged a link somehow intimate with the watch's original owner and Baxter felt suddenly queasy at that thought as his palm began to perspire stickily under its weight and shape. It felt unpleasant to the touch, despite its rarity and refined pedigree. They'd been among the most accurate marine timepieces ever manufactured and he felt almost desperate to put it down and close the trunk lid on its ungovernable life.

He'd heard a theory concerning the story that Ballantyne's pocket watch never wound down. It was claimed that kinetic energy from the alien spacecraft sent to abduct his colonists went on powering its movement indefinitely. This was a quite elegant theory, until it was pointed out that the Breguet never actually got nearer New Hope than Liverpool. It was a relic of its owner's earlier, sea-faring life, prior to his religious epiphany. He'd left it behind among his other abandoned belongings for his ex-wife to dispose of.

He knew another story about the watch. It was that Phil Fortescue had taken it away on loan, had carried it with him for a couple of years following the sudden death of the wife he'd first met seven years ago on McIntyre's New Hope Expedition. Her name had been Jane Chambers and she'd written and presented a prize-winning television series about the Black Death. And Baxter, in the bowels of the museum, in the presence of Ballantyne's sea chest, was beginning to wonder how her widower had ever possessed the desire or fortitude to have the watch in his proximity.

He could still hear it ticking, with the trunk lid back down, with the sea chest locked again, or he imagined he could. Something about that small room impended. It was like laughter stifled or a drowned scream. The sweating had spread from his palms to his temples where it trickled down the sides of his face. His scalp itched with moisture. The boxed pocket watch seemed not so much to tick now as to chuckle with a cold sort of mechanical mirth, mocking and relentless. He felt claustrophobic down there and suddenly and almost overpoweringly, he felt as though disdainfully observed.

He felt the urge to rise and turn and flee. He heard something unstill shift or slither inside the chest and the instinct to do that grew stronger in him. Instead he forced himself to stand up slowly and turn deliberately and exit the room and walk up stone steps and along echoing corridors back the way he'd come. When he saw the Keeper waiting for him in the vestibule beyond the window panels of the last glass door he glanced at his watch and realized with a sick clutch of bewilderment that he'd only been down there alone for a total of about five minutes.

Alone?

'Did you get what you were after, Mr. Baxter?'

'It's not a wind-up?' The joke sounded far braver than he felt. He'd gone there hoping to disprove something that had just confounded him. The question it now begged was how many living mysteries had the New Hope colony's founder left on the island itself?

The keeper shook her head. She said, 'We've never had the need to wind the watch. Much less felt the inclination.'

He tried to smile. He said, 'Thanks for your cooperation. It's been an experience.'

'Rather you than me, with respect,' she said.

But the experience wasn't quite concluded for him yet.

He walked out into the street. It was raining and the cobbles of the dock quarter around the museum were slick and the air above them a rain-tainted grey. Lights from passing vehicles bleared through it when he reached streets no longer pedestrianized. A car horn hooted angrily as he crossed at a busy junction, directionless, paying no heed to the traffic. He passed the stone steps and Deco accents in its masonry of a derelict cinema building.

A faded film poster loomed palely at the corner of his vision out of a tarnished metal frame. It showed a little girl, tawdrily attired in a period nightdress, at the door of a whitewashed cottage, seemingly weightless because her feet didn't quite touch the ground, as her frozen gaze seemed to follow his progress walking by.

A horror film, he thought numbly, half a block on, his coat heavy across his shoulders and clinging to his knees with the rain now soaking it. One of those low budget American shockers that makes back its money over the opening weekend and dies its box-office death once its college kid demographic have been served up their popcorn thrills.

Except, Baxter thought, slowing and then stopping, seeing rain dance above a puddle in the street gutter to his left, the little girl in the poster really had been watching him. He'd seen her slowly turn her head as he passed by, hadn't he?

He couldn't have.

But he *had*.

He turned around and went back. The cinema building looked long abandoned, exposed stone through peeling white paintwork, the steps up to the entrance chipped and cracked, leading nowhere now. He noticed a padlock securing the grand main entrance and saw that the lozenges of decorative glass set into the wooden panels surrounding it were most of them cracked or gone entirely. Buildings of this sort, obsolete, hopeless really, sometimes made Felix Baxter feel a little melancholy. Today, though, he climbed the steps and approached the film poster for a closer look, feeling something instead more coldly akin to dread.

There was a poster in the frame. But the paper, laminated once he thought, was sun-blistered and bleached by a host of city summers and whatever it had once depicted had long since disappeared. It showed nothing. There was not even the ghost of an image discernible there. He shivered. He was an imaginative man. He knew that about himself. His business career testified emphatically to the fact. He possessed vision, he really did. But visions didn't generally possess him.

He looked around, getting his bearings, gathering himself, forcing his mind to clarify and map a mental route to where he'd parked his car. He was certain about who and where he was. But he could still hear the rhythmic tick in his mind of Ballantyne's pocket watch and he was a few blocks on before the strong sensation of feeling watched finally weakened and left him completely.

By the time they checked into the Vincent Hotel on Lord Street in Southport for the night, Phil Fortescue had found his specialist in African tribal magic. It was an esoteric, even obscure area of study, challenging because written primary sources were non-existent. The oral tradition was fine in some sets of circumstances. But the dead languages of vanished tribes created imponderable mysteries and imposed a silence that would last until eternity.

Because it was an arcane area of scholarship, the specialists all knew one another. And there didn't seem to be much professional jealousy between them. It being a Sunday actually facilitated what he was doing because the people he contacted were on their leisure time rather than lecturing. Most of them recognized his name. Various people were recommended or ruled out on the basis of their specialisms in the emails he sent from the passenger seat of the Fiat and the calls he made. One name kept recurring, though, and the name belonged to Dr. Georgia Tremlett.

She wasn't an Oxbridge don. She was a departmental head at Manchester University. She was Professor of

Pan-African Religion and Mythology, which seemed a vast subject area. When Fortescue got through to her, she said she could only see him for 30 minutes the following day and that Wednesday was probably the ideal day that week to schedule some meaningful time for discussion. When he mentioned the Horan journal and referenced Shaddeh's name, she said that she'd have to call him back. She did so after 10 minutes, saying she'd shuffled her schedule around and that she could now offer him the whole of the following afternoon.

At Keele Services on the M6, where they'd stopped for a break, they sat at an outside table where Fortescue sipped coffee and Ruthie smoked and read Georgia Tremlett's Wikipedia entry.

'She started out as an anthropologist. That was the subject of her first degree.'

'How many has she taken?'

'She's a year younger than me and obscenely well qualified.'

'I'll bet she can't drive like you,' Fortescue said, after a pause.

'Careful,' Ruthie said. 'If you were driving, we'd still be the wrong side of Birmingham.'

'You reached warp speed on the M6 toll.'

'No cameras on the toll road.'

'It's convenient my picking up the journal in Liverpool and her being based only 30 miles away. It's ideal.'

'Maybe it's fate,' Ruthie said, wishing she hadn't said it even before the words had left her mouth. She exhaled smoke and stubbed her cigarette out in the ashtray with unnecessary force, thinking that sometimes, most of the time probably, she was a complete idiot. Just mentioning fate was tempting it and she wanted nothing bad to happen to the man she was with. She sometimes dreaded that.

They were in Southport by 4pm, just before dusk. After dumping their bags in their room, they walked along the still-handsome tree-lined boulevard that was Lord Street until they reached Nevill Street, where they turned left to head for the promenade and the pier.

She'd been right, Fortescue thought, it was romantic. The sun had broken through the clouds and Southport had a huge sky and an orange ambience bathed them as they walked the length of the pier to the arcade full of antique amusement machines at its end. They were holding hands and Ruthie walked swinging their arms with happiness and wearing a slight, secretive smile. The last rays of the descending sun gave her heavy black hair a silken shimmer and darkened her lips in a way that made kissing her an urgent need in him.

He stopped and pulled her towards him and did kiss her. The kiss broke. He shaded her from the sun like that and her face was pale and her eyes black in his cast shadow. 'I love you,' he said.

She smiled. 'You'd better,' she said.

They played on the machines with old-fashioned pennies. They put a penny in the slot to hear and watch the Laughing Sailor gyrate and roar with clockwork mirth in his mottled blues. They lowered crane booms with little levers to win liquorice and lollipops. They pinged away at tin targets with pistols firing corks.

Fortescue figured most of the machines were Edwardian. They'd evidently been very keen on having their futures foretold back then. There was a machine on which you placed your hand on a dense rectangle of tiny retractable metal rods to have your palm read. There was another, which printed out your horoscope and a third that predicted your future in answer to some push button questions about your character.

It was destiny quaintly mechanized, but neither Phil nor Ruthie squandered their coinage on these particular attractions. Perhaps they were both thinking about what had been said and regretted earlier at the more mundane and modern-day location of Keele Services on the motorway. He thought that was probably the case.

He could joke about making himself a hostage to fortune by agreeing to be her passenger with Ruthie at the wheel of a muscular car. But fate had so far seemed to play a rudely intrusive part in his life and he thought he might learn things the following day that would propel him powerfully once again on a path not really of his choosing.

He remembered the first time he'd met Ruthie, outside a pub at Portsmouth Harbour overlooking the Solent sea forts. That too had been at dusk. He'd been surprised at how beautiful she was, something that happened to him constantly, a surge of grateful pleasure running through him whenever he laid eyes on her, wherever they happened to be, whatever they happened to be engaged in doing.

Had it not been for his involvement with New Hope Island, he'd never have met her at all. He remembered what he'd said to her then when he'd said he didn't think the island had finished with him and thought it had only just started with her.

They walked back towards the Vincent from the pier, eating unseasonal ice-cream cornets, Ruthie doing that arm-swinging thing she did whenever they held hands, smiling whenever her white-tipped tongue retreated back between her teeth.

He was glad he'd agreed to this little impromptu jaunt. They earned enough combined to be able to afford the odd treat. He was even gladder he'd told her he loved her. It was only the truth. There was no finality about that declaration and nothing fatalistic. It felt like the beginning much more than it did the end of something. He hoped with all his heart they'd be given the time for that adventure together. He wasn't complacent that they would, he wasn't even very confident, in truth. But he knew despite this, that he'd never felt a happier or more fortunate man in his life than at that moment.

She'd finished her ice cream. She said, 'I suppose you know Southport quite well.'

'I used to come here on the train with my brother in the summers as a kid. There was a huge open-air bathing pool, an art deco masterpiece built in the 1920s. It's gone now. It's a multiplex and a Nandos and a bowling alley and their car park.'

'There must be other stuff work seeing.'

'The Atkinson museum and art gallery's a fantastic place. Why?'

'I'll do some writing while you're gone in the morning and then some exploring in the afternoon. I think we should stay another night, drive back on Tuesday morning.'

'That's a very practical suggestion.'

'I'm a very practical woman.'

Chapter Five

Baxter's suggestion that Helena Davenport play guinea pig at the resort complex she'd designed had been as much of a dare as a serious request. She could easily have laughed it off as a joke. She'd done it because she was a bit of a perfectionist. Most architects signed off their building projects before the tiresome problems could begin with cladding or condensation, with water penetration or troublesome acoustics or temperature variables caused by sunlight encountering windows made from the wrong kind of glass positioned at angles not properly considered.

She'd worked extremely hard on the New Hope project, the chief creative on the job because the challenges had made it too risky a commission to delegate. If something went wrong on completion, she felt it only fair that the buck stop personally with her. She trusted to her talent for innovation and despite her little narcotic problem, she was generally extremely thorough when it came to the detail.

Now there was talk in the profession of awards shortlists. She was vain and competitive enough to want her practice to win these. She thought it would be good too for the morale of her staff, for Edinburgh and for Scotland for Davenport Associates to be accorded international recognition. High-profile women architects were still a bit of a novelty and it would help champion that cause. It wouldn't do the New Hope Experience any harm either.

It was late Sunday afternoon and she'd hitched a ride on the back of Derek Johnson's quad bike. His people had their camp at the opposite end of the Island from the complex, just inland from where upper-crust crofter David Shanks had built his cottage in the 1930s and seeing it remained on her New Hope to do list.

She'd already toured Seamus Ballantyne's colony settlement, roughly at the island's centre, trespassing on what was now a World Heritage Site aware that his community had vanished abruptly and without trace. She'd been aware also of a rumour that in response to some earlier crisis afflicting his Kingdom of Belief, he'd indulged in human sacrifice. He would have come across that practice on a genocidal scale while bartering for slaves among the warring tribes of West Africa.

She'd got on okay with Johnson the previous night, on the whole. He'd cracked a beer and improvised a supper for himself of pretzels and nachos and pistachio nuts and they'd watched *300* together while he consumed roughly a year's recommended salt intake. The movies were stored along with music files on a high-end server in her suite's entertainment system and were at least the quality of Blu-Ray on the screen. When *300* had finished, she felt relaxed enough to mention the moment when she'd felt like the woman at the hotel in *The Shining* as he'd hammered at the complex door.

It transpired that Johnson was a horror fan. He told her *The Shining* had originally been a novel written at the end of the 1970s by Stephen King. He said there was a big screen version vastly superior to the TV movie she'd watched and they should see if it was among the stored files. When she did a search, there were three films on the server directed by Stanley Kubrick and so they watched that together too. Afterwards, Helena rather wished she'd sat through *Barry Lyndon* or *Dr. Strangelove* instead.

She hitched her ride on Sunday afternoon partly to get away from the complex. She was leaving the following day and knew she wouldn't be alone there that night because of Baxter's instructions to her burly companion. But the weirdness of the cracked picture window grew stranger every time she looked at it and though she knew it had to be imagined, she thought there was a poised stillness about her suite that posed some impending threat too subtle to identify.

Get a grip, woman, it's not the Overlook Hotel, she told herself. But when she suggested their trip to the other side of the island to her horror-loving chaperone, he seemed as relieved as she was to get away for a while from where they were.

He took a spare helmet from the cargo case mounted on the back of the bike and gave it to her, looking round, his eyes narrowing as he viewed the heights above them.

She said, 'What?'

'Kind of lulls you, all those beguiling place-names the chief's given the Island's beauty spots.'

'It's a beautiful place,' she said. The mild weather was holding. The sky was a spectacular blue, just remote, faint smudges of cloud.

'Eighteen months ago, some people came here on a writers' retreat and none of them ever made it home again. Some of the survivors of the 2010 expedition came to try to find out what had happened to them and half of them never made it back either.'

'Why do you call them survivors?'

'It was kept quiet, but there was a high body count on the expedition in '10. You must have heard something?'

'I was working in New York back then, at a practice based in Manhattan. Hadn't yet come back and set up on my own.'

'A well-known archeologist and cosmologist never came back. Neither did a Jesuit exorcist on the trip.'

'Jesus. They brought an exorcist?'

'They were covering all the bases.'

'And he what? Disappeared?'

'All I know is he never made it back,' Johnson said.

'And in the 1820s, an entire community vanished,' she said. 'There were said to be around 150 of them.'

'And now Cody,' Johnson said. He looked directly at Helena. He said, 'I can think of places I'd rather spend my holidays.'

She put on her helmet. She smiled at him. She said, 'Take me to the Shanks cottage. I'm told it's very picturesque.'

It stood pale and benign above the tide line. It occupied a small granite plateau above the pebbles and then the white sand that stretched to the surf. It looked unblemished by time, but she knew it had been ruined and then restored; sympathetically restored, as the vernacular of property sales would have it. Outside it was spotlessly neat and seemed ready for occupation, inviting, were it not sited at so lonely a spot.

'David Shanks must have been desperate to escape something,' she said.

Johnson only shrugged. He said, 'I don't know much about him. He came from a posh background and he was decorated in the '14–18 war. Maybe he was trying to escape the Great Depression, it was that period when he turfed up here.'

Helena nodded. She'd known about the posh and medal bits, but that was all.

'The chief keeps talking Shanks up, saying that he was a George Orwell type, a significant figure in bohemian literature in the inter-war years.'

'Is that a direct quote?'

'It's word for word. All I know about Orwell is from having to read *Animal Farm* as a set book at school.'

'It's to Felix Baxter's advantage, New Hope having a literary pedigree.'

'He doesn't miss a trick.'

'I'm going inside.'

Inside was a stripped metal cot, a plain table, a Welsh Dresser and two shelves full of books. Lighting was a couple of hurricane lamps depending from hooks screwed into the ceiling joists and neither looked like they'd been lit for months. There was something emphatically cold about the interior of the cottage; not just abandonment but a feral chill that made her want to get out again urgently into the air and the brightness. She had the mad instinct that someone or something had squatted there, baleful and watchful and then afterwards stolen away.

Johnson took her to their camp. The buildings were composed of some tough performance fabric stretched tautly over frames made from high-tensile steel struts. They didn't look permanent, but they looked as resilient as the island's unpredictable weather meant they needed to be.

They prepared a meal and she ate with them. It was lamb stew and she couldn't honestly remember eating anything tastier or more succulent for ages. She imagined their food was all thawed from frozen ingredients, as hers had been in her short time on the island. They were better at preparing their dishes than she was. They'd had longer to practice, but she'd never have made up the gap, she admitted to herself, complimenting them as they clustered around her, men deprived of female company for too long in their tedious New Hope tours of civilian duty. She didn't mention Greg Cody but sensed he was there, at their shared table, in all their thoughts.

Before leaving with Johnson to head back for the complex, she asked to see their transmitter. She'd been sent an invoice in error that had shown her back at her Edinburgh office what the kit had cost. Baxter Enterprises had squandered £20,000 on communications hardware that was apparently mostly useless.

'What worries me when the Experience opens up for business,' she said to Johnson, 'is what happens if there's a kayak emergency or a badly cut child or someone with a ruptured appendix and no contact with Stornoway or the mainland.'

'Get the kit aboard an R.I. and 800 metres offshore and even battery-powered, the signal's not only strong but crystal clear,' he said.

'And if the emergency occurs during a bad storm?'

He raised an eyebrow. 'Fair point,' he said.

'Switch it on.'

'Your funeral,' he said.

He flicked a switch on the big console and various lights lit softly and there was a hum of power surge and the voltage regulator kicked in and the kit became quiet again. Johnson took a breath and leant over the machinery and twisted a dial and very faintly, in a mournful drone, a melody insinuated a strained aural path from nowhere that sounded remotely human.

'Sometimes it sounds like a child,' he said, 'distressed and wanting company. I'd swear it's an actual tune.'

It was a tune. Folk was Helena's thing in the same way horror was Johnson's. He loved Stephen King. She was a huge fan of Karine Polwart and Lisa Knapp. But this wasn't either of them. This was a Kate Rusby song. As faint and distorted as it sounded, it was *The Recruited Collier*.

Around them, a gust of wind blasted against the sides of the comms room with sufficient force to make the fabric ripple and shudder and the steel struts squeal in protest. Sudden rain spattered heavily against the roof above them.

'We'd better get you back,' Johnson said, 'If the weather's about to turn, we don't either of us want to be caught out in it.'

'Is it turning?'

He grinned. 'This is the Outer Hebrides, he said. 'And it's January. Put your cagoule on and then hold tight, Helena. You're in for a rough ride.'

She swallowed. She couldn't help wondering how rough. The New Hope Experience complex had been the biggest challenge of her professional life. She was beginning to wonder if it might also be her biggest miscalculation.

Fortescue was at the staff entrance to the museum at 9am on Monday morning. He'd worked there as Keeper of Artefacts for a full decade before resigning after the New Hope expedition and still sat on its governing board. He was a familiar face and no one challenged him or questioned his right of entry.

He went and fetched the Horan journal from the very spot on the library archive shelf where he'd originally left it and then went to the cloakroom and opened the locker he still kept there in lieu of a desk and took out a bunch of keys.

He hadn't intended to do this. He'd intended only to recover the journal and then to be on his way to Manchester with the hand-written and cloth-bound account of Horan's last voyage aboard the *Andromeda* resting innocently on the passenger seat of the Fiat beside him as he drove.

An early Victorian building housed the museum and those parts the visitors saw had been sympathetically modernized and made spaciously inviting and interactive. But behind its public face, parts of the building were dark and cramped and labyrinthine, something he was forcefully reminded of descending two narrow, veined sets of marble steps to the room at the end of a low corridor itself narrowed by iron pipes from the period when technology hadn't yet permitted plumbing to be discreet.

He found the key he was looking for on the ring and singled it out and gripped its bow between forefinger and thumb, thinking that there'd been a time when what he was about to do would only have been done under duress and would have provoked in him a sick sensation of sweating dread. This was because the room he was about to enter contained Seamus Ballantyne's sea chest.

Inside the chest were Ballantyne's boots and boat cloak and a ceremonial sword of rank and a cutlass for those occasions when a sword wasn't ceremonial but a weapon at sea at the turbulent conclusion of the 18th century. There was a hoard of naval charts rolled and secured by a faded black ribbon. More sinister, at the bottom of the trunk, he knew there were two tribal bracelets made of human teeth, incisors drilled through and strung on fine silver chains, their tiny links exquisitely worked. He couldn't see either of them without rummaging. But that was fine because he thought them safer out of sight.

Most valuably of course there was Ballantyne's watch, a beautiful timepiece of great intricacy and astounding accuracy; the type of instrument which all ship's captains had coveted back then for the role they played in the precise navigation of any voyage. They were highly prized, but he'd been able to afford it comfortably. The slave trade had been a hugely profitable enterprise.

Collectively, the contents of the trunk had brought a series of archive keepers and cataloguers episodes of bad luck. But Fortescue seemed to have become impervious to this, perhaps in the way someone who'd been vaccinated with a small sample of something virulent became subsequently immune to the disease itself. For a while he'd carried Ballantyne's pocket watch with him everywhere, as a reminder of the fortitude he'd once shown on New Hope, this after the death of his wife unmanned him with grief and he'd daily need of proof that he'd once been strong.

Then he'd met Ruthie Gillespie. And a few months after meeting her, he'd quietly returned the slave ship captain's Breguet to what should by rights have been its resting place. Except that Ballantyne's watch was disinclined to rest, he thought now with a grim smile, opening the room's door and then fumbling slightly for the iron key on his ring of them that would unfasten the sea chest's lock.

Ballantyne's chest had his initials inlaid on the wooden curvature of its lid. It was a personal touch that traversed the centuries with the intimacy of a whisper or a hug. All around Fortescue were the sort of marine artefacts of which he'd been this museum's keeper. There were the tattered flags of battle and the oars of jolly boats and beaten drums and muskets with barrels fire-hardened in the ardent clamour of battle.

He opened the chest. He reached for Ballantyne's watch, glittering proud amid the trappings of rank and items of antique plunder. And he felt it tick strongly with its pulse of sprung, impossible life, its blued steel fingers showing as they always did the time now, correct and precise.

He'd needed to do this, he realized, he'd needed this tangible example of something finely crafted and completely practical and totally other-worldly in the restlessly industrious way it toiled on, defying the laws of physics with its rhythmic, unstoppable life. He'd needed this evidence, this cold, hard demonstration that there were forces in the world simply inexplicable. The sceptic in him had sought this proof.

He noticed then a single finger or thumbprint smeared sweatily on the watch's case back. He frowned. The print suggested that the sea chest had been recently opened. Someone had handled the watch, someone less than fastidious in their approach to the past and its surviving relics. Unless they'd just been fearful and careless as a consequence. The atmosphere down there could do that to people, Fortescue knew from his past experience.

He was at his destination in Manchester by 10.15am and by 10.30 the introductions had been completed and Georgia Tremlett had the Horan journal between her manicured hands. She looked very much the modern breed of academic, the sort with a regular gym habit and an eye for designer labels. She wore her hair short and tortoiseshell glasses with round frames. He didn't think the glasses a prop. They didn't make her look particularly studious, but they did look expensive.

'Give me an hour,' she said, leafing through the journal's pages; through Thomas Horan's fastidious copperplate, his steady depiction of an honourable man compromised by a sordid trade and embroiled in a hellish and uncanny episode. 'I can't tell you how much I've been looking forwards to reading this.'

Fortescue was reminded then that Horan had felt moved to hide his account from the world. Writing it had perhaps been cathartic for him; but he'd been so afraid of a family member or friend discovering it, he'd hidden it in a played-out shaft, sealed off and abandoned, at the mine where he'd treated the workers for free; a man so ashamed of his past, by then he'd become someone else. In Barnsley, he was Thomas Garland. By then, he'd taken his wife's maiden name.

He found a quiet spot in the college building's grounds, a cluster of benches around a fountain in the shade of a spread of conifers. He called Patsy Lassiter and told him where he was and who it was he'd shortly be with.

'This is likely to be illuminating, light on darkness,' Lassiter said.

'Do you know who's on the island now?'

'Just a skeleton maintenance crew and a six-strong security team and Baxter's architect, who is supposed to be leaving this morning, weather permitting, which it isn't at present.'

'Who's your source?'

'For meteorological info, I always use the BBC's weather site.'

'I meant for the New Hope stuff. You know I did.'

'I made some pretty good friends in Southern Isles Area Command when I was on the island restoring the Shanks cottage. And if communications systems worked on New Hope I could talk to Derek Johnson, the head of Baxter's security boys there. He was a Met police sergeant until starting his own business in the spring of last year. But my source is actually your stepdaughter. She cooked me dinner two nights ago.'

Fortescue was quiet. Then he said, 'Bet she had you singing for your supper.'

Lassiter chuckled. 'Like a canary,' he said.

'Did she tell you whether she'd finalized her interview with Felix Baxter?'

'She's hoping to do that this week. Do you ever feel, Phil, that our involvement with New Hope's something we don't have total control over?'

'I've felt that from the start, Patsy.'

'Brief me on what your expert has to say about what you've given her to read.'

'You'll be the first to know,' Fortescue said, which wasn't quite true. He'd be a close second, but Ruthie would be first. He thought about what he'd just said to Patsy thinking that if it hadn't been for New Hope, he'd never have loved and then lost and grieved for Jane. He'd never have met or come to love his stepdaughter. He'd never have encountered Patsy, who was the best friend he had left alive. And Ruthie Gillespie would always have remained someone of whom he was entirely unaware.

Georgia Tremlett looked pale, when he knocked at its door and then entered her office. She sat behind her desk with the journal closed in front of her. She rose and offered him coffee and then poured for both of them from a cafetière into mugs on a little wooden tray. They faced each other seated across her desk.

She said, 'There are differing theories as to the origin and nature of what the Albacheians called The Being that Hungers in the Darkness. And there are obvious mythological parallels elsewhere at different times in different regions of every continent.'

Fortescue frowned. He couldn't think of any obvious parallels.

She said, 'They believed it originated in a duplicate world, a world the mirror image of ours except essentially dark and corrupt. You invite it to be born here instead of there and it germinates and grows and becomes sensate and of course hungry. Only someone with enormous power could achieve this voidal transition.'

'And Shaddeh had that power?'

'Horan's journal gives an insight into the character of the man universally regarded as the greatest West African sorcerer of the modern age.'

'What are the other theories?'

'Some scholars maintain that there's a clandestine side to our existing world, a netherworld, if you will. It's here among us but conceals itself. The Albacheian sorcerers discovered or created a portal into it and developed a way to engage with its inhabitants.'

'None of this is very comforting.'

'The third and final theory is that these are alien species. Some of the Albacheian art and iconography supports that argument. So does the long lifespan of the beings and the fact that they're born already carrying their own offspring and are almost impossible to kill. Biologically, they don't much resemble mortal creatures in some significant regards.'

'Tell me about the parallels.'

'The closest would be the Wendigo believed in by the Algonquian people in Native American mythology. Almost equally close is Grendel in the epic Anglo-Saxon poem Beowulf.'

'Beowulf kills Grendel.'

'The significant point there being that of all the warriors in the known world, only the greatest of them, Beowulf, can kill her.'

Fortescue hesitated before saying what he said next. Then he said, 'I saw this creature. The Wendigo and Grendel were both anthropomorphic. The thing I saw was arachnid.'

Georgia Tremlett nodded. 'That's its natural form. It can only become humanoid after a sustained period of study. It would have learned to appear human to Ballantyne's colonists. It would have lapsed and then been still studying David Shanks when he fled the island, which is why he survived it. How long were there people on New Hope for during the expedition you took part in?'

'About six weeks in the run up, to secure the island against spoiler stories in competing media. It was sponsored as an exclusive. The actual expedition only lasted a few chaotic days.'

'Not long enough,' she said, shaking her head.

But Patsy Lassiter was there for six months and felt watched every waking moment.

'I didn't kill it, did I?'

'The recent disappearance on New Hope would suggest otherwise.'

'I recited the incantation Shaddeh made Horan write down.'

'And you're still alive. So maybe you did kill it. But you left its offspring on the island, growing in strength and appetite and growing in cunning too, all the time. The Being that Hungers is a very quick learner.'

'What about Rachel Ballantyne?'

Georgia Tremlett shuddered. 'An even darker kind of magic,' she said. 'That was Shaddeh probably so weak with delirium he was tempted into playing God. The thing Rachel Ballantyne became in her living death's a persistent affront to the natural order. She's a grave insult to nature itself. Death is supposed to be a one-way street, that's emphatically the deal. Her continued existence makes the island a place of dangerous volatility.'

'The weather's pretty untrustworthy,' Fortescue said. 'And radio signals mostly don't exist there.'

Dr. Tremlett laughed, bleakly. 'That'll be the very least of it,' she said. 'The Albacheians believed a creature such as Rachel Ballantyne's become makes death itself contagious. I'm translating freely, but they called any domain roamed by what Rachel is now a Land without Light. They called it a Kingdom of Decay. To them, it was the Region of the Dreamless or the Realm of Anguish.'

'The names sound quite poetic, but I get your drift,' Fortescue said. 'It sounds like they were very familiar with magic.'

'It's the principal reason for their extinction,' Dr. Tremlett said. 'They came to depend upon it. That corrupted and weakened them because it cost them their will for effort and enterprise and the other imperatives that make a society healthy and discipline it into being ethically sound.'

Fortescue remembered that the woman opposite him has started out as an anthropologist.

She said, 'Shaddeh had every reason to hate Ballantyne, because according to Horan's account, the man was basically his executioner. But the revenge he took on him was a terrible abuse of occult power, even by the rather decadent Albacheian standards of the late 18th century.'

'Do you believe in magic personally?'

'I've always kept an open mind,' she said. She nodded at the journal, between the resting elbows supporting her chin. 'This has opened it quite a lot further.'

'An entrepreneur named Felix Baxter is planning to open a New Age resort on New Hope in the spring.'

'I know, quaint habit though it is, I still read newspapers. Plus, I was born in Aberdeen, so I have a patriot's interest in matters Scottish.'

Fortescue hadn't been able to place her accent. Maybe there was a Celtic lilt, under all the layers of education. He said, 'What do you think of that?'

She said, 'New Hope Island has claimed lives ever since the days of the Colony Seamus Ballantyne established there. What you've shown me today gives me no reason to believe that pattern won't continue.'

'Can it be stopped?'

'I've no idea,' she said. 'But I'll do everything I can to try to find out.' She gestured at the journal. 'Could I hold onto this for a while, for further study?'

'You can keep it,' he said. 'It's mine to give, so now it's yours to have.'

Chapter Six

The concierge at the Vincent had told Ruthie that there were four or five really first-rate pubs in Southport but that the stand-out for him was The Guest House, less than half a mile away. It had been built in the arts and crafts style and was completely authentic and intact. He said the pub was quietly atmospheric, the staff courteous, the food excellent and though she didn't look very much like a beer drinker, the brews available varied and immaculately kept.

She'd spent the morning in their hotel room writing. She'd met her word-count quota without too much of a struggle. This new book was a departure for her, because its intended readership was fully-fledged adults. In the past, she'd always written for children or for teenagers. Almost eight years on from her debut, she was stretching herself. The twin challenges were an engaging plot and the right tone. If you were confident of your story, your characters would evolve naturally, or so she told herself. It was relatively early days, but going well so far.

She planned to visit the Atkinson, an arts centre on Lord Street that had re-opened a couple of years earlier after a massive refurbishment job to rave reviews. She also wanted to walk along the seafront and see the Marine Lake and Rotten Row. But first she would walk to the Guest House in Houghton Street and have some lunch. It was one o'clock and she was hungry. Phil had called her half an hour earlier to say that he was going to go back to the museum in Liverpool before returning to Southport, to check something out.

'Didn't you go there on your way to Manchester to get the Horan journal?'

'I did, but something Georgia Tremlett said has got me intrigued.'

'Did she say anything interesting?'

'None of what she said was reassuring.'

'My life has taken a dark turn since I met you.'

'You asked me to meet you in the first place because your life had taken a dark turn already. Then you asked me out. You're a writer. You should be strong on chronology.'

'Ah, but I write fiction, not history,' she said. 'I can believe what suits me.'

'There's really no answer to that.'

'What time will you be back?'

'At about four.'

'Meet me at the Atkinson coffee bar.'

'Done.'

She walked along Lord Street, past Southport's austerely beautiful war memorial and cenotaph; the great trees of the boulevard unburdened by leaves, the wrought-iron and glass canopies of the shop-fronts on the opposite side of the road rusting genteelly, the sky above grey and uniform but the day so far mild, dry and virtually windless.

The pub was quiet. She ordered her food at the bar and bought a large glass of white wine and went and sat in a small, wood-paneled room to the right as you faced the entrance. The single window was leaded and didn't allow much light from the dullness prevalent outside. The paneling had a dark patina and the period furnishings were subdued. There was one other person in the room, a woman reading an old Penguin paperback with its curled and faded trademark orange cover. The stillness there might have struck Ruthie as odd, were she not preoccupied with a plot contradiction she hadn't quite resolved that morning.

A cleaving blow of despondency hit her all at once, suddenly and completely unexpectedly, almost depriving her of breath. It passed, but it obliged her to glance at the woman seated rigidly behind the old paperback alone in the far corner.

This woman more than slightly resembled Ruthie herself. She had the same dark eyes and crimson mouth and the same straight black hair and precisely cut fringe. They both had pale complexions, but there were contrasting reasons for that. Ruthie's skin was naturally pale. The dead woman, when she studied her, had the pallor of a corpse. Now, the ghost shifted her eyes from her book to meet Ruthie's. They were absent of life, yet curious, which was unsettling. The woman was dressed in a double-buttoned coat of black wool. The buttons were metal and lustreless and the fabric fusty, now that Ruthie looked and her hair had a dull, blowsy lifelessness.

If she gets up, Ruthie thought, if she lurches to her feet, I'll scream. But the ghost was here for her, she knew. It was why she felt so desolate. She gulped wine with her glass between the grip of both shaking hands and stood instead herself. She came out from behind her table and glanced out of the room towards the bar, just to ensure that she was still in the here and now. Behind the bar, the polite young bloke who'd served her polished a dimpled pint mug absently.

Ruthie walked over to the spectre and sat in a chair, not close enough to be reached out at and grasped between the grip of dead fingers, but as close as she dared get; close enough to converse. Proximity did nothing for the woman's appearance. The book between her stiff hands was Mary Shelley's *Frankenstein*.

'Has Fortescue not told you about me?'

Her voice was throaty with disuse. Her mouth moved when she spoke, but she didn't shape the words. It was like watching a ventriloquist who wasn't very good.

'No,' Ruthie said.

'My name is Elizabeth Burrows. I once stole something from Seamus Ballantyne's sea chest. When the chest is opened, I'm sometimes summoned back like this. I think that's my punishment. I'm not proud of my dishevelment. I was stylish in life. I watched him for a while, your Keeper of Maritime Artefacts. He was aware of my doing so. I'm not surprised he's tried to forget.'

'Why are you talking to me?'

'Your Professor's just done something very brave and extremely stupid. He might share it with you but he'll probably be too noble for that.' Elizabeth Burrows' ghost rasped out a chuckle. She said, 'He's a good one, as men go.'

Ruthie had an intuition then that Elizabeth hadn't much liked men.

'It was the fashion, politically,' she said, 'I was a student and there was a gender war. My day would seem very quaint to you, dear.'

Elizabeth's arm jerked. For a stretched-out moment of cold revulsion, Ruthie thought she might be about to reach out a hand to cover hers in an act of sisterly solidarity that would scrape dead skin over flesh still warm and living. But that obscene contradiction didn't occur.

'He can't endure the ordeal he plans alone,' the spectre said. 'I tried that and it drove me to despair and eventually self-murder. He listens with you, or you might well lose him to it. Now go, Ruthie, so I can spare you the sight of my departure.'

Ruthie Gillespie walked out of the pub. She did so leaving half a glass of wine un-drunk and a lunch paid for and not yet served. She'd lost her appetite, not to shock, but to a smell still haunting her nostrils.

She'd turned right without conscious thought. She'd walk across Lord Street on up to the Marine Lake and smoke a cigarette and then find a bar, any bar, and order something strong to drink. The odour had been faint. But it had been persistently there and it had not been at all a scent you'd confuse with the smell of the living.

Helena Davenport said, 'So you're not actually on Baxter's payroll?'

'No,' Johnson said.

'That seems a bit odd when he runs a security firm of his own.'

'They're bouncers, they do doors. This is more specialized. I'm ex-Met police and my blokes are all ex-police or ex-army. There's a level of expertise and fitness required and some knowledge about survival and emergency protocols. What I didn't know already, I've learned. It's a bit different from wearing a black bomber jacket and buzz-cut hair and saying you're not welcome at the disco in those trainers.'

'But you didn't have the expertise required to save Greg Cody.'

'Apparently not.'

'Why did you take the job?'

'There's a Met Commander back at New Scotland Yard, bloke named Lassiter. He's a bit of a legend, to be honest. He was on the New Hope expedition in '10 and he came back here eighteen months ago when a writers' retreat came to grief on the island. His wife came with him and was killed with a couple of other people by a freak wave.'

'Jesus.'

'When this gig came up, I called Commander Lassiter. I'd met him once at a lecture he'd given a bunch of promising junior officers. He remembered me, which was flattering but probably characteristic. He told me the island was a hazardous and intrinsically hostile place.'

'And that wasn't enough to put you off?'

'It was meant to, Helena, there's no doubt about that. But all it actually did was intrigue me further. This was a minimum year duration contract. The pay is good and the benefits generous. Felix Baxter seems to believe that you pay peanuts and you get monkeys. He didn't want monkeys here. He wanted vigilant professionals on the job. He very much wants this project to succeed, is my feeling. I was grateful for the Commander's warning but chose to ignore his advice, as I'm sure he knew I would.'

'He didn't know you that well.'

'He's the sort doesn't need to read body language or look into your eyes. He can intuit just through the tone of your voice.'

Helena said, 'If you'd have been the sort of man to accept his advice, you'd never have left the Met in the first place.'

'That's exactly right. I resigned because I couldn't stomach a level of accountability that means you have to practically fill in a form if you want to take a crap. The bureaucracy of modern policing's just unbelievable. So I quit and now I'm doing this instead.'

'And you're your own boss.'

'In charge of everything,' he said, 'except the weather, and Greg Cody's whereabouts and you. I'm not in charge of you, obviously.'

They were in the sitting room of her suite. The lights were on. Outside it was gloomy and wet, scudding clouds, wind in withering gusts scouring the exterior of the complex. She thought that even with its partial crack, her picture window retained sufficient integrity and strength to resist the elements. She was anxious to get it replaced, but that was more of an aesthetic than a practical priority. She'd already asked Johnson how long the storm was likely to last and he'd just shrugged and said there was no real way of telling.

There were two plus points to her extended stay on New Hope. Every hour she spent in its granite isolation increased her resolve to put the coke habit and the toy boy behind her. The island wasn't exactly party central. She'd be put in the way of narcotic temptation as soon as she got back to Edinburgh.

Professionally, she was doing fine. Personally, she was aimless with damaged esteem and the damage had been wholly self-inflicted. It was long past time to get a grip. She said, 'Meeting someone as intuitive as your Commander Lassiter must be a bit intimidating, like stepping into an x-ray machine.'

'It isn't, really. He's a recovering alcoholic and makes no secret of the fact. He doesn't suffer fools, but there's no arrogance about him. You'd like him, if you ever got to meet.'

Thankfully, we won't, she thought, *because he'd see right through me.* Instead, she said, 'Good looking?'

Johnson pondered on this. He said, 'Yeah, I suppose, in a lean, tough, weathered sort of way.' He grinned. 'Plus he's single.'

Their conversation had taken a fanciful sort of turn. What else did you do? She should have been back on the mainland by now but nothing was going to fly in this weather and the swell was too severe for any boat to come and get her off. She couldn't even contact the office by email or phone. Even amid all that seductive five-star New Age luxury, with the freezer full and under-floor heating on, she was aware of the island's remoteness and isolation and the capricious limits it imposed on free will.

To Johnson, she said, 'What do you know about Seamus Ballantyne's Colony?'

Johnson, burly handful that he was, shivered slightly. He said, 'He called it his Kingdom of Belief, but their faith didn't save them. All of them vanished.' Then he said, 'If you've no objection, Helena, I think I'll do a session in the gym.'

'You've got your kit?'

'It's in the box on the back of the quad bike.'

'Be my guest,' she said. 'I might even join you.' She looked at her wristwatch. It was four in the afternoon and getting gloomier outside, dusk-like. The truth was that she really didn't want to be by herself. She was quite seriously spooked and rather dreading the night to come. It would be an ordeal. She kept telling herself she'd been unnerved by watching *The Shining* two nights previously. But it wasn't that, she knew. It was this place.

'You've got family, haven't you, Derek?'

'I've a wife and two young boys, three and five.'

'You must miss them.'

'Every minute of every day, but it's for my family I'm doing this.' He stood and stretched and the bones of his big frame cracked audibly. He said, 'Ninety minutes of lifting heavy metal and then I'll rustle us up some dinner, crack a beer, open a bottle of vino for you, make the popcorn.'

'Really, popcorn?'

'Tonight's double-bill is *Notting Hill* and *Pretty Woman*. We're having a feel-good evening.'

She smiled. She thought that left to his own devices, he'd probably be looking forward to a filmic zombie-fest or a Wes Craven triple-bill. Except that Johnson's Commander Lassiter wasn't the only intuitive man on the planet.

Phil had taken Ruthie to a swanky, brightly-lit pub called The Imperial. It was a world away from the deliberate, authentic gloom of the Guest House. She didn't think she'd see Elizabeth Burrows here. In the glare of the fierce ornamental bulbs above them she'd look as lifeless and bedraggled as a scarecrow.

I'm not proud of my dishevelment. I was stylish in life.

She'd confronted him straight away, the moment he walked into the Atkinson, waiting for him just inside the main door, pouncing because secrets were lies and lies were a betrayal she simply wouldn't tolerate.

He told her there about what Doctor Tremlett had told him about the hazards present on New Hope, the mythology and the mythic creature's potent, enduring antipathy to man. And she told him about her lunchtime encounter with a threadbare revenant only present to issue a warning.

'You'll tell me what you've been up to Phil, or it's the end of us.'

'I'll tell you everything,' he said. 'I'll tell you tonight, over a drink.'

'You've need of Dutch courage?'

'I'm nowhere near as brave as you seem to think.'

'You're too fucking brave for your own good, that's a big part of our problem.'

He looked crestfallen, at that. He said, 'You really think we've a problem?'

'Yeah, we have, I found out today. And we solve it today or it's over between us.'

At a table at the Imperial he said, 'She was a student. Only two people requested access to Ballantyne's sea chest in the whole of the 20th century. David Shanks was the first of them and Elizabeth Burrows was the second.

'She was a postgrad student back at the end of the 1960's at Liverpool University. She was doing a Politics and Philosophy PhD. She was a feminist and a huge fan of the feminist pioneer Mary Wollstonecraft.'

'She was reading *Frankenstein*, when I saw her, or she was pretending to. Wasn't Mary Shelley Mary Wollstonecraft's daughter?'

Fortescue nodded. He said, 'She was reading that when Patsy Lassiter saw her.'

'Jesus,' Ruthie said. 'Patsy's seen her too?'

'On the day I first met him seven years ago. Patsy came to the museum in the run up to the New Hope expedition. He was still an ex-copper back then, doing background prior to the expedition itself, working on a retainer, still drinking. The contents of the chest gave him a start and he went to the pub afterwards for a stiffener and saw Lizzie Burrows and she spoke to him. He got enough clues when he thought about it to place her time-wise. He had an old police colleague on the Merseyside Force. He was able to find out from him about the original investigation into Elizabeth's death.'

'Go on.'

'Elizabeth Burrows was doing her thesis on Rebecca Browning, who was Seamus Ballantyne's estranged wife. Apparently Rebecca was some sort of proto-feminist pin-up, at least to Elizabeth. She gained access to the sea chest, legitimately. But she stole something and the theft led to her downfall.'

'She committed suicide,' Ruthie said. 'She told me so herself.'

'Do you never regret your Goth tendencies?'

'I can't help my hair colour. Black clothes are slimming to wear. My complexion is naturally pale. The last time I drank cider at night in a graveyard I was 17. That's half a lifetime ago for me.'

'That graveyard night, were you listening to The Cure?'

'You're not out of the woods, Phil, and jokes won't get you there. Get on with the story or I'll make you a very unhappy man.'

Elizabeth had stolen a bracelet of human teeth. The Horan journal later informed Fortescue that this was one of two such bracelets found with Shaddeh when the Albacheians had discovered him on a river bank as no more than an infant child. The teeth were drilled-through and all incisors. Ballantyne had taken them from his defiant captive slave and stored then away and apparently forgotten about them years before his harbour-side epiphany and his leaving of his native Liverpool for the island he would christen New Hope.

'Why the fuck would anyone steal a bracelet made of human teeth?'

'Your language isn't pretty tonight.'

'Elizabeth Burrows wasn't pretty in the Guest House, so fucking well answer the question, Phil.'

'She told me that herself the last time I ever saw her. I'd see her from time to time, in cafes and bars, pretending to read her old paperback with the faded cover and the suntan oil stains from beach reading. Then the last time she appeared was at my flat and she told me she'd stolen the bracelet on a whim. She couldn't understand why she'd done it. Had it been a riding crop or broach or hair ribbon, some keepsake to do with Rebecca Browning, she'd have known why she'd stolen it. But it wasn't and she didn't.'

'What happened?'

'The teeth bracelet was innocent in the daytime. But at night it formed the shape of a mouth and spoke to her. It told her secrets she found it intolerable to hear and know. In the end, she hanged herself.'

'The poor woman.'

'Patsy reckoned she'd have suspected she was going mad, a candidate for sectioning and a straightjacket and a rubber clamp to stop her biting off her own tongue in a fit. He figured her too proud and independent to tolerate that happening to her and so she took her own life.'

'And the object that did for her?'

'Recovered from the desk in her college room and returned in time to the museum.'

'And now you've got one of the bracelets, because you want to hear what that mouth has to say. But you had no intention of telling me you'd taken it.'

'I wanted to spare you the experience. I'm telling you now.'

'Elizabeth told me it could be disastrous for you to listen to it on your own.'

'Well, she should know. Nice of her to care, I suppose.'

'How did you know which of the bracelets to take?'

'I don't think it matters. They're identical. The idea occurred to me listening to Georgia Tremlett. She called Shaddeh the greatest African magician of the modern age. She doesn't necessarily believe in magic. I've been given ample reason to do so. I think it was Shaddeh's voice that Elizabeth heard. If he's as regretful as I think he is about what he set in motion on New Hope, he'll speak to us.'

'So it's us, now? I'm invited to join you in the posh seats?'

'Please don't be angry.'

'You get one let off with me Professor Fortescue and that was it. I'll forgive and forget, but don't ever try and deceive me again. Where's the bracelet now?'

'It's in the boot of my car. I'm not spoiling our little holiday by risking anything like that tonight.'

'He's been dead for 200 years.'

'Elizabeth Burrows has been dead for 50.'

'She doesn't look too fresh.'

'But you take my point.'

'It was actually rather a clever thought, not the not telling me bit, that was exceptionally dumb, but the basic idea. It's going to be bloody sinister to sit through if it works.'

'Would you be happy to have it happen at your cottage?'

'Happy is the wrong word. Where did Elizabeth hear it?'

'It spoke in her college room, in a hall of residence in Liverpool.'

'If anything peculiar had happened in that room after her death, it would have been an adjunct to the police report, wouldn't it?'

'Yes, it would. Patsy said the investigation was thorough.'

Ruthie thought about this, about hearing the bracelet speak within her own four walls. It wouldn't be pleasant, but it seemed reasonably safe.

'It bit me once.'

'It did what?'

'I was overcome by fear, inventorying the contents of the chest. I tried to butch it out. I dared myself to put on one of the bracelets. It was pure bravado and then the teeth closed around my wrist.'

'That must've been terrifying.'

'It was, at the time. In retrospect, I think it was just Shaddeh having a bit of fun. I think he was just teasing me. The skin wasn't broken. No blood was drawn.'

'So you'd do it again?'

'What do you think?'

She leaned forward and kissed him on the mouth. His penance was paid, his period of hard labour over. There were arcane rules about kissing in pubs; but looking around her, at the scouse-brows and heavy make-up and microskirts of most of the Imperial's female clientele, she thought hers a forgivable crime.

'Is there a decent Indian in Southport?'

'There's bound to be,' he said.

'Let's find it,' Ruthie said. 'I'm suffocating in perfume and aftershave in here and I could murder a curry.' She took a last look around, standing. She said, 'I can't understand why you brought me here, it's not my sort of place at all.'

He said, 'You were angry. This place is always heaving. I needed witnesses, in case things got physical.'

'You're forgiven,' she said, 'so things could get physical later. But I've got to eat first or I'm likely to faint'

They watched *Pretty Woman* first on the toss of a coin. They'd got halfway through *Notting Hill* and were down to the scrapings of the popcorn Johnson had made when the screen went off and simultaneously, the lights all went out.

'Power cut,' Johnson said, redundantly.

It wasn't pitch-dark. They'd turned down the lights anyway to brighten the image on the widescreen TV they were watching. There was enough ambient light from the rainy sky outside to be able to avoid bumping into pieces of furniture. It was the locks Helena was concerned about. They were electronically powered and she thought with the power out the locks on the main entrance would probably have released. They did that for safety reasons that had her now feeling anything but secure. It was a fail-safe to prevent people from feeling trapped. Except that trapped was exactly how she felt.

They'd had the volume of the movie cranked up high. The sudden silence wasn't silent at all. Sounds they had been drowning out swelled and murmured. Wind ululated, given a voice by the contours of the complex she'd designed, moaning and shrieking with fluctuating force, whipping and hurling rain audibly against the windows of her suite.

Everything was dulled to monochrome. Helena inventoried their debris; the empty crisp and tortilla chip bags and the drained beer cans and half empty bottle of Merlot and the wine glass beside it and the bowl they'd improvised as a popcorn bucket and they were the vestiges of a little kingdom, stray symbols of the siege mentality their shared insecurities about the island had forced upon them. She felt a frigid blast of salt-air and knew with certainty that their defences had been breached. The front entrance was ajar, its hi-tech locks defunct.

'Can't be a power outage,' she said. 'We're using a tiny fraction of the gen's capacity.'

'Teething problem,' Johnson said. 'Isn't that why Baxter invited you to come?'

'I suppose one of the reasons.'

'Unless it's someone playing silly buggers,' Johnson said.

Someone or something, Helena thought, remembering the abrupt eclipse in the room they were in now, in afternoon sunlight, the shudder of something strong and substantial colliding with toughened glass forcefully enough to inflict a crack she had growing doubts about. Would the window hold? Physics told her it would. But the laws of physics were proving less than immutable on New Hope Island.

'I'm no engineer,' she said, 'but I can get the power back on. Even if I can't locate and fix the fault, I can switch over to our back-up generator. It's tested and fully fuelled. It's not a complicated job.'

Johnson nodded. There was another cold gust of Atlantic air and somewhere not far away a door slammed with a sudden loud thump that made both of them jump.

'I'll get my jacket,' Johnson said.

'I'm glad you're here, Derek.'

'It's my job,' he said, she thought matching her for understatement.

She shivered. The air coming in through the open doors had scoured out their man-made warmth with surprising speed. It was January, it was the Hebrides and around them, a winter storm raged.

She walked carefully into her bedroom and took a sweater from a drawer and put it on. She located gloves and a scarf and her rainproof parka. She was lacing on her hiking boots when she thought there some subtle shift in the sound of the gale outside, now insinuating its path through empty galleries and corridors, through the lift shaft and other pockets of more artful space she'd created. Just for a moment, it seemed to croon out a melody. Wind sang a brief snatch of, *The Recruited Collier.* But she knew that was just her fraught imagination playing impish tricks on someone thoroughly scared.

Chapter Seven

The main entrance was open, when they got to it, battening back and forth on its hinges, a quarter of a ton of steel and the sustainably sourced wood covering it, flapping, toyed with by surging, elemental force. Rain puddled inside the complex foyer making the teak floor slippery between coconut mats meant to give the lobby an informal, Robinson Crusoe feel. They'd been the idea of an interior decorator briefed to conjure a period mood of island paradise.

Now they were damp and ridiculous and would reek stagnantly of salt when they dried out, if ever they did dry out, if ever the storm eased and ended, Helena thought. The island wasn't paradise. It was anarchic and delinquent and it was her cruel and hostile prison too. The thought came to her in the gloom of the foyer that she was being punished for what she'd done here. And she wondered, dry mouthed, whether her crime against New Hope would prove to be a capital offence.

Johnson reached for her upper arm and shook her bodily. He said, 'Stay in the moment, Helena. There's no real reason to be afraid.'

'Then why are you whispering?'

'Just take everything one step at a time.'

'Okay,' she said, nodding, thinking that he was talking to himself in saying this as much as he was to her. It wasn't that fear and panic were contagious, so much as that the place they were in provoked those responses so strongly. For the first time, she wondered seriously were there ghosts here.

They got outside. The air was a harsh, stinging assault of rain and spindrift. The sea itself was a dark turmoil of surging water topped by ragged spumes of white. Gusting wind howled outside and careened around and buffeted them and Helena led the way as quickly as she was able along it's façade and left flank aiming for the rear of the complex and the route underground to the bunker housing their twin generators.

Access was via a grey metal hatch coloured and contoured to match the granite around it. If you didn't know it was there, you were unlikely to spot and be offended by this heavily industrial artefact. The idea, Baxter's idea, was that nothing jarred or spoiled the mood. The generators were literally the dirty secret hidden behind and below his Arcadian retreat.

A hex key opened the hatch and Helena had the one that matched the hexagonal slot precisely on her key ring. She opened the hatch, struggling against the wind, both of them together lifting and dropping it back flat against the rock, staring down into blackness she knew concealed a flight of metal steps.

She hadn't brought a torch.

But Johnson had. He played the beam and they climbed down to an eerie stillness and quiet, everything monochromatic in the torch beam, the gouged vault given the dimensions, as light played on the walls surrounding them, of an epic tomb.

There was a snicker of sound and then a throaty gurgle and generator 1 kicked suddenly, powerfully back into life.

Johnson played the torch beam over its housing. The lights above them in metal brackets in twin rows glimmered and then strengthened and glowed. He switched the torch beam off and Helena checked the gauges mounted on the generator's console. She checked temperature and fan strength and pressure and fuel levels. Everything was as it should have been.

'Glitchy,' Johnson said.

Helena shook her head. She'd have to shout for him to hear her over the noise down there now. She said, 'These things are ridiculously over-engineered. They don't just stop and start spontaneously.'

'The ghost in the machine,' Johnson said, smiling.

It was the title of a book by Arthur Koestler. It was also the title of an album by The Police, which Helena thought Johnson much more likely referencing. Either way, it proved she wasn't the only one with phantoms on her mind. She looked up to the open hatch, rain drizzling through it onto the top-most steps, fearful that it would suddenly shut with a clang, trapping them, their having been deliberately lured there.

But that didn't happen. She had one more thorough look at the working generator and then they climbed up and out, into weather she hoped she wasn't deceiving herself was becoming slightly less severe than it had seemed when the lights went out.

They secured all the doors. Johnson found a mop and bucket and mopped water from the lobby floor. By the time they got back to her suite, the wind wasn't quite the incessant howl it had been when the film had stopped and they'd first become properly aware of it. She examined the crack in the picture window and was relieved to see it hadn't worsened. By now it was 1am and Helena was more than ready for bed and sleep.

She was in her bathroom, had actually applied a smudge of toothpaste to the bristles of her toothbrush when she looked into the sink and saw something sitting there.

It was a single tooth, the enamel slightly yellow against the white of the bowl. There was a brownish circle of gum around the root. The tooth was an incisor and the gum, now Helena had seen it there, gave off a whiff of decomposition like the taint of spoiled meat that caused her to gag, because the tooth was human and had been ripped out forcefully and could only have been put there deliberately for her to find.

Edie Chambers got the call from Felix Baxter's office at 11am on Tuesday morning, at almost exactly the moment the boat appeared on the horizon of a calm sea to collect a relieved Helena Davenport from the cobbled quay that passed for a dock when the weather allowed on New Hope Island.

It wasn't from Baxter personally, obviously. But it was to confirm that their preliminary interview would take place on Thursday at Baxter's London offices at noon.

'Preliminary?'

Baxter's PA had introduced herself as Joy, no surname. 'Assuming the interview goes well,' she said, 'he'll want you to see what he's done with the island. We have a stock of excellent pictures of all the major landmarks and exterior and interior shots of the complex and they can be used to illustrate your piece, but Felix will want you to see it all personally before you write about it. That's just being professional and thorough.'

'Sounds fantastic,' Edie said.

'He might want you to talk to his project architect Helena Davenport and maybe to Hugh Mortimer, who's his resort general manager. That's to be discussed.'

'Okay.' Edie didn't want to interview Hugh Mortimer. She wanted to write a profile piece on Felix Baxter, maybe with a substantial sidebar on the New Hope Experience. It wasn't intended as a puff-piece or advertorial for the resort. Though she thought Helena Davenport might be good value and a live subject since she was both Scottish and up for a clutch of awards. Good for a couple of punchy and pertinent quotes, anyway.

She was also interested in discovering if she could what had become of Greg Cody. Baxter had successfully kept that mystery quiet, at least so far. Edie had discovered Cody had a wife, who lived in Epsom. If Patsy was right, what she actually was now was Greg Cody's widow. Calling her out of the blue would be crass and callous and risk censure from the college. But obtaining a contact number would be straightforward and Edie was curious to know why the woman had not gone public on her husband's disappearance.

'Don't be late on Thursday,' Joy said. 'Felix values punctuality. Being late is bad manners and he hates discourtesy.'

'I'll be on time,' Edie said, 'I wouldn't dream of turning up late.'

So she was going back to New Hope. Her first and last visit to the island had taken place 18 months earlier when she'd been shadowing the Chronicle reporter Lucy Church; sent there by the late Alexander McIntyre to find out what had happened to the writers' retreat members who had days earlier vanished from their camp there.

Lucy Church had been her mum's best friend and to her, Auntie Lucy. Her mum and Auntie Lucy had met and bonded in the run-up to McIntyre's expedition six years earlier, on which they'd both gone. Now they were both dead. Her mum had died of heart failure three years ago and Auntie Lucy had later perished on New Hope. As had Aunt Lucy's husband, to Edie, her Uncle Paul.

Now it occurred to her that some or all of this this might be detail known to Felix Baxter. He was such a thorough and calculating man, it was actually inconceivable that he didn't know about her connection to the island; that her step-father was Phil Fortescue, who was Patrick Lassiter's best friend; two men who'd been members of the New Hope expedition, where Phil had first met her mum. He would have known when he said yes to her interview request. Or he would have found out checking her credentials soon after. Not personally he wouldn't, but Joy or someone like Joy would have done it on his behalf.

That's why he'd granted the interview request. Patsy had been wrong about his ego being indiscriminate. It had nothing to do with his ego and everything to do with finding out first-hand about some of the things that had occurred in the island's recent history. Nothing was going to stop his project on New Hope and nothing ever would have; but forewarned was forearmed. That had been Baxter's reasoning in saying yes to her, she was quite suddenly sure of it.

Something she was much less sure about was her own attitude emotionally to returning to New Hope. It had been a fearful place on her last visit, a place of confusion and terror and in the end of crushing loss. It had no happy associations in her mind. Objectively, she was curious, had a born-reporter's compelling urge to see the changed wrought there for herself. And there was something else, some other feeling that wasn't quite resignation, when she tried to identify it properly. Edie discovered, in that moment, that she felt fated to go back there.

On Tuesday evening, Fortescue called Patsy Lassiter. He told him what Georgia Tremlett had divulged about Shaddeh's industrious New Hope magic and then he told him about taking the bracelet from the sea chest in Liverpool and the encounter between Elizabeth Burrows and Ruthie Gillespie in a dimly lit Southport pub. Lassiter had been up close and personal with Ballantyne's sea chest and endured a cameo from Elizabeth later the same day as a consequence. That was in the period when he'd still been drinking, but evidently, seven years on from the episode, he remembered it well enough.

'Frankly, mate, you're an idiot.'

'That definition works for me on a number of levels. Be more precise, Patsy.'

'Keeping anything from Ruthie is just stupid. She's all or nothing and she's all you've got.'

'I've got Edie.'

'I mean romantically. Second-chances don't generally come along in the shape of Ruthie Gillespie. Cherish her, or someone else will.'

'Cheers.'

'I don't recommend being single, not at our age, I don't.'

'Should I take out my violin, Patsy? I keep it close to hand, just in case.'

'I happen to have a date Saturday night, you cheeky Scouse chancer.'

'Let me guess; a Homebase car park, about two hours after closing. Only my opinion, Patsy, but senior serving police officers should steer clear of dogging sites.'

'Does the name Helena Davenport mean anything to you?'

'Of course it does. She's asked you out?'

'Saturday night, here in London and she's Edinburgh based, so maybe I should be highly flattered but I'm not, because she wants something and the something is information. She's been on the island. She was only able to get off it this morning.'

'My feeling is you'll barter information. Something happened while she was there, that's why she's contacted you.'

'Another century, at this rate, and you'd make a half-decent probationer. When do you and Ruthie plan to do your bracelet thing?'

'Not for another couple of days. Ruthie's really shaken by the Burrows business.'

'With her there,' Lassiter said

'There's no bringing that poor Cody bloke back, but no one else has disappeared, so there's no immediate urgency. Have they?'

'Not to my knowledge, though Ms. Davenport didn't sound overly-calm on the blower.'

'The blower, honest to God, Patsy, sometimes you're right out of *The Sweeney*.'

'An observation previously made by the lovely woman in your life, Phil. Don't you go blowing it with her. You'll regret it forever.'

'I know that. Take care, Patsy.'

'When I've got someone to take care of, I'll be sure to follow your advice. In the meantime, be careful with the teeth, Phil. All teeth ever really do is bite.'

Lassiter was at home, the too big now home he'd shared with his wife Alice until her death on New Hope. He ended the call thinking about the bits he'd left out, the things Helena Davenport had shared with him that he hadn't just now shared with Phil.

'I'd like to talk to you, Commander Lassiter, but it needs to be face to face.'

'I'm assuming Derek Johnson put you onto me.'

'He's a nice man, a good man.'

'Too good to lose, but policing the 21st century way isn't everyone's cup of tea.'

'Will you see me?'

'What's your schedule like?'

'No ties that bind.'

'That's an odd way of putting things, Ms. Davenport.'

'Helena, please, Commander.'

'Then since this isn't official business, please call me Patrick.'

'I'm busy until close of business on Friday. After that I'm completely free. My only pressing social obligations were a coke habit and a toy boy to try to keep in tow and neither of those survived my New Hope experience, which leaves me with a weekend to fill.'

What Lassiter said was, 'The price of success, Helena, it's lonely at the top.' What he thought though was that New Hope for her had clearly been a brutal epiphany. He was intrigued, curious enough to agree to meet her in London early on Saturday evening at his home, where he'd get more out of her because she'd be more relaxed and focused than was likely in a bar or restaurant.

'I suppose it's a bit stupid, revealing a drug habit to a very senior cop.'

'Not one you've put behind you.'

'Your faith is touching.'

'I'm a recovering alcoholic, Helena.'

'I know. Derek Johnson told me.'

'I look forward to meeting you on Saturday.'

He read her Wikipedia entry, which he didn't necessarily trust. He did a Google search and read about the involvement of Davenport Associates with Baxter Enterprises and the complex Baxter had commissioned as the centerpiece of his New Hope Experience. He studied pictures of her building. His distrust of the island told him time would make of it an extravagant folly, but there was no denying its aesthetic appeal. It was a masterfully apt construction, cunningly vernacular, cleverly sympathetic to its surroundings.

Lassiter read about the awards for which Helena's practice had been shortlisted as a consequence of the New Hope build. He reckoned she'd get at least one gong; awards were political and the project had been popular in Hollyrood and Whitehall. They'd backed Baxter's scheme – Baxter's dream – with hard cash.

Finally, he did an image search. The euphemism for Helena Davenport's physique was big-boned. She had generous shoulders and hips and a cleavage. She had shoulder-length auburn hair and a strong jaw and green eyes. She was far from conventionally beautiful and 'pretty' would have trivialized someone so persistently stylish in her dress and fiercely intelligent in her expression. Still, Lassiter thought, she's pretty easy on the eye.

On Tuesday evening on New Hope, the six-man strong maintenance crew held a barbecue jointly with the three members of the security team not on duty that night. The break in the weather, the pale sunshine and relative warmth and calm were their excuse for a little celebratory meal out in the open instead of skulking in wind-wracked shelters like modern day cavemen.

They wound-up Johnson, who was present, with speculation about his five-star romance holed up at the Experience complex with glamorous high-flyer Helena Davenport. This was lightly done, because he was both a devoted family man and built on a scale that made it seriously bad news if he went and took offence.

Carter, the crew foreman, pushed him the furthest, probably on the basis of rank. 'I mean *Pretty Woman*, Deggsy. Does it get any lower?'

'She was spooked,' Johnson said, regretting having mentioned his and Helena's feel-good double-bill. 'I mean Christ, Dave, I was spooked myself. A Freddie Krueger-fest wasn't really on the cards.'

'The thing is it does get lower. It gets down as far as Hugh Grant. I mean, *Notting Hill*, Jesus.'

Johnson shrugged, 'It could've been worse, it could've been *Love Actually*, Hugh Grant and Martine McCutcheon.'

'Wasn't Helena a bit put out by your Julia Roberts fixation?'

'Julia Roberts is the wrong side of 50.'

'Not in *Pretty Woman*, she's not. Anyway, you like them mature. Helena Davenport's got to be pushing 40.'

Derek Johnson smiled despite himself. He didn't mind a joke at his own expense and had actually though Helena a lovely woman, warm and genuine and brave. It was the brave bit that bothered him, the fact that the island had required such fortitude of her. He didn't think that boded well for the future of the resort she'd helped create.

And there was a matter of more immediate concern in the incisor surrounded by its circle of torn and putrefying gum she'd discovered in her bathroom sink and wasted no time in showing him. Johnson wasn't a betting man, but he thought the odds on that belonging to anyone other than the late Greg Cody, very long indeed.

Was there a connection between the cracked window glass and the discovery of the tooth? Probably there was and the tooth had been put there after the generator failure had released the locks securing the complex and so allowing an intruder in while they were out attempting to deal with it.

Savagery and cunning were a potent combination, dangerous when you were ignorant of motive because it made your antagonist not just formidable and elusive but really quite impossible to predict. All you could do was hope to react quickly and decisively when the hostile attention was turned to you. Less and less was Derek Johnson convinced that they were being stalked and toyed with by something merely human. Greg Cody had never struck him as an easy man to spook, let alone terrify. But he remembered Cody's last living sound and it had been that curdling scream.

He'd had Dave Carter check out the delinquent generator that very afternoon and capable mechanic/engineer that Dave was, he'd found the plant to be in sound condition and running very sweetly. He'd said it might benefit from having to provide more power, much in the way that a car engine benefitted from a long run. But he seemed to think the idea of breakdown and failure as unlikely with such high-end engineering as to be almost inconceivable.

'It's state of the art,' he said. Johnson couldn't help glumly thinking that the same glib cliché had been employed to describe their mostly useless radio transmitter.

Now they were at their barbecue, sipping from bottles of chilled beer, eating chicken drumsticks from foil plates, smelling lamb roasting sweetly on skewers slung above a charcoal pit. A sunset flushed the headland and the sea to the west in an orange and purple incandescence and the crofter's cottage looked Tourist Board quaint and the sea behind it glimmered in green folds lapping demurely at the sand.

And Dave gently took the piss, buoyant because Captain Sensible's unscheduled departure had left him in charge of the maintenance crew and upped him a pay-grade automatically. And taking the piss was what anyone would do, probably slightly jealous of the cushy number Johnson had enjoyed over the weekend and possibly slightly suspicious that something might actually have gone on between the crisp Egyptian cotton sheets in a king-size bed up there at the complex.

Johnson's perspective was slightly different. The island had spooked everyone based there at least to some extent. Everyone had complained at some stage about their uncomfortable shared sense of being watched without being able to spot their sly observer. There was an ambient level of creepiness abroad on New Hope Island and gradually, they'd all got used to that. They'd accommodated the recent and inexplicable disappearance of one of their number. They'd had to do that. There'd been no alternative. But they hadn't seen the tooth deliberately placed on the enamel of the sink in Helena's suite and he had.

He hadn't mentioned it to any of his companions there. He'd said goodbye to their visiting architect on the quay in the morning and she'd opened her arms and embraced him, hugging him hard with tears bright in her eyes that testified to the trauma of the ordeal they'd shared. Then he'd watched her boat shrink towards the horizon from the suite she'd occupied until it disappeared. Then he examined the crack in the toughened glass of the panoramic window, aware its makers claimed heavy callibre bullets would only bounce off its surface harmlessly. Then he'd taken the tooth from the shelf where they'd put it, wrapped in a scrap of tinfoil.

On the way back to their island camp, he'd halted the quad bike at a spot he knew he'd recognize again and he'd dug a small hole in the shallow ground and concealed the foil package, marking the spot with a bright blue pebble with vivid yellow veins he'd picked out specifically for the purpose. The tooth was evidence of something and maybe it was even proof; but it was a grim keepsake and he didn't want it near him.

After that he continued his journey to the camp, glad to be going back to their humble abodes of toughened fabric and steel that shrilled in the wind; gratefully looking forward to the company of the others, preoccupied by a mystery, determined for now to keep a secret, convinced that once it opened up to its visitors, the New Hope Experience was the last place on earth to which he would ever bring his own precious family.

Now, he looked around. He wondered what capered out there, evading his vigilant, sober, tiny three-man patrols. They were great blokes, they were the best, his boys, but it was Johnson's considered opinion that they were inadequate numerically to the task. Poor vanished Greg Cody had been the demonstrable proof of that. It wasn't a question any longer of protecting infra-structure and securing valuable construction plant. There was an intruder on the island and they hadn't the resources to find and confront whoever that was. Whoever that was, he seemed to have the beating of them.

Beside him, Dave Carter banged his teeth against his bottle-lip tipsily with a clink, swallowing more beer. He said, 'She's voluptuous, that's the word.'

'No argument there,' Johnson said.

Cater belched, 'Buxom,' he said.

'No,' Johnson said, 'that makes her sound matronly, which is wide of the mark.'

'Eager to please, in my experience, when they're carrying a bit of heft.'

'I wouldn't call an ounce of what Ms. Davenport carries heft.'

'Was she? Eager to please?'

Johnson said, 'Keep this above the waist, Dave.'

'No problem, Deggsy,' Carter said.

The sun had gone down. They were in the dark, which was a fitting phrase, in the circumstances. Johnson suspected this was likely to be a lengthy night. He recalled the single note of terror that had been Cody's scream, waking him in the early hours of the previous Saturday. So much for amenable company, he thought.

Chapter Eight

There was more character and expression in Felix Baxter's face than he allowed of himself in photographs, which Edie Chambers thought interesting. Despite his hunger and talent for publicity, it suggested he didn't really like to have his picture taken. Before he heard the shutter click, he shaped his features into that bland mask of neutrality ubiquitous in shots of him. It was interesting because she thought it probably the reflex of someone almost always with something serious and substantial to hide.

His boardroom was opulent with a view, glittering in winter sunlight this Thursday morning, of the river. The coffee he had served her was excellent. There were buttery biscuits with a lumpy, artisan look she thought had probably come from Harrods Food Hall or Fortnum & Mason. She didn't want a biscuit. She didn't want to answer questions about New Hope Island either, but found herself doing so. It was in a way the price of admission. He knew exactly who she was.

'When I was 14, I was visited several times by the ghost of a sailor named Jacob Parr. He was first-mate aboard Seamus Ballantyne's slave ship, *Andromeda*, though he didn't tell me that, my mum found that out after I confessed about his visits to her.'

'What did he tell you about Ballantyne?'

'That Ballantyne had him flogged for drunkenness. He almost died afterwards of septic shock, but still bragged about that.'

'Why did he visit you at all?'

'He taught me a song, *The Recruited Collier*. And he said I had to find a journal written by the ship's physician, Thomas Horan. By this time the expedition to find out what had happened to Ballantyne's New Hope community was on the point of leaving for the island and Parr said it was urgent.'

'Tall order.'

'The *Andromeda* had been registered to Liverpool. I got in touch with Phil Fortescue, the Keeper of Artefacts at the maritime museum there and told him my story.

'The *Recruited Collier* was doubly a clue. It's a song sung by Kate Rusby, the Barnsley Nightingale. Phil traced Horan to Barnsley after he resigned his commission and he eventually found the journal hidden at a played-out pit shaft there where Horan had treated the miners for free.'

'You did incredibly well as a 14 year old just to get through to Professor Fortescue, never mind to persuade him to help you. And he did unbelievably well to locate the journal,' Baxter said.

Edie sipped coffee and shrugged, looking out of the window at the silver sparkle of the river, remembering a grim and testing time, seeing the cat o' nine wheals on his back Parr had proudly exposed to her in the dorm of her school at night.

'Phil's always thought of it as fate. He doesn't think there was much back then in the way of self-determination New Hope-wise.'

'And Horan's journal told him what?'

'There was a sorcerer in the slave hold of Ballantyne's ship who demanded to be treated as the captain's equal.

Ballantyne had him tied to a chair on the deck and took off his hands with a cleaver in front of his jeering crew. The wounds became infected and he died.'

'But he did something before he died?'

'He said that Ballantyne's daughter, not yet born, would die a child and come back to torment him. He said that he'd summoned something he called the Being that Hungers in the Darkness, which would eventually consume Ballantyne.'

Baxter hadn't sat down at his boardroom table. He listened to the answers to his questions pacing up and down the room with his arms folded tightly across his chest, occasionally lifting his right hand to stroke the goatee newly cultivated on his chin. It was grey, like his hair, but paradoxically, Edie thought had the effect of making him look more youthful.

He said, 'Do you think the Horan journal a reliable source?'

'Ballantyne's Kingdom of Belief thrived for more than a decade until the whole community vanished. In 1934 a would-be crofter named David Shanks caught the wraith of Rachel Ballantyne on cine-film before fleeing the island. By the time Phil went to New Hope to confront the thing consuming them, half of the expedition members and most of their support crew had disappeared.'

'So you actually believe all this stuff,' Baxter said.

'Jacob Parr didn't give me a choice.'

Baxter smiled, but he looked suddenly quite pale. He said, 'Tell me about Rachel Ballantyne.'

'I've never seen her.'

'But you know someone who has?'

'Yes, I do.'

'Can you tell me who that was?'

'No.'

'But you trust their judgment.'

'Yes.'

'You'll be aware that last week, my site-manager disappeared on New Hope?'

'Yet there's been nothing reported publically. I'd meant to ask you about that.'

'It's a mystery made the more so by the fact that Greg Cody wasn't the most enigmatic of men. He was cautious and hardheaded and he wasn't suicidal or even depressed. This is off the record, by the way. Officially his status is still missing, but only his widow believes that. The weather was calm. Foul play's been ruled out. It's baffling. What do you think?'

'Why ask me?'

'Because you've been there.'

'New Hope is a hostile and dangerous place, or it can be.'

Baxter said, 'We've built a leisure complex there with the emphasis on ecological values and cultural tradition. We've built a beautiful sanctuary from the destructive distractions of the 21st century where discerning visitors can take blissful refuge. We've catered too to the white-knuckle ride passions of people who yearn for adventure. We've built all this infra-structure at a cost in excess of thirty million pounds and counting. And we've lost one man among a workforce at the height of construction numbering over 200, probably to the rogue wake of a supertanker changing course at speed closer than it should have been to the shoreline.'

As prepared speeches went, it sounded both winningly spontaneous and reasonably convincing. Or it would have, had Edith not been to the island herself. It was an experience she'd barely survived.

Baxter said, 'We're discussing a place characterized only by its vast potential. I intend to fulfill that potential and I'm too impatient to do it to stick to our original timetable. I'm bringing the schedule forward. That's today's little exclusive, yours with my compliments. The weather in the Hebrides can be unpredictable, but nothing, Ms. Chambers, is going to rain on my parade.'

'Can I record this?'

'I want to show you personally what we've achieved on the island. Are you up for that?'

'When do we leave?' she said, aware now the hollow dread was excavating in her stomach at the prospect.

'The forecast for the weekend is good to fair. We depart at about lunchtime on Saturday and return on Sunday evening, assuming that suits you.'

'It does.'

'Excellent.' He sat down. He said, 'Of course you can record this. And nothing you're about to hear has yet been publically aired.'

He began to speak. He outlined his plans, what he termed his vision. He peppered his sentences with buzzwords like legacy and uniqueness. He talked about global recognition and international impact. He referenced youth and tradition, imagination and opportunity. There was no talk of profit, room-rates or bottom-lines. Greg Cody's name didn't feature again. She couldn't honestly work out whether Baxter was genuinely fired by his own idealism or simply full of shit.

She knew she could write up and sell what he was telling her to a variety of news outlets. She'd make money out of it, which hadn't been her main motivation in seeking the interview in the first place.

What was his motivation, though, in giving a humble student this sort of access? That was obvious. He wanted the inside-line on the island's dubious history. She thought that had become more pressing than it had been at the outset, with him. This made her wonder whether something had happened, whether he'd experienced something personally to make it a more urgent priority. She was alert and she was observant and she couldn't help wondering about how pale he looked and how restless he seemed. It wasn't Greg Cody doing this. Cody was an irritation, a distraction only. This was more.

For a second time, he said, 'Tell me about Rachel Ballantyne,' more or less confirming her suspicions.

'It's a mistake to think of her as human,' Edie said, 'by which I mean she's both more and less than that. She's been around for the better part of 200 years and she's tired of her existence. She's angry and petulant and the anger's prone to boil over and when it does she's extremely bad news for anyone in her vicinity. At least, that's what I've been told.'

'Because you never encountered her yourself on the island.'

'No Mr. Baxter, I never did.'

'It's Felix, please.'

'Felix, then.'

He was silent for a moment, his mouth pursed behind the steeple of his fingers. Then he took his hands away from his face and said, 'Can you tell me what she's supposed to look like?'

Edie closed her eyes, remembering, hoping her expression didn't betray the fact. 'She died at the age of ten. She's a waif or urchin in appearance, wearing an old-fashioned nightdress. She's frail looking, but the frailty is a lie. She's incomplete, like a figure badly drawn or only vaguely remembered. Her features are just sort of hinted at under a scrappy halo of blonde hair.'

'She sounds quite picturesque,' Baxter said.

'I'm reliably told she's anything but,' Edie said. 'I recently heard Rachel described as an affront to the natural order. I think it's fair to say she creates a bad atmosphere. Some of that's deliberate. The rest I think she just can't help.'

'So she's right out of a horror film,' Baxter said.

'Rachel earns her X-certificate and then some, Felix.'

'Yet none of my people on site have seen her.'

'She sings, apparently.'

'None of them has heard her either.'

'Maybe Greg Cody heard her. Maybe that's what got him out of bed.'

'We'll never know,' Baxter said.

'Are you annoyed by that, by the loose end he represents?'

'I'm philosophical, Edith. New Hope's been a massive project. My strictly off-the-record opinion is that you can't make an omelet without breaking eggs.'

She thought that sounded callous. She said, 'Nothing macabre, then, nothing ghostly or demonic?'

Baxter smiled. The smile looked genuine but he was still pale and the restlessness gave his limbs a coiled, restricted look. To her he looked slightly trapped. He said, 'We might both of us draw different conclusions after the weekend. Right now though, I'm inclined to think New Hope well named.'

Ruthie sat in the dark and the rain at her table in her garden early on Friday morning, reading the news pages of *The Chronicle* on her phone, emptying her cafetière of coffee and smoking four cigarettes in succession, secure in the knowledge that no one was there to disapprove of her doing so because Phil was away on some consultancy job in Bristol and she wouldn't see him until 7 o'clock that evening.

The biggest selling of the mid-market tabloids had run Edith Chambers' taster story as a full-page exclusive. Ruthie was thrilled for Edie and the story was punchily written, but she didn't think they'd have given it quite the prominence they had without the Chronicle's New Hope history.

The paper had been Alexander McIntyre's flagship title and had sponsored the expedition in '10. That said, she thought the average reader would find the story entertaining enough. Felix Baxter's vision was ambitious and his enthusiasm, to most people, probably contagious. There was plenty of gloom and doom in the news and the New Hope Island Experience story was by refreshing contrast upbeat and optimistic. Ruthie thought the doom and gloom would come to it eventually, though. They just hadn't yet arrived.

She waited until 7am and then called Phil.

'I've seen it,' he said.

'You must be very proud of Edie, though?'

'That's like asking a Titanic survivor did they enjoy the voyage otherwise.'

'It's bad, isn't it?'

'Edie approached Baxter because she's ambitious and learned a bit about opportunism from her Auntie Lucy. But Baxter probably gets interview requests every day of the week and routinely turns them down in the old-fashioned belief that time's money. So why say yes to a student journalist?'

'Her surname rang a bell and he checked her out,' Ruthie said. 'He knew her mum went on the expedition. He probably wanted to pump her for what she knows about the island.'

'Edie called me last night,' Fortescue said. 'She called me after she filed the Chronicle piece. That's exactly what he did, yesterday morning, before the interview proper.'

'What did she tell him?'

'New Hope's a dangerous place.'

'Not what he wants to hear.'

'She's flying there with him tomorrow, weather permitting, coming back Monday.'

'Well, like you said, she's an ambitious girl. Did she tell you anything else?'

'Yeah,' Fortescue said. 'She thinks something's happened recently to Baxter. She thinks he's had an experience that didn't fill him with hope, new or otherwise.'

'He was in Liverpool last weekend,' Ruthie said. 'He mentions that in Edie's piece. Maybe Lizzie Burrows had a busier schedule than just me.'

'He asked Edie specifically about Rachel Ballantyne. She said he didn't look at all comfortable doing it.'

Ruthie said, 'Nothing's going to stop him going ahead, not now it's not. A quitter's the last thing he is.'

'He's a megalomaniac,' Fortescue said. 'I reckon he's probably a lot like Seamus Ballantyne was.'

'That thought occurred to me this morning.'

'Spooky.'

'Speaking of which, Phil, we should do the bracelet thing tonight, The Bite of Fright?'

'The tooth is out there,' he said.

'It's us going plaque in time.'

'Or plaque to the future,' he said.

'Either way, we'll get to the root of it.'

'A slightly gum prospect.'

They'd joked and punned around this sobering eventuality since journeying back south. It was a way of trying to trivialize and domesticate what they intended to do. It hadn't really worked, though. And she was right, he thought, they couldn't put it off indefinitely.

They concluded their call. Ruthie had gone inside to make it. She brewed more coffee. It was 7.30 and not yet light. She spooned Coffee-Mate into her mug and tore the cellophane off a fresh pack of cigarettes. A growing part of her wanted to give up, but now didn't seem a realistic time. She opened her kitchen door and went back outside to sit and smoke and contemplate in her snug parka under her table umbrella in the rain.

She thought about the Ghost of Elizabeth Burrows. She remembered her fusty elegance and her papery voice and the way the words had left her unmoving mouth. Like ventriloquism but without a dummy to complete the trick, she'd thought at the time. She wondered what kind of effort it took for someone dead to deliver a warning to someone living. What unknowable forces were at work to enable that?

She remembered then something Phil had told her Shaddeh had confided in Thomas Horan when boasting of his prowess as a magician. *I can make puppets of those who take their own lives,* the dying sorcerer had said. And the ship's physician had remembered that claim and written it down in the journal he had kept on what was to be his last ever voyage aboard the slave vessel Andromeda.

Shaddeh had regretted what his dying spells and curses would eventually unleash on New Hope Island decades later. He'd been sorry, but too enfeebled to reverse what he'd set in motion. Or so Thomas Horan had written. And Shaddeh had died in the fervid stink of a ship's hold and been buried without ceremony at sea.

Ruthie shivered. She knew that Georgia Tremlett at Manchester University had called the slave-sorcerer the greatest African magician of his time. Perhaps two centuries of rest had now revived him. He'd been very powerful. Perhaps hc'd made a puppet of Elizabeth Burrows, who'd taken her own life by hanging herself in her room at a Liverpool University hall of residence. Perhaps their warning about the bracelet of teeth had really come from its original owner, regretful about his dubious accomplishments and trying to make amends or pay some kind of penance to the living.

Ruthie didn't really want to know. She did know she never wanted another encounter with Lizzie, however well meaning it was. She didn't think she would ever forget the ghost's stiff fingers or forlorn touch of lost pride in how beautiful she no longer was. She would never forget her voice and would always remember the faint whiff of her odour corrupting the Guest House air.

Could anything be worse? An encounter with Rachel Ballantyne would be worse, of course. Rachel's return after her death from diphtheria had been Shaddeh's curse inflicted upon her father. But she'd stuck around after her father's demise and after 200 years on New Hope spent mostly in solitude, had grown powerfully malevolent in her own right, according to a legend Ruthie had personal cause to believe entirely convincing.

Felix Baxter's New Hope questions to Edie had mostly centred on Rachel, at least according to Phil. And Edie thought he'd been given a recent shock. He'd made a point of insisting not a single man or woman among all the people who'd worked on the New Hope Experience had ever seen or heard the island's resident wraith.

That didn't mean their boss hadn't.

Ruthie wondered what Baxter had been doing in Liverpool. He could have been viewing commercial properties; potential nightclubs or leisure centres or car showrooms or just office blocks to add to his bulging portfolio. Except doing that wouldn't do anything to provoke little Rachel into making a guest appearance.

What, then, would?

She stubbed out her cigarette and exhaled at the clouds now visible in outline in the lightening sky and lowered her head to look at her watch, and remembered with a frown the first time she'd met Phil, outside the Spice Island pub on Portsmouth Harbour in the days when he'd carried the Breguet in his bag that had once belonged to Seamus Ballantyne.

That was it, she thought. That's where Baxter had been last weekend. Enlightenment came to her with the clarity of dawn breaking. He'd been to the museum where Phil had once worked and from where Phil had recently taken a bracelet of teeth. He'd rummaged through a trunk of her father's belongings and little Rachel had taken exception to that. Somehow she'd allowed him a baleful glimpse of herself, despite physically residing hundreds of isolating miles away.

If she could do that, she was very powerful indeed. If she could do that, why hadn't she shown herself in a similar way to the equally rummaging Phil? *Maybe she's on the side of the angels,* Ruthie murmured under her breath to herself. And then she shivered again, because even that was a pretty disconcerting thought.

Derek Johnson had become a bit proprietorial about the New Hope Experience complex. It was his team's responsibility to check the place out and to do so at regular intervals. But meeting and warming to its architect and the unnerving ordeal they'd shared when the lights had gone out had made his interest somehow personal. It wasn't that he'd become infatuated with Helena Davenport or even that he had a crush on her. He was almost ludicrously happily married. But he liked and admired her and she'd inspired a sort of loyalty in him that compelled him to try to protect her proud creation as best he could from any threat.

This didn't mean that he felt any real fondness for her Island building. On the contrary, it had given him good cause to think it a distinctly unpleasant place. Duty was duty, however. You didn't fulfill it by taking shortcuts or turning a convenient blind eye. There'd been a recent death on the island he categorized as highly suspicious, unwilling to collude in the convenient belief that Greg Cody had strolled screaming into the sea.

He went to give the complex its routine tour at noon on Friday. He took king of the dubious barbecue wisecracks Dave Carter with him. Dave wanted another look at the generator, still mystified as to how it could have cut out and then reactivated without a bit of deliberate tinkering. And Johnson was honestly glad of the company. He tried to tell himself that there was nothing intrinsically sinister about the building, that all sizeable buildings were a bit unnerving empty and that it was just a consequence of viewing *The Shining* there late at night. He was unconvinced, though. Horror movies had never scared him before.

Plus, the complex had no history. The Overlook Hotel in *The Shining* had been corrupted by its own past, contaminated by the evil deeds done there. But that was grasping at straws as a line of argument, he knew. The chief had given the island all those quaint place names. On a clear day, from anywhere on the island, you could see Kingdom Heights. Their base was at Shanks's Reach. Where they were headed on the quads wasn't far from Ballantyne Cove. But the labels didn't charm Johnson as they were intended to. They just reminded him that New Hope's history was bloody and mysterious.

It didn't matter that the complex was a new build. It didn't matter that its creator was clever and striking and charmingly human. That it was up for a slew of awards was immaterial, if it wasn't outright ironic. All that mattered was where it was sited.

'Location's everything,' Johnson said to himself. In so doing he was parroting what they always said on those junk property shows a period nursing a fractured ankle had taught him were popular on daytime television, in programmes where it was a mantra and a truism both. New Hope was a corrupt place and the complex had caught a dose of its sickly contagion. Baxter paid his wages. But it was for Helena's sake he hoped the sickness wasn't terminal.

At least the weather was tolerable. On calm days it made sense to travel from their compound to the complex in a clockwise semicircle from one end of the island to the other along its shore. In fine weather, the ground there was the least treacherous on New Hope; shingle giving way at low tide to hard-packed sand. Even that seemed sort of symbolic in his current mood to Johnson. The island was safest at its extremities; venture inland and the hazards began to accumulate.

He looked at Dave Carter, riding grinning straddling his quad to his right. The bikes were routine to Johnson's boys but to Carter, probably still a bit of a novelty. He was enjoying the ride. Why shouldn't he? The day was bright, the views breathtaking and they were being handsomely paid for doing not very much more than just being there. What wasn't to like? Johnson resolved to try to ignore his nagging doubts and gloomy presentiments and live a bit more in a moment just then innocent and sunny. He'd have to do that. He'd crack up otherwise and start hearing and seeing things that simply weren't there.

They arrived at the complex. The main entrance was locked, which meant that the power was on. They were in the lobby when Carter said, 'I'm going to go and check the genny anyway, since that's what I'm here for.' He turned on his heels and was gone.

Johnson felt for a moment an absurd surge of disappointment. He was being ridiculous; he stood six-four in his socks and weighed 18 stone and not an ounce of it was flab. He'd been a fixture in the second-row of the Met's first rugby 15. It was how he'd got the ankle injury that had taught him all about daytime TV while he recovered from it wearing a cast. He was no one's idea of a pushover, least of all his own. He'd tour the place, take in the bars and restaurants, the cinema and recreation rooms, the master suites, including the one Helena had occupied.

He got through all this grinding his teeth as he told himself it was just a routine inspection. His big mistake, he realized too late, was leaving the visit to Helena's suite till last on his to-do list. It meant that by the time he swatted the passkey through the lock on what had been her door he'd fulfilled every other obligation. That made this the pinnacle or climax, didn't it? That made it a hurdle, the final one to overcome and therefore the biggest, in his mind. He should have done this first, he thought, opening the door on trepidation mutating into fear.

There was a smell. It was faint, but undeniable, sweetish and rank and not the ghost of some expensive perfume with which its recent guest had adorned herself there. And as he entered the suite, he sensed that the smell strengthened in the direction of the bathroom. He looked around the sitting room. He felt disembodied in a curious way, exiled from the real, so that the panorama through the picture window looked more a vibrant painting, pellucid and still, rather than the real world trembling with exterior life.

There was something old about the smell. Decay wasn't the whole of it. It hinted at an antique time, was the odour of life lived centuries ago; linen and camphor, carbolic and tallow, dirty skin clothed in rags soiled and musty.

'My imagination,' he said out loud, 'has to be.' But to his own ears his voice sounded tremulous, dry with the terror making his heart thump audibly in his chest. 'Get a grip,' he said, disgusted with his cowardice. He forced himself to walk towards the bathroom, towards the source of the smell, to where it grew rank and fetid with its own potency, turning from an odour as he reached the open bathroom door, into a ripe stench.

A single word had been written on the bathroom mirror. It had been scrawled there in soap and grime. It read:

EVAEL

A hand touched Johnson's shoulder lightly. He jumped and twisted in one fearful reflex and it was Carter, staring now at the soapy message and growing pale as he did so.

'You left the door open, mate. Had to see the place, didn't I, your and Helena's passion pad?' He nodded his head at the writing. 'What the fuck's that?'

'I've no idea.'

'Someone can't spell evil. And what's that stink?'

'It isn't misspelled, Dave. It's 'leave,' spelled backwards. What I mean is I've no idea how it got there.'

'You think it's a warning for us?' Dave Carter was a Welshman, from Cardiff. It wasn't usually obvious, but shock or distress had caused his accent to thicken suddenly. Suddenly he sounded almost caricature welsh.

'I don't see what else it can be,' Johnson said.

'But no one can get in here, it's impossible,' Carter said, 'and that smell is like something dead.'

'I think we're about to start earning our pay,' Johnson said.

Carter licked his lips. His eyes had grown in his head, the pupils shrunk to pinpricks with fear and alertness. He said, 'Seriously, Deggsy, what are we going to do?'

'We're going to open all the windows and air the place,' Johnson said. 'I'm going to find some bathroom cleaner and a cloth and wipe the mirror down. Then we're going to get out of here and have a serious talk. Is the generator okay?'

'It's running as sweet as.'

'We have to decide whether to tell the others about this. I don't want any panic, but we're the two blokes in charge, we're not alone here, Cody's death was no accident and the island isn't safe.'

'Is that a warning, or a threat?' Carter asked, nodding at the mirror again.

Johnson looked at the grimy, waxy scrawl. 'I think it's intended to be both,' he said.

Chapter Nine

Doctor Georgia Tremlett had worked something out that Friday morning she thought might be of interest to Professor Fortescue, should he feel compelled to return to New Hope Island. She thought she had discovered a flaw or weakness in the mythical monster sometimes termed The Being that Hungers in the Darkness. It had surprised her, this conclusion. Then the insistent logic of it made it seem obvious and therefore something she felt she should actually have come to suspect much sooner than she had.

There was some mitigation for this uncharacteristic lapse in her intellectual alertness. She had been sleep-deprived by the details she had read in the Horan journal, as much a confession, she thought, as a description of the surgeon's final voyage aboard the *Andromeda*. She'd found it brutal and shocking and quite haunting, all told.

And when she could sleep, she'd been troubled by bad dreams. She'd dreamed of the slave vessel's first-mate Jacob Parr, flogged for drunkenness in Horan's bloody account, his back sliced to ribbons by the tongues of the lash, his life saved only by the cold sea water with which Horan had bathed his wounds to combat shock and septic infection.

Parr sang a song in these dream visitations Georgia Tremlett was enduring. The song was always the same and was one of course from the era in which he'd lived. It was entitled, *The Recruited Collier.* It was odd hearing Parr sing it, for though his voice was tuneful enough, the words of the song were a woman's, her sweetheart drunkenly lulled into joining the army, brutalized into a stranger to her by the incessant cruelty of the battles he subsequently fought. It was a sensitive and melancholy song.

Parr would boast in the dreams when he wasn't singing of his closeness to Captain Ballantyne, the martinet commander who'd had him flogged to within an inch of his life. She supposed sailors of the period had been philosophical about punishment. Life before the mast was notoriously hard. At least, this was her reasoning awake. Asleep and dreaming, she was more concerned, and revolted, by Parr's unwashed stink and grog-soaked breath and the brown tobacco stains on what few teeth he possessed from smoking his ever-present clay pipe.

It was a bright and gentle day for early February. She'd decided to eat her sandwich lunch outside. She didn't know it, but the location she'd chosen in the college grounds was the same one at which Phil Fortescue had waited and called Patrick Lassiter, whiling away the time it took her to read the Horan journal prior to their talk together in her office. The cluster of benches under the stand of pines tended to be a secluded spot because the bench slats sometimes became tacky with resin from the falling needles and cones. It put people off sitting there. February, though, was an un-sticky month in their life.

She wondered would Professor Fortescue by now have stumbled on the same conclusion she had concerning the Being's flaw or weakness. She thought probably not. He'd struck her as an intelligent and thoughtful man troubled by a failure to properly control his own destiny. She'd do a little more research, she decided, before telling Fortescue anything. Early the following week would likely be soon enough.

Meeting him had affected her in one very surprising way. It had made her nostalgic for the fieldwork she hadn't had time to indulge in for years. He'd made her realize that she missed it. Academic eminence brought substantial rewards both to the ego and the bank balance, but learning new things while getting her hands dirty was something the maritime Professor had made her remember fondly and hanker to do again before time and procrastination took their toll and she became hampered in the wild by a Zimmer Frame.

She unscrewed the cup of her coffee flask and poured and put her hot drink steaming in pale wreaths above its rim on the arm of her bench. She unwrapped her sandwiches and the smell of sweet-cured ham and strong cheese on rye bread stung her nostrils and provoked a swell of saliva under her tongue. She was hungry. She bit into a sandwich and began to chew.

Pale in the distance, she noticed a young woman. She was tall and wore her black hair cut with geometric severity and the skin of her face had a white pallor under her hair. From this distance she was dark-eyed, tall in a black coat with a double-row of gilt buttons. She seemed to stare at Georgia for a moment with eyes that at the distance the two women were apart, looked dark enough to be black.

Georgia felt a pang of envy. The pale woman looked very striking. Georgia wasn't striking, she knew. She had her hair expensively cut and the gym had firmed her figure and a Betty Jackson habit saw to it that she was always stylishly dressed, but she just wasn't physically a statement sort of woman. That had recently been brought home to her when she'd held her internal debate about asking Philip

Fortescue out for a drink. He had a ravaged handsomeness and a rangy muscularity she thought strongly appealing.

Maybe she'd get her opportunity to do that yet. She felt that he'd be intrigued by her fresh insights into the malevolent forces apparently present on New Hope. She thought they gave her every justification for another face-to-face encounter. That would preferably take place somewhere quiet in the evening over a glass of something that would slowly but surely disinhibit them both.

Georgia dropped a brittle shower of rye breadcrumbs into her lap and looked down to brush them away. Mercifully, the spot was too quiet generally to attract a regular pigeon population, so she didn't worry overmuch about the debris. There was no flying vermin there to have to feel guilty about encouraging. Remembering her smart, still observer, she glanced up again. But when she did so, there was no sign of the striking woman left in sight.

It was Friday evening when Phil Fortescue took the cloth bag containing the bracelet of teeth from the boot of his car. He had deep misgivings about doing what they were about to. When it had been done before, it had eventually cost the person doing it her life. He had reservations about doing it in Ruthie's cottage, which had been a blessed refuge for him ever since their romance had begun. He'd nearly lost Ruthie over the bracelet. More accurately he'd almost lost her over his decision not to tell her about it, or what it was he was to attempt to try to do with it, or have it do with him present. And now they were going to do that together.

She really didn't like deceit. That made him curious about her past romantic history. She was 35. It was plenty old enough for the heartbreaking back-story of love and betrayal she might be keeping to herself. She had a right to her privacy, but he was intrigued by the past generally and because he loved her, tantalized by hers.

Almost losing her over it was a very good reason to think the bracelet bad news and his taking it from Ballantyne's chest nowhere near the smart masterstroke he'd thought it the previous Monday. He could feel the teeth slip and chatter in the bag in his hand. It was eight o'clock now, long dark, and he felt like something strong to drink to steady his nerve and shift his prevailing mood of gloomy foreboding.

It wasn't as if they could do this at a table at the Spyglass, surrounded by burnished ship's brasses to a backdrop of cheery banter from the bar. It was going to be a sobering and perhaps frightening vigil. The only thing he could think to compare it to was a séance, and Fortescue had never felt the inclination to attend one of those. His phone rang in his pocket, making him jump just as he got to Ruthie's front gate. He saw Patsy Lassiter's name flash on the screen.

'We're doing it now, tonight.'

'That's why I've rung. I suspected tonight would be the night.'

'It must be a bit like being God, having your powers of deduction.'

'Alice used to say that. I can assure you it's not.'

'It makes everything predictable.'

'Alice's death wasn't something I could predict. If I had done, I could have stopped it.'

He'd mentioned his dead wife twice in two sentences. It wasn't something he did. Fortescue felt his mood plunge from foreboding into despondency. He said, 'Mate, have you been drinking?'

'No,' Lassiter said, 'the temptation's there, I have to be honest and say it's always there, but I haven't been drinking.'

'Do you ever sense Alice?'

There was a silence. Then Lassiter said, 'All the time.'

'Patsy, Jesus.'

'It's not what I called you to talk about, Phil. I don't mind talking to you about the loss of Alice or about the booze because I've no better friend in the world.'

'And both have been on your mind.'

'Yes they have. But they're not why I'm calling now. On balance, I think Liz Burrows is on the side of the angels. She's disconcerting. Frankly, she's frightening, but not deliberately so. Her intentions I think are basically good.'

'So you rang to reassure me?'

'No. I rang to warn you. The dead aren't the best judges of what's good for the living. I think what you're about to do is probably extremely dangerous. If you don't like what you hear, bag the bracelet, plug your ears and throw the fucking thing as far as you're able into the sea.'

'How did you know I was on the coast?'

'You're a maritime historian so you're always on the coast. But right now you're at Ruthie's place in Ventnor. You're doing this with her at her insistence, so where else would you be?'

'I'm scared, Patsy. There's no pretending otherwise.' The bracelet roiled under cloth in the palm of his hand like something gleeful.

'Just keep an eye on Ruthie. She's too brave for her own good. Both of you are. Good luck, mate.'

Fortescue had a key to Ruthie's cottage door. They'd reached that stage. But if he knew she was in, out of courtesy, he always knocked. It was her home, not his. Just before he did knock, he thought about the question he'd asked Patsy just now about the booze. He thought it must be terrible to live always with that suspicion even among the people who thought most of you. It was a high price to pay in humility and distrust for sins you probably prayed daily would stay firmly in your past.

When he kissed her, Ruthie's breath was a toxic cocktail of charred tobacco and white wine and recent Colgate toothpaste. Her faith in toothpaste was touching but misplaced, verging on delusional, maybe even mystical in the power with which she credited the stuff. She'd lit candles. Of course she had, she'd had a few glasses of Chablis and she'd reverted to Goth. From somewhere, the gloomy rumble of some black-clad, pale-faced band was present in angst-ridden chords. He could smell something that wasn't her signature scents of Berkley Menthol cigarettes or Calvin Klein Eternity perfume and thought it probably a joss stick. He wasn't having it. Matters were creepy enough without the atmospherics. He flicked on the lights and blew the candles out. He switched off the music.

Ruthie hiccupped, 'Spoilsport.'

'How many have you had?'

'Just the one, Professor, needed to steady my nerves.'

He knelt and emptied the bag out in her fireplace surround, on the tiles in front of her wood burner, where they could both face it seated on her sofa. He did so as gingerly as if it had been a tarantula or a scorpion, unpredictable and deadly released from the confinement of its cloth prison. The bracelet slid and clattered and then was silent and still. He got up and retreated backwards and sat beside her, where Ruthie held his hands in both of hers as they stared at the ivory jumble of white incisors with which the great African magician had once adorned his scrawny arm.

They waited. After 20 minutes of stillness and silence, Fortescue could endure no more without a drink and he got up and went into the kitchen and poured and drank two inches of chilled vodka. He sat back down with the rosy glow of the spirit spreading through him, feeling better, or at least less bad.

'I don't think it wants to speak to us,' Ruthie said, after 40 minutes of silence.

'There's no one else,' Fortescue said.

'There's Patsy Lassiter,' Ruthie said. 'There's Edith Chambers. Maybe it should really be talking to Felix Baxter.'

Fortescue nodded. What she said made perfect sense, if you took it on trust that a jumble of human teeth strung through by a silver chain was somehow capable of speech. For a moment, he wondered had Liz Burrows simply been a victim of a breakdown or insanity. Then he remembered the teeth closing on his own wrist in the museum basement in Liverpool and he dismissed the suspicion.

After an hour, he put the bracelet back into the bag and took the bag back to his car where he put it in the boot. The walk there felt longer than it should have. He thought the bracelet might writhe and whisper confidentially in his grip en route. It might wish to confide in him alone. That didn't happen, though. Ruthie was waiting for him wearing her coat at her porch, hugging herself against the damp night chill when he returned. He said, 'What now?'

'The Spyglass,' she said. 'A few tequila slammers wouldn't go amiss. That was horrible, Phil.'

He nodded. It had been horrible. But he thought they both knew it could have been much, much worse. And under the immediacy of relief, he felt disappointment welling. He'd hoped to learn something of value. After provoking Monday's row with Ruthie and enduring five fraught days of anticipation, all he'd done in the end was waste an hour of their precious time together.

'Tequila slammers it is,' he said. He didn't often feel like getting drunk, but tonight was an exception. He'd hoped to learn something before his stepdaughter left for New Hope the following day aboard Baxter's monogramed chopper. He'd hoped actually to learn something that might stop her going.

Walking hand-in-hand with Ruthie to the Spyglass, he wondered whether anything would have done that. Journalists didn't shirk from danger. Instead they sought it out, because danger meant stories. They didn't hanker after a humdrum life. They took risks with their own safety. At least, they did if they were of the intrepid variety. Edie's model and mentor in the profession had been her Auntie Lucy. The fearless curiosity of Lucy Church had in the end got her killed, but that hadn't put Edith off, had it?

Telling her not to go wouldn't work. She knew first-hand how dangerous New Hope could be. Some of the hazards present on the island when she'd gone there 18 months ago were no longer a threat, but it was never safe and had claimed its most recent life less than a week earlier. Greg Cody's disappearance would only have sparked Edie's interest further. Telling her not to go – ordering her – wasn't something Fortescue could do in dealing with a mature woman of 20. She might not laugh at him. Love and respect would prevent that, but she'd certainly disobey anything resembling a command.

He stopped walking. Ruthie stopped beside him. He called Patsy Lassiter.

'I'm all ears, Phil.'

'It was a waste of time.'

'So why have you called?'

'When you had dinner with Edie the other night, did you tell her anything useful about New Hope?'

'I told her about some places there she'd be wise steering clear of. She was definitely listening.'

'Good.'

'I've been thinking all day about calling her and asking her not to go.'

'It wouldn't work, Patsy.'

'I'd beg her if I thought it would do any good.'

'It wouldn't.'

'I know.'

'Do you believe in the power of prayer?'

'Not usually,' Patsy Lassiter said, 'but I'll be saying one for Edie tonight and expect you will too.'

In calm weather, Dave Carter and his lads had taken to doing exactly what Derek Johnson had told Helena Davenport could be done to make their radio transmitter function effectively. They'd haul the kit aboard an R.I. and head for a point 800 metres offshore and drop anchor and fire it up battery powered to report into Baxter Enterprises H.Q. away from whatever interference contaminated the island's atmosphere, the signal crystal clear, strong and completely steady.

Thus they got four hours warning that the chief was paying them a visit. This short-notice was completely characteristic of the man. He paid well enough that people shouldn't be sleeping on the job. Any disorganization or dishevelment, any sign of poor practice or sloppy maintenance and someone would pay for it with dismissal, shipped back to the mainland ignominiously and without a penny's compensation.

There was no chance of that happening. Their barbecue had been Dave Carter getting as sloppy as he ever did and that had been on their own time, off-duty. Professionally, he was punctilious and more than competent. So when the helicopter chuntered into sight on the eastern horizon there was no panic or nervousness among the little delegation gathered by the old colony dock to greet it. They were actually looking forward to seeing Felix Baxter. He was a lively character, down-to-earth, full of energy and brimming with wisecracks, generous with the bonuses he tended to splash about.

They'd cranked up the heating at the complex. The windows there, subdued in sunlight because of the glass Helena Davenport had deliberately chosen, nevertheless sparkled. The façade was free of bird shit and spindrift scum and salt. It looked immaculate in its splendid isolation, Johnson thought, except it didn't really look isolated, because it looked so much as though it belonged. Helena was a talented woman. Terrible taste in movies, but a genuinely gifted architect.

They'd told no one about the message left on the bathroom mirror. After considering it for the forty minutes it took to reach the spot on the way back to the camp on their quads, Johnson pulled up and first told Carter about the discovery of the incisor and then dug out and showed it to him. He thought it irresponsible and amateurish to do otherwise, really. If the maintenance crew faced a real hazard, their leader should know about it, he reasoned. This was particularly true since the tooth had probably belonged to the man Carter had recently replaced.

Carter had winced looking at the tooth, smelling the pungent stink the rotting circle of gum gave off close-to.

'You're an ex-copper, Deggsy,' he said. 'Your boys are all either that or they're ex-forces. You're trained for what people like you call hostile scenarios. I'm not. If that was pulled out of Greg Cody's jaw, I'm completely out of my depth.'

'We're all out of our depth,' Johnson said. 'The message on the mirror proves we're not alone on the island. Cody's disappearance suggested the intruder means us harm and this only goes to prove it. And none of us has seen anyone. A three-man patrol isn't much, given the size of the island and the cover available for concealment. But my lads are hand-picked, highly mobile, it's 24–7 and we've seen absolutely fuck all.'

'You're going to radio in for reinforcements?'

Just after 24 hours after that exchange, Johnson watched the approaching helicopter still unsure of what his answer was. He might take Baxter to one side and have a quiet word and the chief was the sort of mercurial bloke who might just quietly kill the messenger. He could be nice, but instinct told Johnson he was never going to be open to bad news concerning the costliest gamble he'd ever taken in his entire business life.

He could imagine the exchange:

We've got unwelcome company on the island, chief.

What kind of company?

I don't really know except that it's hostile.

Have you actually seen them?

No.

So you haven't challenged them?

No.

But you're sure they're here?

Yes.

Then you're not doing the job I pay you for.

Whoever had written the message on the mirror knew far too much for comfort about him personally. The meaning had been plain; it meant go and it meant do so now. But it had been written backwards in tribute to the *redrum* warning scrawled on a wall at the Overlook Hotel in *The Shining*. That had been 'murder' written backwards and the leaver of their bathroom warning had somehow been aware that the story had been lately in his thoughts.

There were only two ways in which this could be possible. Either the mirror messenger could read minds; or had spied on him and Helena when they'd watched the Kubrick film together. Neither possibility offered any shred of comfort.

The helicopter got closer and then swooped and hovered over the concrete pad put there for its landings. It came down and the rotor-blades slowed and the weight of the craft settled. The fierce localized breeze it had brought with it weakened. A door opened and Baxter got out dressed casually in jeans and a black blouson jacket and helped a lithe young woman with blonde hair down to the ground. She was dressed in a leather jacket and combats and hiking boots and carried an overnight bag.

She looked around, sheltering her gaze from the lowering sun with a raised hand. You could tell by the body language that they weren't an item. She was nearer his son's age than she was the chief's. She reminded Johnson of someone. Ever the gentleman, Baxter reached up to his window and performed the ritual post-flight courtesy of shaking hands with his pilot.

Johnson realized who it was the girl reminded him of. It was the TV doctor Jane Chambers, the telegenic virologist who'd done a hit series for the BBC about the Black Death. He remembered being stunned a couple of years earlier, stumbling across her obituary surfing the web on his phone. She'd been shockingly young to die. He remembered she'd been one of the experts on the expedition to the island in '10.

Chapter Ten

When Patrick Lassiter opened the door to Helena Davenport, he was treated to a surprise. She had between her hands a large and colourful bouquet of fresh flowers. He said, 'They can't be for me.'

'Don't you like flowers?'

'Everyone likes flowers.'

'But you've got none in your house.'

'It's February.'

'You wouldn't have flowers in the house in July, Commander. You wouldn't think to. And you're wrong, they are for you, so invite me in and we'll find a vase for them.'

He ushered her inside and took her coat and she found a dusty vase on a kitchen window sill and washed it out and arranged her bouquet and found a place for it on a table near the window of his sitting room where its winter blooms lustred richly and would lustre even more in daylight.

'There,' she said, flashing her green-eyed smile. He was aware of her perfume, her tailored dress, of the soft Scottish burr of her speaking voice. He hadn't liked a woman so much on meeting one since Phil Fortescue had first introduced him to Ruthie Gillespie. Perhaps that was proof he didn't have a type. Perhaps it just demonstrated that likeable women came in all shapes and sizes. He felt strongly physically attracted to her and he hadn't felt that for any woman since before the death of his wife.

'I'm assuming you're a meat-eater.'

'I imagine you've looked me up.'

'Not your dietary preferences, I haven't. The flowers threw me, but usually I'm quite adept at people.'

'It depends, really,' she said, 'I haven't eaten a burger or a bacon sandwich since my undergraduate days.'

'So you're a high-end carnivore.'

'You've got me in one.'

'Good, we're having roast lamb.'

He poured her a glass of wine and got a Diet Coke for himself. Then he took her through to his conservatory, which he used as his home office. The rather battered pair of leather armchairs there were the most comfortable seating he owned. There were shelves of books and there was a desktop computer. A vintage Anglepoise shed a cone of yellow light. Magazines were piled atop a nest of Eames tables and the small oils on the walls looked to her eyes originals. It was a homely space but also businesslike, with his hung citations and career souvenirs. There at the rear of the house, beneath timber and glass, an old bronze radiator provided ample warmth, creaking and gurgling softly. There was no traffic noise.

'You have a lovely home.'

'It was my wife's home. I didn't have her for anything like long enough.'

'You're very direct.'

'I think that's trying to make up for lost time.'

'The time you lost to drink?'

'Tell me why you're here, Helena, why you've come all this way.'

She took a sip of wine. She said, 'I studied the history of New Hope Island before taking on the commission. So I know that what happened to Seamus Ballantyne's

Kingdom of Belief was at best a tragedy and at worst an atrocity.'

'I'd stick with the latter description.'

'I know you were on the expedition in '10. I've heard a rumour it was you discovered the lost cine film David Shanks shot of a wraith he claimed was Rachel Ballantyne.'

'It was me that found it. It was more than a wraith.'

'I thought you'd left the island a safe place after the expedition?'

'Recent events would suggest otherwise.'

'I stayed in the complex I designed for a few days at Felix Baxter's invitation. It was more in the way of a dare, I think. Architects are prone to take the money and run with really innovative builds, just in case the actuality reveals flaws the computer software didn't at the blueprint stage.'

'So you picked up his gauntlet,' Lassiter said.

'There were a couple of strange occurrences. Three, actually, I'd like to tell you about. But first I'd like you to tell me about your time on the island when you rebuilt the Shanks cottage. You were there for six months, weren't you?'

'Yes, almost to the day. Was that your intention in coming here, learning more about New Hope?'

'To be perfectly frank my intention in coming here has shifted since you opened your door to me and invited me in. My motive in coming here is simpler. The island frightened me. I'm proud of what I created there but don't want to collude in some kind of impending tragedy. I want to know is the island a dangerous place. Tell me about it.'

'I thought grief-stricken was a hackneyed cliché, Helena, until I was personally stricken by grief. I was a mess when I took refuge on the island. I might not be the most reliable witness to events there in that period.'

She stared at him levelly without speaking for a long moment, licking her full lips, teasing a loose strand of her hair, coiling it glossily around a finger. She said, 'Derek Johnson totally undersold you. He said you were good-looking in a hard sort of way. I already think you're the most attractive man I've met in my entire adult life. I suspect you're probably also the sanest. Tell me what happened on New Hope. Please don't leave anything out.'

'You might find it hard to believe.'

'I'm not the skeptic I was.'

'Just the same.'

You've an honest face, Patrick. Talk to me.'

So he did.

He told her about the secret places he'd found and the secret place that found him when he was lured there by what had once been Rachel Ballantyne. He told her about his audience with Rachel and the promise he'd made her. And he told her how curiosity evolved into hostility in his silent, secret observer after his discoveries and how when he left the island, it was because his instinct for self-preservation compelled him to go.

'Now tell me your story,' he said. 'Start with the stuff you're certain about.'

She sipped wine and smiled. She looked down into her lap and then up again to meet his eyes. She said, 'The only thing I'm absolutely certain of is that I'd like to go to bed with you tonight, if it's something you'd like too.'

'I don't think you need have any doubts at all about that,' he said, 'but we've dinner to get through first. Now you talk to me Helena, and I'll try my best to concentrate on what you say.'

Georgia Tremlett was struggling to think of a way to overcome her disappointment. She'd discovered that Professor

Fortescue wasn't quite single after all. He'd been made a widower several years earlier when his rather famous and successful wife had died. More recently and improbably, he'd shacked up with a Goth children's author from Ventnor on the Isle of Wight.

It was improbable because he was a respected academic and she wore elaborate tattoos and to Dr. Tremlett, looked quite druggy and possibly even a bit of a tramp where matters sexual were concerned. *Slumming-it* was the phrase they used in Manchester for what Fortescue was doing with Ruthie Gillespie. But Ruthie was pretty in a sluttish sort of way and Georgia knew that men thought with their dicks disappointingly often.

It was Sunday. She'd been to the gym and she'd done a bit of expensively ineffective retail therapy. She thought she might have another read of the Horan journal. It was priceless as a source and she already knew most of the text by heart. One of the many significant details it revealed was that Shaddeh could not use the power he possessed for magic to help himself.

He'd been able to lull those slaves chained around him into a trance-like slumber to ensure that his conversations with Thomas Horan in the vessel's hold were confidential. But when he'd claimed occult powers and been challenged by the ship's surgeon to use them to free himself of his bonds, he'd said the magic didn't work that way. It was fascinating. Esoteric scholars had speculated for years on the paradox of his being taken into slavery. But that was without knowing the details Horan had made her so vividly aware of.

She could feel a Shaddeh monograph coming on. She could sense a paper on the Being that Hungers in the Darkness and see in her mind the stir that would cause when she cited all the circumstantial evidence for its existence on New Hope. She'd quote Fortescue as a witness to its presence there. She thought a quid-pro-quo of that sort only fair after the way she had enlightened him about the Being when they'd met.

Or she could go to New Hope, where her hankering for fieldwork would be satisfied and where first-person experience of the island would give her the material basis not just for a paper, but for a whole book. It would be scholarly but readable, atmospheric and actually quite definitive. It would also be sensational enough to become a bestseller on the non-fiction chart. All those Wendigo and Bigfoot sightings vindicated. Cynicism revoked in page-turning chapters of her unimpeachable prose and fastidious footnotes. It would make of the world a darker and more mysterious place than most people complacently supposed, but that was no bad thing. There'd be film rights, inevitably.

If Phil Fortescue wanted to get down and dirty with a Goth nobody with a loser's taste for ink, then that was actually his business. He was welcome to his squalid private life. Georgia had business of her own. And she needed to get on with it. She was aware of Felix Baxter and his Celtic Disneyland plans for New Hope. If she was going to go, she had to get there before that ghastly New Age circus did and despoiled the island completely.

She could embark on this trip the following day. She had two seminars planned for the week ahead. She could delegate either or postpone both. She was head of Department and hers was anyway the sort of trophy appointment long on prestige and rather shorter on practical work. Research was the buzzword in centres of academic excellence these days and her research pedigree was flawless. She could wangle a week away at short notice to investigate something in her area of expertise that wouldn't wait.

Suddenly she felt quite buoyant. A romantic fling with the ruggedly put-together Philip Fortescue would have been nice, but it didn't compare to the peer-group glory and financial profit she could see a surreptitious week in the Hebrides providing her with. She decided she'd spend the afternoon writing a proposal to her American publisher, the Manhattan-based imprint that had paid her handsomely two years earlier for her book on African tribal magic. That had sold strongly. This would sell on a wholly different scale. She'd ask for a healthy advance and they'd pay it, promptly.

She wondered for a sobering moment whether going to New Hope would expose her to actual physical risk; not from the natural hazards of the island but from the unnatural phenomena for which Fortescue and Horan's journal insisted Shaddeh was responsible.

She was still open-minded about the possibility of something real and tangible having resulted from his spells and curses. But she thought the chances of something stalking and then devouring her pretty outlandish, all in all. Baxter's people had been there for months and the only fatality among them had almost certainly been accidental, a site-worker washed out to sea at night by a freak wave. That death might more grimly have been a suicide, it was naïve to think that totally impossible. What it hadn't been, was deliberate or malevolent.

Georgia fired-up her laptop and got down to the business of writing her proposal. An hour later, she had a strong and fluent synopsis for the book she planned to write. She glanced at her wristwatch. There was still time to pop down to the Arndale Centre and buy some camping kit for when she reached her destination after her journey to the Hebrides the following day.

Edie Chambers had a go at kayaking. She put on a wetsuit and tried windsurfing, though there wasn't much wind and the direction from which it came when it came at all was trickily inconsistent. She tried out a jet ski, circling the island in Felix Baxter's wake with a giant named Derek Johnson bringing up their rear in case of mishaps. It was exciting, being part of a convoy and if the mood of the sea was unseasonably calm, her jet ski was fast and it was still the Atlantic Ocean spuming in her wake and filling her nostrils with brine.

Her aquatic adventures over, she scaled the heights and attempted a rock climbing pitch described in the brochure as difficult. She thought 'impossible' more accurate. Then a man named Dave Carter strapped her into a safety harness and she experienced what Baxter claimed was the longest zip-wire ride in Europe. Hurtling along on that was more thrilling than anything she'd ever experienced at any fairground or theme park she'd ever been to in her life and the views were nothing short of breathtaking.

She sat down to Sunday lunch at the Experience complex at 2 in the afternoon exhausted and impressed. The complex was a wonderfully atmospheric and sympathetic construction and her suite was the last word in luxury. She'd almost overcome her reservations about New Hope. She was almost optimistic about the future promised by what Baxter had built there. But she remembered the evening recently spent with Patsy Lassiter and a phrase Patsy was fond of repeating in this regard. *The island's got form*, Patsy would say. And that was undeniably the case, Greg Cody the proof, his death still a sobering enigma.

Their food wasn't the fare the guests would enjoy when the Experience opened proper. Guest menus were to be prepared by a team of top chefs. They'd already been headhunted from Scotland's best restaurants. Today by contrast, they were sitting down to pre-cooked meals microwaved from frozen. But they weren't at all bad and she was so hungry after her action-packed day that to Edie, everything she ate tasted delicious.

Baxter was Baxter, relentlessly energetic and charming and predictable in manifesting those qualities until halfway through their dinner together when he placed his knife and fork carefully to either side of his unfinished plate and said, 'You lied to me.'

She knew immediately what he was referring to. Rachel. 'Yes, I did.'

'Why did you?'

She said, 'It's not something I wanted distracting you from answering my questions when I finally got the chance to ask them. I wasn't the one being interviewed and profiled. I was trying to be professional.'

'But you have seen her, haven't you, Edith. You've seen Rachel Ballantyne.'

'I have, Felix. I think you have too.'

He said, 'Describe her to me.'

'I've already done that.'

'Not the first-hand version you haven't.'

'I was here 18 months ago. I was with a group including my stepfather, trying to find out what had happened to the people who'd disappeared here on the writers' retreat held on New Hope back then. We were in the stone cellar where Ballantyne's colonists stored the whisky they distilled before its buyers shipped it to the mainland.'

Baxter smiled, though he'd grown pale, the ruddy-cheeked colour exposure to the day's adventures had given him drained now from his face. He said, 'That cellar's going to re-open as our souvenir and gift shop. Not that we'll call it anything so crass.'

'It was gloomy, poorly lit. There were three of us down there. And then suddenly, there were four. I saw her first, seated on top of one of the big oak barrels. At first you think she's cute looking, picturesque with her blonde curls and urchin costume. But then you start to catalogue the detail and she becomes disturbing and horrific. She was a child who died of a fatal illness 200 years ago and yet she's animate. Her face has a vague, unfinished look, as though poorly remembered. She creates a kind of disturbance in the atmosphere, a sort of dismay. She's an affront to nature and she knows she is.'

'That's very eloquently put.'

'Words are going to be my living so I try to use them precisely. And I've had a year and a half to think about it and I have thought about it, because she's not a presence easily forgotten.'

'I saw her only for a moment,' Baxter said, 'and in two dimensions. You're bang on, though, saying she provokes dismay.'

'Did she speak to you?'

'I've done a bit of reading on ghosts and demonology since. I don't think she was actually there. It was just a glimpse and then gone again and a long way from home. I think it was just a projection. It was in Merseyside, a week ago.'

'It's quite possible she was born in Liverpool.'

'I know that,' Baxter said, 'but it's here she lives, if 'lives' is the right word.'

'So you believe in her existence?'

'I know what I saw. I don't think I'll ever forget the effect it had on me.'

'Doesn't that concern you?'

Baxter looked at her. He'd kept the goatee, which suited him. He looked youthful in his jeans and denim shirt, with his grey hair tousled, seated here, at the heart of his burgeoning empire. To her surprise, Edie found herself feeling a bit sorry for him. He was glib and manipulative and rich, but she couldn't help thinking that he was out of his depth, with not the remotest idea of just what he was letting himself in for.

He said, 'There's plenty of room on the island. The last thing my visitors will wish to do is despoil or intrude. They're going to be here to celebrate the solitude and they won't just appreciate the wilderness environment, they'll revere it.'

'Jet skis and zip wires don't exactly celebrate solitude.'

'We mean Rachel no harm. I think her tormented spirit provides one of the island's most potent and enduring myths. It's one we'll respectfully celebrate.'

Edie said, 'You're going to turn Rachel Ballantyne into a tourist attraction?'

Baxter smiled. He'd quite recovered himself. He poured pricey wine from their open bottle, topping up their glasses. He said, 'I'm in the business of maximizing opportunities, transforming negatives into positives.'

She remembered one of his celebrated platitudes. *Failure of nerve is a dream's only obstacle to becoming reality.* And she remembered her recent visit to Patsy Lassiter's house and Patsy's recounting of his meeting with Rachel in the sepulchre under the old Colony settlement. She sought peace. She hankered after final rest. She wouldn't welcome the intrusive babble and jostle of curious company, however well meant.

'I know what you're thinking,' Baxter said, 'or at any rate, I think I do.' He was smiling now, but his whole demeanour had darkened. 'You're thinking I'm misguided or foolhardy, but that's because you're not seeing things from my perspective. Aren't you impressed by this complex?'

'There's a cracked pane in the glass fronting one of the VIP suites. How did it get there?'

'It might have been faultily fitted and subject to too much tension.' He shrugged, 'I'm no engineer, but it'll be replaced during the coming week. What's your overall impression of the build?'

'I think it's brilliantly done,' she said. 'It couldn't be more in sympathy with its surroundings. Helena Davenport's a genius.'

'Didn't you have a good time today?'

'I honestly had a blast.'

'Wasn't last night fun?

His maintenance crew and security boys had hosted a barbecue outside their compound, on the beach. The pale bulk of the Shanks cottage had seemed less sinister than serene in its isolation there, somewhere she knew Patsy Lassiter had found a refuge from the torment of his grief. There'd been karaoke and then a Scots electrician had plucked at a ukulele singing sea shanties in a lovely tenor voice as they sat in the warmth drinking beer around the roasting pit until midnight.

'Yes,' Edie said, 'last night was a lot of fun.'

Baxter sighed and nodded. He folded his arms across his chest tightly and bit his lip. He said, 'What you have to realize, Edith, is that it's far too late to stop now.'

The final bit of business after lunch didn't involve Edie. Baxter needed an hour with Dave Carter to go through the items on a maintenance roster and approve a couple of budgetary and procedural proposals. He suggested Edie take a quad, chaperoned of course, for a last blast of sunset adrenaline before the chopper arrived to take them away.

It was her chance and she knew it was and she took it, as the bike ticked cooling beneath her, Derek Johnson in the saddle to her right, Shanks' Cove picturesque before them and the quiet charged as the sun descended in the sudden absence of engine noise.

'What happened to Greg Cody?'

Johnson didn't return her gaze. He sat bareheaded, toying with the buckle of his helmet as the sea breeze teased the tresses of his thick black hair. He said, 'I had the biggest teen crush on your mum. She was intrepid as well as beautiful. I remember her roaming around that plague pit in her TV series with the bacillus still active in the teeth and bones of the victims.'

'Your point?'

'You're her daughter. So I knew you'd ask one of us that question if you got the chance, just as you know we're none of us permitted to comment on the matter.'

'I didn't know, Derek. I suspected it and know now.'

'I'm sorry.'

'Let me ask you another question. Do you think New Hope a hazardous place?'

Johnson did look at her then. He glanced briefly and twitched a smile and put his helmet back on, twisting his head to look at the sky in the direction of the mainland to the east and their rear. He said, 'Your ride will be here in less than an hour, Edie. I only wish to God I was hitching a lift on that helicopter and out of here with you.'

He didn't say anything else. He gunned the motor of his quad, its belligerent roar making further conversation between them impossible.

Phil Fortescue had a week's work scheduled at Portsmouth Harbour. They'd booked him into his hotel from Sunday.

He'd come back to stay with Ruthie for the following weekend on Friday. That was the plan, anyway.

She drove him in the Fiat to the ferry terminal at Fishbourne on Sunday evening and said goodbye to him and got back into the car intending to drive it back to Ventnor and park it and forget about it there. Phil wouldn't need it in Pompey and she didn't really have any great need to drive on the island. February wasn't a month for sightseeing and she wanted to get back on schedule with her word-count. She only remembered the bracelet of teeth in the boot when it began to speak to her.

It was dark and the road was quiet and the only noise was the rumble of the car's engine. When she heard the sibilant hiss of something over that, she thought at first it must be the radio. She glanced down and saw that the radio was switched off. Then she realized that the noise was coming from behind her and it registered as a human voice, accented and cold and slightly girlish. It was too faint to make out individual words, but there was something insistent and urgent about it that made her pull up and switch off the ignition and get out and open up the boot.

She hadn't seen another car travelling either way. The sky was overcast, no moon or stars, so there wasn't much light. There was enough, though, to enable her to see the cloth bag containing the strung teeth ripple and recoil with movement. This had happened to Lizzie Burrows, who in death had commented on the resemblance she'd shared with Ruthie in life. And the experience had driven Lizzie to suicide. Ruthie, however, didn't think she was going mad. She might resemble how Lizzie had looked physically, but there was one significant difference between them. She had a healthy and proven belief in magic.

That didn't mean she was complacent or unafraid. She picked up the bag and weighed its unstill burden in her hand with a shudder through her of cold revulsion. From inside the bag, the teeth shifted and shaped chattering and the mouth formed there whispered something. Instinct made her want to drop the cloth envelope rippling with uncanny animation against her palm and fingers. She willfully resisted doing so. She had to hold it close to her ear to make out the sense of what was being uttered.

'Not here,' it simpered. 'Take me to the wood.'

Brightstone Forest was the nearest wood to where they were. It was sometimes rumoured to be a place of enchantment. It was dense and secluded and at 8 o'clock on a winter night there would be no one at all there up to any good. Ruthie didn't think parking up and wandering into the forest in the dark remotely an attractive or sensible idea. But if that was what was required of her, she'd do it. She felt afraid. Of course she did. But she needed to hear what it was the sorcerer had to say.

She put the bag back into the boot for the drive along the coast road to the forest. It was too loathsome an object to bear putting into her pocket or even on the passenger seat next to her. Driving on a night as dark as this, when you were unaccustomed to night driving, was sufficient of a challenge without occult distractions.

When she got to where she was going, she pulled off the road and retrieved the cloth bag. She wished, holding it, that the bracelet would keep still until they reached a quiet spot at the forest's heart. The task was difficult enough without the teeth grinding and squirming in the way that they were. At least the bracelet's voice stayed silent, as she crunched over dead leaves and wind snapped twigs and tried to avoid tripping over fallen branches, picking a path between the trunks of skeletal trees hair-trigger sensitive to any noise not natural to this ancient, secluded place.

'Here,' whispered the bag, eventually. Ruthie stopped. She unzipped her coat and squatted on her haunches and emptied the bag onto the loam; white against black, a pale, glistening mouth shaping itself in a hellish circle, words emanating from it more strongly here, audible, disembodied and like a solemn mockery of life.

'The Being bred,' the bracelet told her, 'its progeny far stronger for being born here than its progenitor was on the strength only of my summoning. This is how the magic functions. The incantation I gave the good doctor will not destroy this creature now. Its power is immense. Its hunger is insatiable, its spite depthless.'

'Can it be stopped?'

'There is but the one way in which it can. You must discover that for yourself.'

'You can't help?'

'I cannot interfere.'

'Can you tell me anything?'

'It waits, now. It lurks, learning. When its moment comes, it will sense that. It is mighty already. And it is cunning.'

Ruthie shivered.

The bracelet chuckled, or seemed to. Shaddeh said, 'Your professor is right to believe in fate. We cannot escape our destiny, any more than we can live beyond our allotted span.'

'You seem to have managed.'

Shaddeh chuckled again and the teeth whispered and chinked with his dead mirth. It was a horrible sound in the silence of the night wood. 'That is not of my choice. My torment now is my punishment for what I began then.'

'We risk our lives to sort out your mess and you get rest?'

'I will be given rest only if it is your destiny to succeed. That is why I cannot interfere.'

'In fiction, in situations like this, you'd at least give us some clues.'

'Your professor was given his clues when he spoke to the scholar now intent on proving herself a fool.'

'You mean Doctor Tremlett?'

'He has his answer if he can but recall what was said to him and determine to do what the knowledge enables him to. He should confide what he's learned in his friend.'

'Patsy Lassiter?'

Shaddeh chuckled again; 'The only friend he has left living.'

'His other friends were claimed by New Hope. They all of them died there. You shouldn't take pride in that.'

'Not pride, Ruthie Gillespie. Not even consolation. Talk to one another, as allies in all your destinies. Plot carefully and then go back there and end this, finally.'

He knew her name. He knew all their names. It sounded like a game to him. The great game, she thought, wondering where she'd heard that phrase, to what it alluded. Maybe just to this. She said, 'You can shed no more light?'

There was a sigh from the lipless, gleaming oval shaping itself on the loam, an exhalation of breath she knew was impossible but heard distinctly nevertheless. 'I have brought only darkness,' the sorcerer said. The mouth of teeth sagged and collapsed with a bony tinkle and Ruthie knew it would speak to her no more.

She got out of the forest without mishap. A few burrs clung to her coat, but that was okay, it wasn't the indignity of falling flat on her face, or giving into panic and running screaming into a tree. She put the bag once again containing the bracelet back into the boot of the car. She drove home and called Phil in his hotel room and told him what had happened, what had been said to her.

'You're very brave, Ruthie, and I'm none the wiser.'

'You need to think really carefully about what Doctor Tremlett said to you. Go over and over it in your mind. Maybe speak to her again?'

'I've left about five messages. She's not picking up her calls.'

Ruthie coughed. It wasn't her perennial smokers' cough, she was deliberately clearing her throat. She required clarity. She said, 'I married someone in my mid-20s. It was a disaster. On paper it lasted five years, in reality a lot less. One day I'll tell you about it. But if I seem touchy sometimes about honesty and betrayal, that's the reason, what happened to me then. It's not you, I trust you. I couldn't love you if I didn't and I do, I love you, Phil.'

'And I love you,' he said.

'Shaddeh was wrong about one thing, mistaken to call Patsy your only friend. I'm your friend. I'm your friend too.'

'And I'm yours, Ruthie,' he said.

'Now I'm going to have a drink,' she said. 'I'm going to have a large drink all alone. Is that really terrible?'

'Not when you've earned it,' he said. 'And you have.'

Chapter Eleven

Patrick Lassiter thought it was the small stuff, the incidentals, the shifting colours of the sky, its brightness and shade, the smell of grass, dust-motes in sunbeams through glass, the rich resonance of a chord struck plangently in a familiar song still with the power to stir your heart. He'd missed all that stuff, the minutia of human feeling, since his wife's death. With Alice gone, he'd had no reason to log in his consciousness the detailed intricacies of everyday life. He'd lived by rote, functioned mostly on autopilot.

Helena's presence had brought that home to him. She'd left, reluctantly, just after lunch. He felt her absence keenly now, having known her altogether for less than 24 hours. In one way it seemed ridiculous, like a schoolboy infatuation had taken hold of him. In another way it seemed entirely natural, exactly what he'd needed and truthfully, heaven sent. He'd endured his share of personal torment but as Sunday afternoon matured and mellowed into evening, he felt like the luckiest man in existence. He was blessed. He'd been invited back into the warmth and the light. He was fully among the living again.

She'd told him about the events on New Hope, the dark eclipse and following collision in her suite, the toughened glass cracked by impact. She'd told him about the inexplicable failure of the generator powering the complex. And she'd told him about the tooth in its rotting encirclement of torn gum she'd found in the sink of her otherwise spotless bathroom. He'd listened without comment, lying beside her, because they hadn't made it to dinner time before she'd taken his hand firmly in hers and led him up to bed.

'Our dinner will burn,' he said, laughing, pulled after her up the stairs.

'No, it won't,' she said, 'I turned your oven down a minute ago on the way back from the loo.'

'I don't believe you.'

'Forward planning,' she said.

She told him about the sense of being watched she'd experienced on the island and of Derek Johnson's sharing the same instinct. She told him that Johnson believed the animosity aimed towards them by their elusive observer had been cranked up a notch.

'I'm sure Greg Cody would agree,' Lassiter said, 'If he was still around to do so.'

'I became really scared on the island. Derek was an absolute lifesaver, especially when the weather closed in. But when the lights went out, he was as scared as I was. The island's such an isolated place. Half the time it isn't even in radio contact with the rest of the world. More than half the time.'

'Felix Baxter promotes the fact as part of the island's charm.'

'Felix Baxter is full of shit,' Helena said.

'With you on that,' Lassiter said.

She smiled and kissed his shoulder. 'How tired are you?'

'Not tired enough.'

'Good.'

Later, because he had to, he told her about the presence on the island he was no longer confident had been destroyed. It had consumed half their number on the expedition in '10. They'd thought it gone, eradicated. Everything happening now suggested it wasn't.

'Will you go back there, Patrick?'

'I might not have a choice.'

'Don't you dare come into my life only to leave it by losing yours. Don't you dare.'

He thought there was some debate about who had actually come into whose life, because he thought it was Helena had done that rather than him. But he took the point.

'I'm quite resilient,' he said, 'hard to get rid of.'

'Good.'

Now, he shook himself out of his reverie because his phone was ringing. It was Phil Fortescue.

'Professor,' he said.

'You sound knackered.'

'I've every right.'

There was a pause while Fortescue processed this information. He said, 'Congratulations, not before time.'

'What can I do you for?'

Fortescue told him about what Ruthie had heard earlier that night. He said, 'I can't think of anything Georgia Tremlett told me that gave me a single clue about ending the nightmare that sorcerer dreamed up. Every word rang alarm bells. There was no cavalry coming over the hill in anything she said.'

'Call her back.'

'I've tried. She's dropping her calls. Why would she do that?'

Lassiter was tired and love-struck. The pondering was unusually hard for him, but after a moment, he got there. He said, 'She's on her way to New Hope Island after academic glory armed with Horan's journal and everything you've told her. She's got to do it before the Baxter circus trundles into town, so she's not wasted any time.'

'You're joking.'

'Contrary to popular opinion, I do possess a sense of humour, Phil. But New Hope's not a fit subject for wise cracks.'

After Phil's call he thought about the promise he'd made and felt honour-bound to keep to Rachel Ballantyne. He reckoned he'd worked out a way to provide her with rest. It didn't require magic, but he didn't think he could achieve the end she sought alone. It would be a collective effort that might jeopardize their lives. Sometimes though, you just had to do what was right, regardless of the consequences.

He did something then he hadn't done once since returning from the cottage on New Hope he'd rebuilt. He went to listen to some music. It was by now quite late on Sunday evening. His hi fi had become dusty with neglect in the long absence from song in his life. He knew what he wanted to listen to, an album that had become a favourite before his island sojourn, after Edie Chambers had advised him to learn a few folk songs as a precaution should Rachel Ballantyne wish to pluck them from his mind.

He switched on the player and looked for the CD he'd chosen to listen to on the shelf where they were listed alphabetically. He ran a finger along their spines. The one he wanted was Kate Rusby's *Sleepless*, which had on it *Sweet Bride* and her gorgeous version of *The Wild Goose*. But it wasn't there.

Then he noticed something on top of one of the speaker cabinets he definitely hadn't left there. He was by nature and habit methodical, punctiliously neat. He walked across the room and saw that *Sleepless* had been singled out already and put there for him. On top of it was a single bloom plucked from the vase of them Helena had brought him. He knew that Helena hadn't put it there. He thought he knew who had. He'd only met one person in his life possessed of an authentic psychic gift, one woman who would have known which album he'd intended after all these months of willful silence to listen to.

Tears of grief and surprise and gratitude suddenly bleared his sight and smarted and then trickled down his face. The solitary flower was the sign that Alice approved. She was happy for him. He'd embarked upon a new and for him unexpected chapter. He felt found and that feeling inflicted upon him a sudden sensation not of loss, but of parting. Patrick Lassiter knew he'd sensed his late wife's presence in that house for the last time.

Dawn on Monday morning broke anxiously for Derek Johnson. The fine weather had held. Dave Carter and one of his boys, Alan Newton, had decided to break the monotony with a night's fishing aboard one of the R.I.'s they had as part of their haul of equipment on the island. The chief's visit had gone without mishap. He'd been helicoptered off the previous afternoon all smiles, with his not quite docile pet reporter in tow.

He'd been full of praise for the job they'd done and were continuing to do. There was an extra grand added to the pay of every man there at the end of the month. That amounted to twelve thousand pounds, which Johnson, perhaps more jaundiced than the rest, thought a drop in Baxter's considerable ocean. Dave Carter had been pleased and possibly relieved, though. He'd needed some encouragement after the story of the delinquent generator and the grisly relic of Cody's incisor. The chief had provided it.

Carter's belief, only briefly discussed, was that however theoretically malevolent the island might be, the sea surrounding it was benign. His reasoning concerned their expensively unreliable radio transmitter. It functioned haphazardly on land, given to all sorts of snarls and cutouts and weird distortions; but it worked perfectly well once you got it a decent distance offshore.

It was a plausible theory, and one in which Johnson had felt no faith whatsoever. Personally, he'd no more have spent a night anchored off New Hope in a rubber boat than he's spend another night alone at the elegant complex the voluptuous and much-missed Helena Davenport had masterminded on the island.

Johnson was missing Helena. This was not as a consequence of any salacious intent on his account, but because he thought women sometimes got to the bottom of things much quicker and more directly than men. If she were still there, he figured he'd be less clueless about the strangeness of the island than he was. He'd also feel less lonely. In a short period chronologically, he considered she'd become a genuine friend.

He tried to get a response from the shortwave he was carrying, but there was no sign of life from Carter's end. Alan Newton was from Barmouth on the Welsh coast and had been an RNLI volunteer there for a five year stint. Their R.I.'s on New Hope were the same model the lifeboat crews handled and so Newton was an experienced sailor familiar with the craft he was aboard. If he was still aboard it, Johnson thought, looking out to sea from a point just beyond the Shanks cottage, sweeping the horizon with a pair of Zeiss binoculars that generally missed nothing.

How far out would they have risked going? Quite a distance, because Newton was so bloody confident and because every foot for Carter, subconsciously at least, was a foot further from the unnatural hazards of the island. Plus the bigger fish favoured the deeper waters. And there were abundant fish-stocks out there. They weren't depleted. The trawler men of Mallaig and Stornoway generally avoided the area close to New Hope out of long-held superstitions. They thought it an unlucky place.

Morning had broken dully, sunless with a raw chill and a strengthening wind that whipped at the hem and cuffs of the cagoule he wore. They'd had almost a week of spring-like weather, but it was still February and the unseasonal spell looked and felt at an end. There was a rising chop on the water, not yet a swell, but it would get there given an hour or two. Johnson felt the anxiety in his stomach tighten a notch.

If something fatal had befallen those two men, severe weather would only make their fate more ambiguous, the ex-copper in him insisted. The North Atlantic was inherently hazardous, a hostile environment and the home to countless natural calamities. If those boys had disappeared it would seem much less mysterious in the teeth of a rising storm than Cody's vanishing had done.

Johnson's anxiety lasted until just before 11am, when one of his team called in having spotted debris washed-up on the shore of a cove a mile roughly to the northwest of the crofter's cottage.

'Bodies?'

'Nope, you need to see this though, boss.'

'Moving.'

He took a quad there, overland, the coastal route too dangerous by then in the gathering swell that the squall hitting them had fostered, the engine deafened by the withering screech of the wind and the rain smearing the goggles he'd been forced to put on in the face of its needling assault.

The descent to the cove was rocky and steep and he almost tumbled down over it, seeing his headlamp swap a view of turf for the void of empty air only just in time to brake and bring the bike to a shuddering, skidding halt on the brink of the decline.

He clambered down, buffeted, hampered by the spume and spindrift reducing visibility to only a few feet in light shed gloomily from low, sullen cloud. He was agile for so big a man and grateful for it, thankful for all the scampering drills the rugby coaches had forced him to endure over the seasons of his sporting life.

There wasn't much to see. There was a bait box and a smashed oar and a large section of pulverized rubber; but it was enough. The rubber bore the stenciled serial number of the craft Carter and Newton had taken out.

Ricky Hurst had found it. He was a former Royal Marine, hard as nails, three tours in Helmand Province, a veteran of minefields and coastal assaults, of firefight ambushes and close I.E.D. encounters he never really spoke about. He was a Glaswegian and naturally pale under his crop of red curls, but today his facial skin had a taut stretch to it and looked almost translucent under hair plastered to his skull. His eyes too were pale and studiedly neutral.

He said, 'Collision with something colossal, boss. Maybe dragged under the hull and into its propellers. Catastrophic damage, they wouldn't have known what hit them and they wouldn't have had a chance.'

'No chance at all,' Johnson said. *They wouldn't have known what hit them.* He was thinking about the crack in the glass of Helena Davenport's picture window, the dark eclipse and thump of impact she'd described to him.

Hurst fixed him with a stare. Then he glanced back at the wreckage. 'No offence to you, boss, but this is some sorry fucking mess,' he said.

Johnson just nodded.

There was nothing tangible to discuss. They'd been confronted by the certainty of death in the violence of the tempest. Marine tragedies occurred. Everyone knew the risks of small boats on big and busy seas. The circumstantial evidence wasn't so much persuasive as overwhelming. But men with Hurst's proven talent for survival also possessed a well-honed instinct for danger they tended always to trust. Neither of them said anything further, only because neither of them needed to.

Johnson got astride his quad and rode back to the compound. He walked straight to what was laughably called their communications room and fired up the wireless transmitter. Its display of lights glowed green as the twin power metres surged and settled and he was reminded of that American phrase about all the lights being on but there being nobody home. It was a definition of madness, as was the habit of repeating the same action and expecting a different outcome; but he had to persist, had to try to do his duty and call this into Baxter Enterprises HQ and alert the coastguard if he could.

A moan ululated out of the set so wretchedly child-like in tone it made him physically recoil. For some reason he was reminded of the word scrawled on the bathroom mirror at the Experience complex. Was he listening now to the scrawler, was that her crooning away in the ether? Leave, she had warned them, a warning unheeded and too late now for poor dead Dave Carter. Carter, who'd never make him wince again at some dubious barbecue wisecrack. Johnson closed his eyes and gritted his teeth with his headphones clamped and persisted in slowly twisting the knob, praying for an audible frequency and an end to that spectral voice.

Georgia Tremlett got to Stornoway aboard the ferry on Monday evening. The crossing was rough and the vessel smelled sourly of vomit from seasick passengers that hadn't all made it to the crowded latrines in time. She spoke to a deckhand who told her it was much worse further out but she wasn't discouraged by that. She'd booked a room in a Stornoway B&B with no intention of travelling on to New Hope with anything other than several hours of daylight left to her in which to set up camp.

She thought Seamus Ballantyne's old colony settlement the best place to look for an evidential trail. She'd establish camp close to its sheltering wall. She knew it had been declared a World Heritage Site, but though she'd be guilty of trespass without official permission to visit and in the absence of a guide, she would be careful in damaging nothing and taking no trophies or souvenirs away. She'd always been fastidious and scrupulous in her past fieldwork and those habits wouldn't change just because this was unsanctioned and a less orthodox mission than those had been.

She was much more excited than afraid. She was slightly daunted by the ambition of what she intended to prove, but not really concerned for her own safety. One presumed fatality in all the time Felix Baxter's infrastructure had taken to assemble didn't amount to the presence of a ravenous monster to her. She wasn't looking to confront something capering, demonic and hungry. She was looking only for evidence that it had been there in the island's bleak and mysterious past.

Perhaps she would find hair and skin samples in what had been its lair. Perhaps she would find a pile of gnawed human bones, the flesh devoured by some species its recovered DNA would insist was a stranger to the known world. She was confident she would find enough even without hard physical evidence to substantiate what she intended to write. She thought in short that she was on to a winner.

Rachel Ballantyne, her persistent folkloric myth, would provide Georgia's compelling sub-plot. She didn't really expect to come face to decomposing face with the revenant of Seamus's daughter either. Even if the story was true and her antic spirit was there, she'd have no business with a visiting academic. She'd left Baxter's people alone, presumably indifferent to their presence, unless she enjoyed their company from an elusive distance.

Georgia thought about calling Professor Fortescue and sharing with him her theory about the Being's solitary weakness. Then she decided against doing so. She would save that revelation for the book she intended to write. Fuck Professor Fortescue. She'd have enjoyed doing that herself, but he was shacked up in Ventnor with his black-clad, tattooed tramp. 'Good luck to them,' she said to herself, actually wishing them just the opposite.

She dumped her rucksack in her room. She went to find the harbour bar where the fishing fleet did their drinking. She didn't think many of them would be going out into the exposed ocean on a night as rough as this one was. She wanted to find someone who'd take her to New Hope just as soon as the weather improved. That might be by dawn the following day, she knew meteorological conditions could and did change swiftly in the Hebrides. She reckoned a two-hour window, given the distance, all she needed.

At her third attempt in the busy harbour, Georgia found her bar. She got four flat refusals before an elderly salt drinking something from a pewter mug with whisky chasers turned overhearing her and said, 'Adam Cox is your man, miss.'

'Why's that?'

'He went before, 18 month ago. Story is he did it for the price of his diesel. He can only say no.'

Adam Cox did his drinking in another bar on the other side of the harbour. The walk there was rainy and windy and cold, but Georgia was just glad he wasn't teetotal and she could locate him at all. She felt lucky so far in this enterprise and hoped her luck would hold.

She saw a young man who answered the old sailor's description. He was in conversation with two other men roughly his own age. She asked him could she have a private word and they went and stood in the pub's porch and she explained where it was she wanted to go to and he told her he wouldn't take her.

'Apparently you've taken people there in the past.'

'I took one person 18 months ago and I took her against my better judgment. And when we got there, I tried to dissuade her from going ashore. And that was in the summer, when it barely gets dark. It wasn't the middle of winter like it is now.'

'How much did she pay you for the crossing?'

'It's none of your business and it's not relevant.'

'I'll double it,' Georgia said.

'The answer's still no.'

Georgia was intrigued. 'Who was she, 18 months ago, Mr. Cox, and why did she go there?'

'She was a woman named Ruthie Gillespie. She was scared, which made her very brave, if you get my drift.'

'Oh, I get your drift alright.'

'She went because some friends of hers on the island were in trouble. That's what she said. They needed help and she went there to help them.'

Georgia took stock of what she'd just been told. She wondered had Professor Fortescue been one of the people in trouble on the island 18 months earlier. He hadn't let on to her that he'd been back after the expedition in '10.

Maybe he'd simply not thought his return worth remarking upon. But he was in one piece. And Ramshackle Ruthie, his Goth party animal squeeze, was also in one piece. If no harm had come to someone as hapless as her on the island then it really couldn't harbour any serious threat.

'I'll give you five hundred pounds Adam, for a one-way ride.' She was thinking of the advance she'd asked of her American publisher on emailing the book synopsis. She'd suggested eighty thousand dollars would deter her from shopping around further.

'It's not a ride,' he said, looking out over the stone of the quayside to where the whitecaps welled and seethed in the sea beyond. 'It's a voyage. And no one's going out in this.'

'Agreed,' Georgia Tremlett said. 'But tomorrow's another day and the weather might have calmed and I'm actually thinking 750 of our English pounds might prove a welcome temptation in a thin season.'

He looked at her sharply. He said, 'How'd you know times are hard?'

'You and your friends were drinking halves in there,' she said. 'I teach students. So I know young men your age don't drink halves unless they're having to.'

'Maybe we're in training for something.'

'Or maybe you're about to have your boat repossessed.'

'Let's see how tomorrow's weather leaves us,' he said.

And Georgia smiled, knowing that she'd booked her passage.

Chapter Twelve

Felix Baxter felt haunted. He'd felt that way ever since his misguided trip to the museum in Liverpool and its weird aftermath. The pale, crumpled visage of the urchin on the horror movie poster he thought he'd seen outside the derelict cinema building might have bleached to nothing in life, but was still vivid in his mind, the head turning and following his dazed progress through the rain along the street with its vacant eyes.

He thought he knew very well who she had been. She was the wraith caught by the New Hope crofter David Shanks on cine film in the 1930s he'd always airily dismissed as faked. He'd had a change of heart and mind about that. He didn't think it faked anymore. Edith Chambers had seen whatever Rachel Ballantyne had become over two centuries of antic, impossible life. Edith was a bit naïve and still possessed the innocence of youth, but she wasn't delusional and she wasn't a liar either. She said she'd seen Rachel 18 months earlier on the island and Baxter believed her.

He'd been fearful during his weekend there. He'd put on a pretty good show for Edith and he didn't think she'd seen through the bluster to the jumpy, anxious reality. He'd studied the faces of Dave Carter and Derek Johnson, his team leaders there and he'd seen strain and sensed a degree of collusive secrecy he'd dismissed at the time as paranoia, except in retrospect it didn't seem like that at all. He thought the strain came from the effect on their nerves of the things they were hiding from him only in order to protect their precious livelihoods.

Given longer there and given the privacy from Edith to do it, he'd have tried to get it out of them. He might not, though, have succeeded in this. He had a reputation for killing the messenger. Carter and Johnson both of them knew it and they were family men with the financial obligations wives and children bought.

Or they had been. Half an hour earlier, his PA Joy had called him and told him the bad news. Johnson had managed one of his intermittent transmissions on that expensively unreliable radio kit they were equipped with there. And he'd used it to deliver a sobering report. Dave Carter and an electrician named Alan Newton had disappeared aboard a rigid inflatable. Bits of the boat had washed up earlier that day. They'd set off for a few hours of night fishing in calm weather as a break in their routine and conditions having worsened, their vessel had washed ashore in fragments of wreckage. Or some of it had. Most of it, like the two men, was still missing.

New Hope Island was becoming an increasingly accident-prone place. He was reminded of the words of that detective, Patrick Lassiter, questioning him about the island in the aftermath of Cody's vanishing.

I was left alone there.

That phraseology was both ambiguous and disturbing if only because not every resident on New Hope seemed to share the police commander's good fortune.

He'd have to go back. Unhampered by his pretty and ambitious journalist student chaperone, he'd seek out the unambiguous, uncensored truth. He'd bring with him a big dose of rationality, a large serving of skepticism, a welcome dash of hard-headedness. Except that he truthfully felt none of his brasher character traits really suited these particular circumstances. These *peculiar* circumstances, he thought, because they seemed not only unique to New Hope Island, but somehow determined by the Island itself.

He'd felt watched there, if he was going to be completely honest with himself. And not just by his alert and curious student companion. She hadn't so much observed as studied him there and he'd had the curious sense she wasn't the only one doing it. This covert surveillance – and that's what it had felt like – had made him feel self-consciously uneasy whenever out exposed on the open ground. And he'd sensed his people there felt it too and didn't much like it either. They'd endured it for longer. They hadn't got used to it. It might prove a deterrent to his paying guests if it persisted. He'd have to go back to see if he could sort matters out and put his perfectionist mind at rest.

Baxter was in his Manchester flat and Manchester was 30 miles from Liverpool, where Rachel Ballantyne might well have been born. That thought occurred to him now. Her father had lived there before his New Hope epiphany and his departure for his Hebridean Kingdom of Belief with his doomed followers. A large and growing part of Baxter expected to encounter her again and he dreaded that in a way so fearful he would never have been able to explain it to anyone.

He'd always been fired by self-belief and his hard-earned status as a business visionary was something he'd felt was deepening and expanding with the progression of the New Hope project from ambitious dream to breathtaking reality. Now though, he was having these serious doubts.

But would he pull the plug even if he could? The question wasn't one seriously worth asking himself. Schemes enacted on this epic scale had their own colossal momentum.

He was in too deep with too many interested parties to extricate himself at this late stage. If he tried to do it, he'd alienate the investment partners he'd worked so hard to cultivate and needed for any sort of commercial future. If he pulled the plug he'd bankrupt himself financially and destroy his business credibility at a stroke.

That was the rational side of his thinking. The irrational was the impulse that had impelled him to close the curtains of every window in the flat as darkness descended half an hour earlier. The night glitter of Mancunian life was something he generally enjoyed in this buoyant northern English city. Only London bettered it for energy and enterprise. But he feared he might see a child-like figure on the other side of the panes, someone ragged and forlorn, her features unfinished or just forgotten over time, pale and curious and undeterred by the fact that his was a penthouse eleven floors above the pavement.

His phone rang, making him jump.

Joy, his PA.

'Not more bad news?'

'Just checking in with you, Felix. By your standards, you're being unusually quiet. Anything I can do?'

'Yeah, please, doll. Charter a chopper for Wednesday morning to take me to the island.'

'You only got back from there yesterday.'

'Left a couple of loose ends need tying up a bit more neatly. I'll probably stay just a single night.' Baxter checked the weather in the vicinity obsessively, three or four times a day. He knew it was rough now but also knew the forecast was encouraging.

He could and would carry on as though the misgivings he had were nothing more than the neuroses a project of the magnitude of the New Hope Experience would naturally engender in anyone sane in overall charge of it. But psychologically the acid test for Baxter concerned his son, 18, on his gap year, enjoying travelling in Central America and the only person in the world he really cared about.

Would he let Danny take a student job on New Hope; let him earn some pocket money bar-tending or as a field-guide or waiter or lifeguard? Not in a million years, he wouldn't. He wouldn't risk his precious son's wellbeing for a single moment there.

He thought he heard a noise, then. He thought he heard a smudge of sound from outside, a soft, dull, beckoning thump against his sitting room window. He swallowed bile and fear and on legs that felt they didn't properly belong to him, walked over and pulled back the heavy drapes and took a look. There was nothing there, when he did. There was just empty space and below the distant twinkle of the night city. He'd have a drink, he decided. He didn't generally drink alone, but knew he wouldn't sleep this evening without a nightcap.

'I thought maybe an eagle, or possibly an albatross.'

'Neither creature would have the mass. And at that velocity there'd have been a mess left behind, albatross blancmange smeared right across the pane.'

'Charming thought.'

'I can't think of anything living with the strength. Maybe a gorilla with a sledgehammer could do it, if great apes used tools and were native to the Hebrides. But I honestly don't think even that would work.'

Helena Davenport was outside Aberdeen early on Tuesday morning with Miles Stanhope, managing director of Rampart Glass and a worried man because his company had profitable contracts with security services around the world occupying offices that were required to be fortifications as well as places of work. They also manufactured and supplied windscreen glass to a variety of heads of state and royal households. They did a lot of lucrative business in the Middle and Far East and their reputation, so far, was untarnished.

Stanhope was a small, neat man in an immaculate suit and with what looked to her like an expensive recent haircut. The overall effect was spoiled by a sort of pecking agitation, like a bothered hen.

He'd arranged a demonstration for Helena, which she thought unnecessary. She knew all about the durability of the product, but she also knew what she'd left behind at the complex on New Hope. Something had achieved what Stanhope considered impossible there. She thought the demonstration set up as much to reassure him as to persuade her.

She had no intention of telling anyone about what had happened. She'd asked Derek Johnson to keep it to himself and Felix Baxter didn't sweat the small stuff. He'd mentioned it in a phone call the previous day after his own return from a flying visit to the island and she'd told him Rampart Glass would make good the damage at the company's own expense this week and he seemed satisfied with that.

The demonstration involved the sort of old-fashioned ball and chain suspended from a crane boom that used to be used to demolish houses. It swung through forty-five degrees gaining momentum as it did so and collided with the secured vertical sheet with a booming off-key thud of impact. The iron ball juddered on its chain. When everything came to a halt, the glass wasn't even scratched.

'Very impressive,' Helena felt obliged to say, which it was. It was a hitherto unstoppable force meeting an immovable object you could see through with absolute clarity. Rampart's product was a remarkable feat of technology and manufacturing skill.

'That pane on New Hope must have had an inherent flaw and our testing procedures failed to reveal it,' Stanhope said, the line he'd been taking ever since she'd shown him the photos of the crack taken on her phone. 'We've already revised them,' he said.

She nodded, knowing there had been no inherent flaw. Impact had done the damage. 'When will you replace it?'

'Tomorrow,' he said. 'We'd have done it sooner but for the difficulty of communicating with the maintenance crew and security boys on the island. And the weather's been uncooperative over the past couple of days. But we'll do it tomorrow, without fail and of course at no charge.'

'That's great,' she said.

He cleared his throat and said, 'Would this experience put you off using us in the future?'

Helena couldn't think of a build anywhere else requiring the strength and durability characteristic of the New Hope complex. But she answered him honestly. 'I'd use you again without hesitation,' she said. 'Your product's the best of its type in the world.'

It hadn't been an eagle or an albatross or a great ape wielding a sledgehammer or a pickaxe. It had been substantial enough in size to cast the entire room she'd stood in into shadow. It had been immensely strong and nimble enough to get out of sight quickly. And if it hadn't been flying, it had been an agile climber because the suite she'd occupied had been sixty feet above ground.

Had it really wanted to get in, it would have, Helena thought for the first time with a shiver. It was only testing the obstacle to its doing so. It hadn't quite breached the defences, but it had learned that it could. And then it had found a less direct and cleverer way by stopping the generator and disabling the locks.

Whatever it was, it was smart and elusive as well as imponderably strong. It had killed Greg Cody and left them the evidence as what? Perhaps just as proof it had a grisly sense of humour. They'd been toyed with, her and Derek Johnson. They'd been very fortunate to survive the experience. Had the thing lurking on the island chosen to attack them, they would have been its helpless victims.

The reason she'd keep the failure of a pane supplied by Rampart Glass to retain its structural integrity on New Hope Island was quite simple. Helena didn't think anything natural had inflicted the damage. She couldn't really blame the company for a crack put there by something with no rightful place in the world.

Patrick Lassiter had told her about his pledge made to Rachel Ballantyne. He'd been adamant the revenant preacher's daughter had not put the crack in the pane. She was powerful but physically petite and it simply wasn't her style to steal about unseen. Evidently she was content to leave some people alone on the island. Helena had gained the strong impression that Rachel actually liked Patrick Lassiter, felt a fondness close to human for him. Antagonized, she became a cavorting, gleeful, murderous nightmare. The difficulty apparently was in predicting what might antagonize her. And her fondness for Patrick would not endure the insult of a broken promise.

It occurred to Helena then that if Patrick kept his promise and successfully delivered Rachel the rest she sought, the sly, furtive, pane-cracking monster would have New Hope entirely to itself. She had no idea why, but this notion troubled her. There was no logic to it, but she thought if that happened, the island would become an even more potent hazard to any people there than it already was.

Fog and calm marked Georgia Tremlett's arrival on New Hope Island. It was only a sign to her that her good fortune was holding. Unless it was actually fate, she thought. Professor Fortescue's arrival in her professional life had come completely unexpectedly and there were half a dozen other specialists in the field to whom he could just as easily have gone. Through him she'd acquired the priceless source of Thomas Horan's journal and been given the opportunity she was now exploiting. Was there a strong element of destiny involved?

If there was, she might not altogether have finished with him personally. Ruthie Gillespie's charms were both limited and superficial and clever men when they were also physically attractive had low boredom thresholds. She'd likely be extremely busy for the foreseeable future with this new project she'd embarked upon. But in three months or six months, the maritime professor would likely begin to find Ruthie's company tedious; superficially picturesque, but deeply unsatisfying.

Adam Cox was taciturn on their crossing to the island. Clearly he needed the money she was paying, but her generosity didn't encourage him to communicate beyond what was necessary. She thought that perhaps her jibe about him and his drinking buddies only being able to afford halves had hit home. Young men had their pride and she'd hurt his by being right about his scrimping.

Eventually he asked, 'Do you know the island?'

'I've studied the topography.'
'Where is it you want to get to?'
'Ballantyne's colony settlement.'
'Jesus.'
'I'm not expecting him to be there.'

But Cox didn't respond to the joke. He said, 'There'll be some security on the island, has to be, with all that new development there. But they won't see my boat in this fog. I'll paddle the dinghy to put you ashore but I'm not hanging about, Miss.'

She wasn't too concerned about the security. She wasn't trespassing on the island, Baxter didn't own it and the bits he'd developed she had no interest in at all. When she'd got what she wanted she'd make contact with Baxter's people there only as a means of getting off New Hope. Their presence enabled her to do that pretty much at the time of her choosing. That was another piece of luck, unless it was again the helping hand of fate.

He rowed her ashore at a spot about a mile to the east of the New Age Experience complex and on the other side of the island from the crofter's cottage, where he said he thought the workers' compound was likeliest to be sited because it was the best spot weather-wise on the whole of the island.

'You're going to the worst spot, weather-wise. It's on the heights, so it's exposed to gales and storms.'

'A wonder he chose it,' she said.

'No, it's not, Miss. Seamus Ballantyne was sorry for what he'd done in his former life. Living there was deliberate. It was his penance.'

'You know a lot about it, for somewhere you avoid.'

'It's knowing about it makes me avoid it.'

She hefted her rucksack to the diminishing lap and gurgle of his oars as he rowed back into the fog out of sight and then hearing, leaving her alone on the shore. She could see little of her surroundings but the pebbles and scrub at her feet. It was very quiet and in the mist, everything appeared still, petrified. She knew if she kept going upwards she would likely reach her intended destination eventually.

It was ten o'clock on Tuesday morning. There were about seven hours of daylight left before darkness. It was more than ample time to orient herself, establish her camp and do a bit of preliminary exploration. She would start with Ballantyne's infamous windowless church. She wanted to immerse herself in the culture of the colony in a way that helped her write, when the time came, vividly and evocatively about New Hope.

She set off daydreaming about the casting of the movie they would make about this one-woman expedition and its sensational findings. She thought that given a chic trim, Gemma Arterton would be great casting, though the part would probably go to an American actress to give the film greater appeal internationally at the box office. Jennifer Lawrence was probably a bit young, but there was such a thing as artistic license and she had the right steely, determined look about her.

Georgia was fit from her regular gym habit and so despite having done no fieldwork over recent years, found the going tolerable. Her rucksack weighed about 60 pounds, heavy because it contained her food rations and her tent. The load was well balanced and she could carry it if she rested at intervals. She had a litre bottle of water clinking metallically on her hip, knowing she could replenish that at any time from the freshwater tarns on the island.

She began to think about her quarry. The Being was a shape-shifter, able to assume the appearance of a human but probably much larger in its dimensions when it did so, at least according to the Algonquin mythology. The Wendigo of their tribal legends was both elusive and deadly, hard to spot but extremely bad news when you did see it, because it didn't leave its witnesses alive to describe the experience.

Of the various explanations for where it came from, she thought somewhere alien to earth the most rational. Species originating on earth had shorter lifespans than that generally claimed for the Being. They weren't born carrying their own offspring. And man apart, no animal native to earth was deliberately vindictive. Some predators – great whites, polar bears, big cats – were capable of extreme savagery. But they didn't any of them kill solely for pleasure.

The question she'd never be able to answer, was how Shaddeh had summoned the creature, coaxed it into mortal existence. From what she knew of him, he'd been born with the occult powers he possessed. Over his lifetime he'd refined them and he'd been feted and almost worshipped for what he could accomplish for his people. But Georgia thought his powers probably as much a mystery to him then as they were to her now. He could make the dead restless. He could affront nature. Or so it had been persistently claimed.

That thought made her wonder whether there were some mysteries that were simply better left unsolved. That was a sensible and pragmatic position for most people to take. But to her, professionally, it was also heresy. All her academic training insisted it was not just her job but her vocation to shed whatever light she could on these dark and esoteric enigmas.

She became aware of a slight feeling of self-consciousness, labouring upward in her hike. It was almost as though someone spectated, observing her progress with cold amusement through the grey blanket of the mist. She knew that was only her imagination, but it made her wonder did she look slightly ridiculous in her combat fatigues and watch-cap with the burden of the rucksack on her back. She'd tried on the outfit she was wearing at an outdoor store on Sunday afternoon in the Arndale Centre and thought she looked dashing and svelte. Now, she wasn't so sure.

Georgia began to wish the fog would clear. Yes, she might have to deal with one of Baxter's jobsworth security patrols, but a wilderness you were unfamiliar with was unnerving when you were blinded to its hazards. Studying the topography on a contour map was nowhere near the same as being physically familiar with a place. She was totally unfamiliar with New Hope Island and the fog inflicted a degree of helplessness and risk she really didn't like.

And it distorted sound. She kept hearing things for which the mind could find no rational excuse. She heard a small avalanche of stones trickle downward somewhere off to her left and then abruptly cease. She heard the cry and feathery swoop of some large avian creature and wondered was she approaching a protective eagle's nest. She heard the mournful blast of a foghorn amplified from miles away over the still sea through the petrified air and wished for a moment she was back in the reticent company of Adam Cox, headed for the warm refuge of Stornoway aboard his chugging boat.

By now the feeling of being watched was doing more than make Georgia Tremlett feel self-conscious. It was making her skin crawl. She was no longer remotely concerned with her appearance. She was itchy and cold with gooseflesh coarsening on her upper arms, unwilling to take the break from her rucksack burden she needed because she was afraid to stop on the exposure of the slope she walked up. She felt exposed herself, vulnerable, almost as though naked. She knew it wasn't a rational way to feel but she was fighting with every step the instinct just to abandon what she was carrying and turn and flee.

Something man-made loomed into her vision. It was the perimeter wall of Ballantyne's colony settlement. She'd reached her destination. The realization calmed her. She'd suffered an hour and a half's sensory deprivation in the mist reaching the spot. Isolation had led to panic, that was all. Fatigue had exacerbated it; she'd been carrying a substantial weight on her back up a steep incline. She'd take out her camping stove and brew some coffee and she'd be absolutely fine, she knew. The practical tasks – choosing a likely spot, pitching her tent – would refocus her thinking and make her feel comfortable and confident again.

She walked its perimeter reluctant to enter the settlement through the breach in its wall in the fog. She would wait until that cleared. She concentrated on finding somewhere flat and offering a degree of protection from the elements. Eventually she chose a place flanked on one side by the wall and opposite that, the edifice of a granite crag. It was quite sheltered for somewhere at that altitude, the crag obstructing the prevailing westerly wind from blowing her tent away in a gale.

The feeling of being watched had returned to her. She erected her tent acutely aware of the sensation, trying to fight the panic blossoming with a hollow bloom of dread in her stomach. So determinedly did she concentrate on the job that it wasn't until it was accomplished that she noticed the fog was finally lifting. The sky was a pale blue above its thinning grey reach and the sun a pallid orb at about its zenith. It was just before one o'clock.

Georgia ate a power bar and brewed coffee like someone auditioning for her own life; quite unable to shake the feeling that to alert, unseen eyes this was a performance providing a degree of interest or even amusement. She wondered had Baxter's security people spotted her. They might be filming, surveiling her. It was possible. Except that she didn't think being the subject of a camera lens would have the effect of making her feel quite as wretched as she did. She felt a powerful sense of foreboding there at the wall, in its bleak shadow now the sun had strengthened and the fog lifted fully.

I'm not going to get the part, she thought. *I'm failing this audition.*

She had to get a grip. The coffee she'd drunk was a strong one and she could feel the caffeine raise her heart rate and deliver her a febrile sort of energy. She needed to give the moment some sense of purpose to try to shake the groundless suspicions and vague negative instincts she was prey to from overwhelming her. She secured her rucksack in her tent and grabbed her camera and walked around to the breach where its great wooden gate had once been in the settlement wall.

The settlement buildings were silent and still and seemed somehow poised. The hovels squatted and the bigger structures loomed. Roof slates were absent like missing teeth in a grin. Doors were canted oddly against black, lightless interiors. The door to the windowless church was intact, though, balanced on its hinges, a massive oak obstacle that was no barrier at all, because it was unlocked, open a chink, a slit of gloom between the wood and the masonry flanking it.

She opened the door and went inside. She allowed her eyes to adjust from relative brightness to this large and sightless space. There was a figure in one corner, an effigy, she saw. She assumed it was a statue because of its size. Then, in the darkness, its grainy visage cracked as it leered at her and shifted.

Chapter Thirteen

Johnson heard the scream. It rent the still island air for hundreds of metres from its source. He was on the heights when he heard it, halfway up the climbing pitch Edie Chambers had struggled to conquer, roped and sweating with effort, doing what he was as an alternative to the tedium of free-weights and press-ups. He'd been on the face since before the fog lifted. It was more fun than running was when you couldn't see the view. For the first time in weeks on the island, he'd completely lost himself in the task, until he heard Georgia Tremlett's scream.

He abseiled down to the base and started to move in the direction from which the scream had come. He thought it ominous that there'd been no repetition. It had been an expression of primal terror and had chilled his blood, but someone that scared went on screaming if they were capable of doing so. They didn't stop voluntarily. Generally, they wouldn't stop until the screaming fit had done its therapeutic job and exhausted itself.

He summoned back-up on the shortwave. Ricky Hurst responded, which was good. Ricky had approached him quietly in the compound after the discovery of the R.I. wreckage and confided that he'd brought a few souvenirs back with him into civilian life when he'd left the Royal Marines.

'Might be out of my mind telling an ex-police officer this, but it's what the situation requires.'

'Horses for courses?'

'Nothing to do with matters equestrian.'

'No, Ricky. It's firearms you're talking about. You've got a loaded gun with you here on the island.'

'Bloody hell, you must've been some copper.'

'I wasn't the best,' he'd said, thinking of Commander Lassiter. 'But I wasn't bad.'

It turned out Ricky Hurst had a Sig Sauer P224 subcompact semi-auto loaded with 11 9mm rounds. He took the calculated risk of telling Johnson this because he figured matters on New Hope were escalating in a manner that was hazardous and deliberate. He hadn't worked out the nature of the threat on the island, but he knew it was a hostile environment, didn't believe Carter and Newton had met their deaths accidentally and thought it highly unlikely that Greg Cody had met with some innocent accident. A couple of the boys were speculating that Greg might have topped himself. Hurst thought the suicide theory stank.

Cody and Hurst had rubbed along pretty well together. They'd both been bike enthusiasts. Men about to kill themselves don't pay the deposit on a brand new Harley Davidson, as Greg confided he had in Ricky. He'd bought the bike on his last leave, just before his departure from home for the island.

'Why did you bring the hardware?'

'I carried a side arm in the field for better than a decade. Feel a bit naked without it to be honest. And it seemed practical. We're a team of six. Anyone coming here aboard a boat looking to steal plant is going to be organized criminals and they're going to be tooled-up.'

'It's a blatant firearms offence. You make it sound like a sensible precaution.'

Now, approaching the sound of the scream, Johnson saw a distant, approaching, scrambling dot he knew was Ricky Hurst. Johnson would get there first. It would be more comfortable to enter Ballantyne's stone labyrinth with someone covering his back, but there wasn't time to wait. The scream had been too urgent.

He reckoned the bigger buildings likelier locations than the hovels. He checked out the distillery and the tannery and the stable where they'd kept their mules. He checked the sheep pen and the schoolroom and found nothing in any of those places.

Hurst had reached him by the time he approached Ballantyne's windowless church. He'd have just scrambled miles, much of it peat bog, the rest of it uphill, and he wasn't even breathing hard. He was formidably fit and together they were a handful and one of them was lethally armed. And Johnson didn't think he had ever been more afraid in his life. And he heard Hurst swallow drily beside him and saw the tremor in the hand holding his pistol and knew they both felt the same way.

Johnson heard himself say, 'No point both of us falling for it if this is a trap, mate.'

'Can you use a gun?'

'Did a twelve month stint in diplomatic protection.'

'You're in charge.'

Hurst handed him the pistol. The weight of it felt comforting and familiar in the grip of his right fist.

I'm in charge for now, he thought. He took a breath and opened the door and walked into the gloom with the pistol extended at the end of his arm with the safety off. The interior of the church was absolutely quiet and still. An ocean of blood had been spilled there, if the legend was true. Seamus Ballantyne, in his torment and madness, had resorted in the end to human sacrifice. There was no sign of ritual violence now. There was just a smell, oddly feral, as though something wild had made the place its lair.

He looked around and as his eyes adjusted, the bare walls stared blandly back. It had been done here, his intuition told him. The scream had come through the open door of the church, amplified off these walls. The killing had followed. First, though, the killer had pried open his victim's mouth and torn a tooth from their gum. From *her* gum, Johnson reasoned, the screamer had been a woman.

He could look around the floor for the signature incisor in its circle of fresh pink gore, but didn't think it would have been left there. Logic suggested Carter and Newton's deaths at sea had been a tragic accident. This latest event would likely be viewed the same way. Certainly there would be no evidence to the contrary. The killer was rationing, carefully, trying with these ambiguous deaths to leave the people behind the New Hope Experience undeterred.

'Looking forward to the feast,' he said out loud.

He realized Hurst had entered the church, sensed the man's tense, muscular presence at his back.

Hurst said, 'Can you smell that stench?'

'Yeah, don't recognize it, though.'

'Like the bear enclosure at the zoo,' Hurst said, 'only stronger.'

Johnson remembered the cracked glass in Helena's suit. Their killer was a lot more agile than any bear.

'Any ideas, boss?'

'Nothing useful,' Johnson said, 'except that I don't want you calling me boss anymore. I've got your back and you've got mine, Ricky and from now on you call me Derek.'

'Dave Carter used to call you Deggsy.'

'I'll answer to that too.'

Half an hour later, they found Georgia Tremlett's tent and shortly after finding it, knew who their vanished screamer had been.

Felix Baxter rated Derek Johnson very highly. He thought Johnson's six-strong team vigilant professionals and all the security needed to guard his infrastructure against theft or vandalism prior to the opening and occupation of the New Hope Experience complex. He didn't, though, think that a scream amounted to a murder and told Johnson so 20 minutes after his helicopter touched down at lunchtime on Wednesday.

Missing didn't necessarily mean dead or even injured, Baxter felt obliged to remind Johnson, there with some other guy named Hurst to greet him when he touched down. And dead didn't always mean unnatural causes. The island had natural hazards aplenty and Professor Tremlett had no right being there unannounced, alone and without a viable means to communicate.

They'd find her or she'd find them, he predicted, as Johnson and Hurst shot glances at one another nervous for two so big, tough-looking men. Carter and Newton was a shame but they'd been foolhardy. It had been a classic case of overconfidence on Newton's part and he'd paid the ultimate price for his nonchalance about the sea. They'd strayed into a shipping lane and been churned in the night to shark chump by the propellers of a cargo vessel. That wasn't quite how Baxter put it, but that was what his words clearly implied.

The mood was buoyant at the complex when they reached it, despite Johnson's gloomy earlier speculation on the lost academic's fate. A team of contractors was on site replacing the cracked windowpane in the suite Helena

Davenport had occupied. They abseiled around the fascia in bright blue overalls with belts busy with alloy carabiners, flashing and chinking in the late winter sunshine.

The pane itself, the new pane, was suspended on belts roped to a pulley on the complex roof. The whole operation looked slick and spectacular and full of positivity and optimism and Baxter watched, sipping an iced beer one of the maintenance crew had known where to look for in one of the big kitchen refrigerators yet to be properly stocked with fresh food for the paying guests.

The job was completed as evening approached. By then Baxter felt exhilarated. The buoyant mood was provoked by spending time touring what he was now confident would come over time to be regarded as Helena Davenport's masterpiece. The weather was positively spring-like. Easter would soon be upon them and he was determined to open well ahead of schedule. The logistics – the staff and the supplies – could be speeded up by a couple of computer clicks. Everything would kick in smoothly and if it didn't, any kinks would very soon be ironed out.

The doubts he'd harboured over an uncertain evening at his Manchester penthouse had not proven a match for his natural inclination since then towards positive thinking. The vanishing of Captain Sensible admittedly remained a mystery. Ballantyne's Breguet too was a puzzle apparently defying the laws of physics. He hadn't really rationalized the sobering apparition depicted on that Liverpool cinema poster. And he still wouldn't have let his son come within several deep and briny nautical miles of New Hope Island. But the RI mishap had been an accident waiting to happen, frankly. And Georgia Tremlett was too dowdy a woman for her being listed as missing to provoke much tabloid interest.

Baxter sat down that evening with Georgia Tremlett's laptop in front of him. He'd ordered it retrieved from her tent as soon as he'd been informed of her disappearance. That wasn't strictly something the police would approve of in the case of a missing person but he doubted anything in her personal computer files would help anyone find the lost university lecturer any quicker than they were going to anyway.

The optimist in him hoped to find a suicide note written there. If he did, he could have one of his boys stumble on the laptop somewhere less incriminating on the island than the desk he sat at now and alert the police to its existence innocently.

Or he could tamper with the time and date on the machine and forge a suicide note. That was a simple enough thing to do. There was sufficient stuff written by Doctor Tremlett online for him to mimic her writing style. It was just a matter of repeating her favourite phrases and her stock vocabulary in a missive telling the reader that she'd decided to end it all. She was in her early forties. At least, she'd been in her early forties if she was indeed now dead. The positive there, was that she'd never age another day, and you had to look for the positives, didn't you, in any given situation?

Early middle-age was a tricky time for a woman whose photograph spelled out spinster in the way that Georgia Tremlett's did. Every successive day was another weary anticlimax. Her social diary was a lonely rebuke. The calendar was a graph describing only the mundane. Old age and isolation were what she'd honestly had to look forward to. It didn't really amount to much of a life, did it?

He'd looked up her Wikipedia entry guessing that her date of birth would most likely provide her computer password.

'Bingo,' he said aloud as he tapped the numbers in and the screen clarified and he saw her icons shape themselves in punctiliously neat rows.

One file in particular caught his eye immediately. He recognized the name, *Fortescue*. He swallowed. It reminded him of the chest in the museum, of Ballantyne's permanently unstill pocket watch, of the ragged little apparition studying him afterwards from the framed film poster that managed to erase itself when he went back to it, steeled for a closer look in the drenching rain.

It had been Rachel Ballantyne, hadn't it? He was unsure of the how, but had become certain of the who it had been when Edith Chambers had finally relented and described her to him. He shivered, though it wasn't cold where he sat. He took a fortifying swallow of the single malt in the glass at his elbow. And he double-clicked on the Fortescue file.

Professor Philip Fortescue has strayed from his maritime specialism in his researches into the monster he believes lurks on New Hope Island. The creature name Grendel in the epic poem Beowulf is sometimes in its blank verses referred to as the Sea Hag. It can swim. Sea going vessels are not safe from it and the mythology of the oceans is an area Fortescue has spoken about in past years compellingly on television.

But his interest here is personal. He believes Seamus Ballantyne unwittingly bartered into captivity the greatest sorcerer known to West African tribal legend in the time when the practice of magic was at its most potent there. Shaddeh was chained into a stinking slave hold and then demanded he be freed and treated by Captain Ballantyne as the slave-ship master's equal. Ballantyne's response was to bring Shaddeh manacled up to the main deck where before his jeering crew and rope-bound to a chair, his hands were severed by cleaver blows and nailed to a mast as a grisly demonstration of the captain's unquestionable authority.

I believe all this happened as described in Fortescue's source, an account clandestinely kept by Thomas Horan, the ship's physician aboard the Andromeda. This source seems to me impeccable. Horan was first cousin to Ballantyne's wife. I've established the blood tie genealogically myself since the account came into my possession.

Horan describes how Shaddeh's wounds became infected back in the fetid squalor of the slave hold, where he began to lose his life to septicaemia. Before he died he doubly cursed the Andromeda's master. He said that Ballantyne would father a daughter who would die young before returning to life to torment him. But it is the second, greater affliction that is of interest to me. He also told Horan that he would unleash a creature his Albacheian tribe believed in as, the Being that Hungers in the Darkness. This monster would be birthed at Shaddeh's occult bidding, would mature and grow and gain appetite and eventually would consume Captain Ballantyne.

Fortescue believes that all this came to pass. He believes the creature was eventually born on New Hope and consumed Ballantyne's community there, perishing one by one in their terror and isolation. He believes it because so many also vanished on the recent expedition in '10 mounted by Alexander McIntyre in attempting to finally solve the New Hope Enigma. That expedition claimed the lives of the forensic archaeologist Jesse Kale and the cosmologist Karl Cooper and the flamboyant Belgian Jesuit Priest, Monsignor Degrelle. They died. Or at least, all trace of them disappeared, a fate shared by a senior staffer on McIntyre's flagship newspaper title there only to write about their attempt to solve the original mystery.

Horan writes towards the end of his account about Shaddeh's remorse concerning the harrowing train his dark magic had set in motion. That was almost immediate, but the sorcerer was too weak by then to try to reverse what he'd done. Instead he had Horan write down words phonetically that used in a ritual would destroy the Being. It provides the journal's footnote.

Fortescue claims that he performed this ritual in '10 in the New Hope Island Colony's settlement church and that he thus duly killed the creature. And this is the bit I have most trouble believing. Without Shaddeh's intervention, I don't think that could have been done. And Shaddeh had been dead by '10 for just over 200 years. He claims that the journalist Lucy Church witnessed this confrontation. Conveniently for Fortescue, she perished on New Hope 18 months ago and so cannot contradict his account.

Mythologically this creature is Grendel. Or it is the Wendigo or it is Bigfoot or the Abominable Snowman. It was described on their walls by cave dwellers of the Neolithic period. It seems to be as old as time, or at least as old as is humanity. The Albacheians believed it born arachnid, but capable of learning over time through sly study to become humanoid. In all the stories and depictions it is however much bigger than a mortal man.

If it is still living on New Hope, this creature shelters in places there lost to history. I think it was there in Ballantyne's time and that its bones, if I'm extremely lucky, are the most of it after two centuries left to be recovered and subject to forensic analysis and DNA testing to determine whether it is indeed some fearsome undiscovered species.

Fortescue really believes there is a monster on the island. And this isn't the same sort of monster rumoured to inhabit the peaty depths of Loch Ness. Nessie has become domesticated, a folkloric Highland mascot almost, only because it is a creature that doesn't exist. The thing Professor Fortescue thinks secretly inhabits New Hope Island is the Being that Hungers in the Darkness and its appetite is said to be insatiable. This monster devours people. It was arachnid when he says he saw it, calloused, rough, huge and able to violate the mind with what passes for its thoughts. It's a shapeshifter. It's an abomination. And I think his belief it still lives will compel him shortly to go back there.

Felix Baxter finished reading these notes thinking that hysteria and meddling and scare stories about monsters were not at all conducive to the middle-class family values he was trying to promote as integral to the New Hope Experience package. He preferred Ballantyne's community abducted by benign visitors from a distant galaxy. It played better than having them consumed by a creature that had terrified mankind since before the Stone Age, summoned into existence by a vengeful magician. The latter story wouldn't play at all well with his affluent New Age punters.

Then there was the Colony's founder himself. Baxter didn't want Seamus Ballantyne the martinet commander of a floating dungeon, meting out barbaric punishments to those of his human cargo who offended him. He wanted the version of Seamus who had seen the light, sincerely repented and established a model community somewhere remote, beautiful and still unspoiled. He preferred the spiritual visionary to the demagogue butcher. The former had more cultural mileage and made much better business sense.

He couldn't legally prevent Professor Fortescue visiting New Hope. He'd leased the land on which he'd built his visitor complex and attractions and the compound built for the service and maintenance staff. The old Colony settlement was a World Heritage Site. But anyone had free access to the rest of the place and that included him.

How he reacted depended on whether Doctor Tremlett was right in her prediction concerning Fortescue's impending trip. If she were wrong, he'd do nothing. If Fortescue arrived without fanfare, Baxter would just have him quietly and discretely monitored while he wasted his time and energy looking for something so outlandishly unreal as he apparently intended to.

But he might seek publicity. Baxter vaguely remembered the TV series he'd fronted about superstition and the sea.

It had been five or six years since then, but the ratings had been respectable and the maritime professor might hanker once more for the media spotlight. Sometime people did. If he did that with this New Hope monster quest, he'd meet with an accident. The accident might prove fatal and it might not. But it would certainly incapacitate him and put an abrupt stop to his publicity seeking antics.

Felix Baxter knew people who knew people. Years earlier, the mother of his son had left him for a Premiership footballer. He'd felt humiliated by that. But matters concluded satisfactorily when a subsequent hit and run collision wrecked the player's right knee. The offending car had never been recovered, the offending driver never been identified and therefore no one ever charged. And that had taken one untraceable phone call and afterwards the anonymous delivery of a sports bag filled with well-laundered cash. When you knew people who knew people you could get things quietly done for you. And Baxter did.

Ruthie Gillespie sat outside the Spyglass Inn at Ventnor on Wednesday evening, sipping at a glass of white wine and hugging herself against the night chill off the adjacent sea inside her parka. It was off-season and there were few customers inside the pub. She was the only person seated outside, there so she could smoke as she drank and ruminated on the novel she was writing.

New Hope kept interfering with her efforts to plot her story. Reality kept intruding into her thoughts. She'd heard a brief mention in a radio bulletin the previous morning about the two men missing at sea off the island. She knew that in the story of Beowulf, the monster Grendel was sometimes called the Sea Hag. It was Ruthie's belief that Shaddeh's Being that Hungers could definitely swim.

The Grendel comparison had been made by Professor Tremlett when Phil had gone to see her at the beginning of the previous week. She'd gone to New Hope, inspired to do so by what she'd read in Horan's journal, or so Patsy Lassiter had suspected and told Phil. And he'd been right, because half an hour before leaving for the pub, Ruthie had read about, 'Concerns there for the missing woman's welfare,' scrolling though the BBC News site on her phone.

There'd been a file picture of her taken years earlier on a field trip to somewhere remote and exotic, a plain woman precisely made-up decked out like a female version of Indiana Jones in a scuffed leather jacket and a bandana and a photogenically battered fedora hat. Ruthie had never met Georgia Tremlett, but felt a pang of sympathy for her, looking at that picture. Women who saw their lives as the starring role in an unfolding drama were made vulnerable by the delusion and Ruthie recognized Georgia straight away as one of those.

She scrabbled out her cigarette in the ashtray on her table and lit another straight away with a familiar stab of guilt and swallowed wine and looked up, aware that she now had company there. A stiff figure sat alone at a corner table, moonlight catching the double-row of gilt buttons on her coat, making them glimmer.

'Oh, fuck,' Ruthie said to herself, exhaling smoke. It was her Southport friend, her Guest House confidant. It was Lizzie Burrows, dead for close-on 50 years, far from home, unlikely to be travelling light. She wished Phil was there with her, but if he had been, she wouldn't have been sloshing back the white and practically chain-smoking, exiled from the pub's interior by her anti-social habit. She'd have been doing something more acceptable altogether. Not quite baking bread, but along those domestic wholesome lines, possibly wearing a Cath Kidston pinnie.

She got up and walked across and joined the dead student at her table. Maybe there were compensations to an early death, she thought. Elizabeth Burrows hadn't aged a day since her demise. At least not superficially, she hadn't. The detail, though, didn't bear close scrutiny. Her black bob was thick but utterly lustreless with absence of life. Her features were static and dusty and dull and when the ghost spoke, she still resembled a bad attempt at the ventriloquist's clever art. Her speech wasn't clever, it was unnerving and grotesque.

'You're smarter than you look, Ruthie. You've worked out what it is you need to do.'

'What did Shaddeh say to you, to make you despair so completely?'

'He's penitent now. He was still boastful then. And your maritime professor has rightful access to the contents of Ballantyne's chest. I stole from it and was punished accordingly.'

'What did he say?'

'He bragged about his accomplishments. He told me about Rachel. He had Rachel visit me in my dreams. I thought my mind was conjuring it all. I thought I was going mad.'

'Patsy Lassiter thought as much, said it was why you killed yourself.'

Lizzie Burrows' head shifted with a click and her dead eyes fixed on Ruthie, who jumped and thought she might scream; 'He's strong, Lassiter. He's going to need to be strong. All of you are.'

Ruthie swallowed. 'So we're going back there?'

'I'd smile, but the sight would appall you, Ruthie. Hasn't that penny dropped yet? No one escapes their destiny, no one.'

'What's in it for you?'

Lizzie did smile at that. She blinked lazily through the rhyme gummy around her vacant pupils and her lifeless lips stretched to expose her teeth. She said, 'I took pride in how I looked. Not unlike you, I was once quite beautiful. What's in it for me is an end to this indignity.'

'Shaddeh has promised you that?'

'There isn't much time. Not for you, there isn't. The challenge grows more formidable by the day.'

'If I don't do it, I expect I'll be seeing more of you.'

'It was why you saw me in the first place. It was why the master spoke through the bracelet only to you. It's why I've been sent now. It was always you because it's you who've worked out what it is that needs to be done.'

'And if I don't do it –'

'Yes. And I doubt that gets any easier, Ruthie.'

'Will we succeed, Elizabeth?'

'I'm not the owner of a crystal ball. The dead own no possessions. I don't have the answer. If I could, I'd pray for you.'

Ruthie smoked and waited for words both necessary and almost unendurable to hear.

Lizzie said, 'Leave, now. I'll have to walk away from here and the sight of that is something I'd rather spare you. Do what is expected of you, Ruthie, if you want this to be our goodbye.'

Ruthie left Lizzie Burrow's vacant table and walked home on legs that felt like they belonged to someone else unfamiliar with such matters as balance and direction and bearing a body's weight in motion. Her skin felt tender under the rough touch of her clothing as though a rash blistered there or she'd been badly burned. It was just after 9 o'clock in the evening.

She got to her cottage door and struggled for a couple of minutes to try to get the key between her convulsing fingers into the lock. Her breath shuddered, shaking her. She dropped her key twice and groped around on the ground for it in the darkness fighting all the while the strong urge to weep.

She got in eventually and switched on the light. Everything there possessed a familiarity that seemed entirely fraudulent. Her things wore the still aspect of stage props. Her furniture and hung pictures seemed poised and expectant, as though awaiting the entrance of the actors, prepared for a performance that would never come.

She walked to the kitchen without taking off her coat and opened the freezer compartment of her fridge and took out the vodka bottle and tried to unscrew its lid. But the bottle was slippery with cold and her fingers disobedient and the bottle slipped from her grip and smashed loudly on the stone flagged floor. The smell of liquor rose and glass shards crunched under her boots as she flapped uncertainly at space, wheeling about, lost for what to do next.

Ruthie counted very deliberately to ten. Then she took off her coat and hung it on a kitchen peg, the glass fragments now embedded in the soles and heels of her boots squealing and crunching with each step. She fetched a brush and pan from the cupboard where they were stored and squatted down and swept up the pieces of the broken vodka bottle. She ran a cloth under the hot tap and washed the wet floor until the smell had gone from the stone.

But the strong vodka odour was still in her lungs and her nose making her heave and she barely made it to the loo off her kitchen before vomiting mightily into the pan. White wine and pistachio nuts welled up sourly from her stomach into her mouth and she retched until emptied and then spat and rinsed out nut gravel and gargled at the sink, eyes smarting, gasping for breath.

When her home finally began to resemble that properly again, she slumped into an armchair in her sitting room shaking and stared at the stars through a window with its curtain still un-pulled against the night. Eventually her heart rate slowed to something closer to normal. Eventually, the rawness became less painful prickling her skin. She very deliberately avoided thinking at all about the sight and sound and loathsome scent of what had in life, half a century since, been a young woman named Lizzie Burrows.

It was one thing in Merseyside. It was a bad experience in a charming place you might never willingly visit again. It was something quite different and much worse on your own doorstep. There it was despoiling, a violation. And it undermined everything she had and valued. She didn't honestly know how many such encounters she could undergo and remain sane. Not many, she didn't think. Anticipation would become dread and the dread would be permanent, with no respite from it.

Ruthie had to try to put a stop to it. She knew she had no alternative. These present circumstances were intolerable. She'd had to fight just now not to break down completely. She had to do whatever it was she could to bring these visitations to an end. And she believed, as had been stressed to her, that there was now very little time in which to act before it became too late.

Eventually, after two hours of trying to regain some semblance of composure, she called Edie Chambers. She said, 'I know you were on New Hope with Felix Baxter over the weekend. Phil told me. How did he seem to you?'

'Are you okay, Ruthie?'

'I'm fine.'

'You don't sound it.'

'Don't worry about me. Tell me about Baxter.'

'He was jumpy. He did a pretty good job of hiding it, but he was nervous and he wasn't the only one. A couple of his people there struck me as seriously spooked.'

'Three people have gone missing there since you got back.'

'I know, and all totally explicable, an accident at sea and an academic out of her depth in the wilderness. You'd honestly wonder what it's going to take.'

'I'm not going to let that happen, Edie. I'm going back there. I think I know what needs to be done.'

Edith was silent. Then she said, 'Phil won't let you go alone. He'll insist on going with you. So you'll be putting him in danger and doing it deliberately.'

Ruthie closed her eyes. She said, 'It's not Phil I need there. It's Patsy Lassiter. If I'm right, he's the key to this. It's Patsy has to come.'

'Are you really okay, Ruthie? You don't sound much like yourself.'

'I'm fine,' Ruthie said.

'I like you,' Edie said, 'I'm the one who got you and my stepdad together in the first place, but Phil and Patsy are all I've got left in the way of family. You risk their lives and I'll never, ever forgive you.'

'Phil and Patsy are grown-ups, Edie,' Ruthie said, closing her eyes tightly, concentrating so her voice wouldn't wobble into a sob. 'They make up their own minds about what they do or don't do.'

'Fuck you,' Edith said, after a pause, terminating the call.

She called back ten minutes later. She was crying. They both were. She sniffed and said, 'Bring me up to speed, Ruthie. Tell me what you think's got to happen on New Hope.'

So Ruthie did.

Chapter Fourteen

They convened at Ruthie Gillespie's cottage at Ventnor on Wight on the Saturday. Phil Fortescue had been there since the previous evening. Patrick Lassiter arrived with Helena Davenport. She was his guest for the weekend and had an interest both in New Hope and now in him. They'd adjourned to a table in a quiet corner of the Spyglass at 11am when Edith Chambers surprised them. Phil and Patsy rose and hugged her in turn. She was introduced to Helena.

To Ruthie, Edie said, 'A gatecrasher's probably the last thing you think you need but I'll have something to say about this plot you've dreamed up, and I've every right to say it.'

'How did you know about today?' The words were spoken to Edie, but Ruthie was looking at Phil.

'He didn't tell me,' Edie said. 'Patsy's at work in London, except at weekends. When I spoke to you on Wednesday night, I didn't get the feeling you were inclined to wait much longer before doing something. So I reckoned on today.' Edie looked at Helena. 'You're the only surprise,' she said. 'I told Felix Baxter you were a genius. Seeing you here I might have to revise that judgment.'

'We should all listen to what Ruthie has to say,' Lassiter said, 'without heckling, Edie. I'm sure there'll be ample time for discussion when she's finished.'

Ruthie had pondered long and hard on what the late Georgia Tremlett had told Phil at their meeting in Manchester. Dr. Tremlett had described the magic used to bring back Rachel Ballantyne as vastly more potent than that used to summon the Being. She thought this significant. To her it meant that Rachel – the thing Rachel had become – was intrinsically more powerful than the Being was.

There was a clue to this in the names given by the Albacheians to the domain inhabited by a creature such as Rachel. They described it as the Land without Light or the Kingdom of Decay or the Realm of Anguish. They described it too as a place where death itself was contagious; but the clear implication was that New Hope was hers to rule, or to misrule. As her father's daughter it could be claimed she had a dynastic right to govern the island. But it was her power now, rather than the bloodline she'd possessed when naturally alive, that really signified.

'I think it's within Rachel's power to destroy the Being,' Ruthie said. 'I strongly suspect that it keeps out of her way.'

To Lassiter, Phil said, 'The Being tolerated you because all the while you were there it was learning from studying you how to appear in human form. Then it got very pissed off when you discovered a couple of its hiding places, so pissed off you had to scarper.'

'I'd think of it more as a dignified retreat,' Lassiter said.

'I get your reasoning,' Helena said to Ruthie, 'but I don't see how knowing this, even if it's true, has any practical application'

'I do,' Edith said. 'Ruthie thinks that Rachel took such a shine to Patsy when he was there that she'd happily put herself out for him.'

'There's no need for the sarcasm,' Ruthie said, 'no one thinks Rachel Ballantyne does anything happily. But from what Patsy's told Phil, he was tactful and kind when she spoke to him in the sepulchre.'

'All I've done so far for Rachel is fail to deliver on a promise I made her,' Lassiter said. 'That's not much of a basis for getting her to do anything, let alone battling a monster.'

'I don't think it would be a battle,' Ruthie said. 'I happen to think that particular encounter would be rather one-sided.'

'And we take your word for that, which is all we've got, and we go back to New Hope and risk all of our lives on the strength of a hunch,' Edith said. 'Fucking brilliant, Ruthie, and I have to say fucking typical of you.'

'Calm down, Edie,' Fortescue said.

Edie said to him, 'Divided loyalties, Daddo? Or not even that?' Her eyes were shining now with unshed tears.

'What none of you except Helena knows is that I've been in regular contact with a source on the island,' Lassiter said. 'I say regular, though it's actually intermittent because wireless transmissions aren't dependable from there. But I've had several long conversations at New Scotland Yard when the wavelengths have permitted it with Baxter's head of security.

'He saw the trophy an intruder left for Helena after Greg Cody's disappearance. He saw the wreckage that washed up after two men vanished aboard a rigid inflatable. He heard Georgia Tremlett scream when she was taken in the windowless church and he smelled the feral stink afterwards of the thing that took her. He's a frightened man in need of help and I'm inclined to offer it.'

Helena said, 'And your promise to Rachel?'

'I think I know how to keep my promise to Rachel and I think Ruthie is right to suspect she'll be disposed to help us if she knows I'm going to do it.'

'Couldn't help but notice that plural creep in there, Patsy,' Edith said. 'How many of us are you committing to this?'

'I can keep my promise to Rachel, but don't believe I can do it alone. I'll need help for that. But I'm obliging no one.'

'I'm there, mate,' Fortescue said.

'I'm in,' Ruthie said.

'I'll come,' Helena said.

Edie was quiet. She sniffed. She rubbed at her nose with the back of her hand and said, 'Ruthie here told me late on Wednesday night about a little visit she'd received earlier in the evening from a woman named Lizzie Burrows reluctant to stay dead, or anyway to stay restfully dead. In your place, Ruthie, I'd quite likely be driven to what you're planning. I mean if I thought my sanity was at risk. You want to stay sane, you reckon you don't have a choice.

'You're committed, Daddo, because you feel an obligation to protect Ruthie, regardless of how hair-brained her misjudged scheme. I don't like that, but seven years ago it was the same instinct made you to help me when I was a snot-nosed adolescent calling out of the blue.'

Fortescue smiled slightly. 'You weren't that bad.'

'What about you, Patsy? You're usually such a sensible man.'

Lassiter frowned. He said, 'If I hadn't taken my island sabbatical rebuilding the cottage, I'd have started drinking again. I'd never have made my promise to Rachel Ballantyne. I'd never have met Helena.'

'So it's love or it's infatuation,' Edith said. 'Jesus.'

'It's fate,' Lassiter said, 'the island's unfinished business for some of us. Not for you though, Edie. I'd rather you didn't come.'

'That's just hypocritical.'

'No it's not,' Fortescue said 'At worst it's a double standard. It's one I share. You shouldn't come.'

'What about you, Helena,' Edith asked. 'You I don't get at all.'

'I had some bad experiences on New Hope,' Helena said, 'mostly in the company of Derek Johnson, who was heaven sent. But I'm more concerned about the thing from hell, Edie. I believe it's there. The complex was built to my blueprint, every joist and board and screw. I don't want to collude in a catastrophe.'

'What about you, Kiddo?' Fortescue said.

Edie sniffed again and in a wobbly voice said, 'If any of you think you're leaving me behind on my own you're even more misguided than I think you are.'

'Getting there in a hurry, from here, is going to be horrendously costly,' Helena said. 'Has anyone even thought of that?'

Ruthie and Edie looked at Phil. He cleared his throat and said to Helena, 'Have you heard of Alexander McIntyre?'

'He was the media tycoon who financed the expedition you and Patrick went on seven years ago. A year and a half ago, he died on the island.'

'Violently,' Edith said.

'I'm the main beneficiary of his will,' Fortescue said. 'I haven't touched the money, haven't felt entitled, to be honest. But it's there. And I don't think Alex would argue with me spending some of his legacy on this. I can charter us a helicopter for this afternoon. We can be on New Hope by tonight.'

'We'll have to get some gear together,' Ruthie said. 'It's late February. Even what passes for good weather there will actually more likely be atrocious.'

'Its fine there now,' Fortescue said, 'I checked this morning. But that's only going to last until about midday tomorrow.'

'Daddo?'

'Edie?'

'That helicopter's already booked, isn't it?'

'Yes, Edith, it is. It's chartered and fueled up and waiting for us now.'

'We only need clothes,' Helena said. 'There's food and accommodation at the complex. I've still got a passkey and the bloke in charge of security won't chuck us out.'

'He'll think we're the cavalry,' Fortescue said.

'Then he's deluded,' Edie said. 'How long do you think we'll be there, Patsy?'

Lassiter smiled at her. He said, 'Are you familiar with the theory that nothing ever goes to plan?'

'Unfortunately, yes.'

'If we haven't succeeded by tomorrow night, we'll have failed.'

'And if the weather turns, we'll have no way of escaping,' Edie said.

Ruthie said, 'Then we'd better not fail.' She looked through a bleared windowpane at the neglected seating outside. It was cold and raining which was why they had sat where they were. She recalled her recent encounter with Lizzie Burrows, the scalding of her skin and harrowing of her soul that confrontation had inflicted.

Then we'd better not fail.

Ricky Hurst had positioned himself on the heights. He had found a spot both sheltered and concealed from below by a scatter of boulders on a shelf of rock. He had a view of the whole of the old colony settlement, its perimeter wall, even the sad red crumple of Dr. Tremlett's abandoned tent, almost directly below him 300 metres distant. He had been there for two hours and dusk was close to falling.

He'd trained as a sniper during his decade of service in the Royal Marines. He hadn't done it prolifically in combat zones, had only two confirmed kills to his name, but remembered the field-craft required. He was disciplined at keeping still and his eyesight was excellent. His breathing was regular and close to inaudible. He was warmly clothed and comparatively comfortable. The knowledge that he wasn't going to find himself in the crosshairs of an enemy's scope sight might have been a comfort. But present circumstances on New Hope meant that it wasn't.

He'd climbed to the spot he occupied because logic told him that whatever was picking them off was probably based at the centre of the island in the seclusion of the settlement. The boundary wall meant you couldn't see movement inside it from below. And almost everywhere on the island was below that wall. So it offered concealment as well as shelter. It was a World Heritage Site, which put it out of bounds to visitors, except by prior arrangement. It was a creepy place, even worse if you knew about its bloody history, but he didn't think whatever responsible for the recent deaths either squeamish or superstitious.

Being at the centre of the island put you at its hub. It meant you could reach the other significant locations moving downhill and therefore rapidly. He didn't know precisely what he was looking for, but would if he saw it. He wasn't there to kill it or even to try to take it on. He thought that the Sig Sauer semi-automatic snug under his arm in its shoulder holster gave him a measure of personal protection. He couldn't make a shot with a handgun at this distance though and that wasn't his intention.

He just wanted to see it; to know what they were up against and to have his theory about its hide proven to him so that he could go back and tell Johnson and between them, they could come up with some feasible plan of action.

Hurst rated Derek Johnson. The big ex-copper was brave and shrewd and led by example. They were in a serious predicament they knew nowhere near enough about, but he was grateful that Johnson would have his back when things got lively, as he expected they would. Or as he hoped they would, because thus far they couldn't even lay claim to chasing shadows.

Now, the shadows around him were not just lengthening but growing indistinct as the sun dipped on the horizon. Soon he would have to give this up. He'd have another crack at it tomorrow. He couldn't see in the dark and staying where he was when night fell was just too hazardous a risk to take in the dim hope of hearing something that would give their antagonist away. Hurst didn't relish fighting this particular battle but if it was to be fought, wanted it done in daylight.

He was about to move, cautiously, deliberately, when he thought he heard something. He'd been aware of the ambient sounds; the shrill whistle of wind gusting through granite apertures, the cries of seabirds. But this was different, a snarl of pain or fury that sounded at once human and impossibly old, ancient, even primeval; a mythic voice not meant for mortal ears, an utterance from dark legends. It reverberated loudly through the heights and faded to nothing.

Something unfolded from the rocks below him and closed the distance to the settlement's stone perimeter in a blink where the eight-foot wall momentarily gave it scale before it vaulted over and was lost to sight among a cluster of buildings.

Hurst rolled onto his back and stared at the darkening sky and let out a long, silent breath with both fists clenched tightly at his sides. He could smell it now, sour and feral, the spoor drifting up on the lightest of breezes. He'd never seen anything human move at anywhere close to that speed. He'd never seen anything human built to that scale. It seemed impossible. But he had to believe the evidence of his own eyes. It had looked like a man, powerful and naked, agile and huge.

And hungry, he thought. He thought what he'd heard, that single expulsion of sound, nothing other than the raw bellow of its impatience. It was waiting. It was rationing itself, as Johnson had feared and confided in him. This was the fast, but the feast would soon enough follow.

He wondered if the creature scented him now, late in the darkening winter day, would it be able to resist its own strong, un-sated appetite. The thought of being consumed wasn't a comfortable one. And he had no doubt the creature he'd just glimpsed could easily do it. He had no confidence the bullets in the pistol he carried would penetrate its hide. That was if he managed to get a shot off at something so preternaturally quick. In spite of its size, it had moved with the sleek suddenness of a cobra strike.

Carefully, Hurst rolled back onto his stomach. He rose to his knees and elbows. Slowly and deliberately, he stood, at a wary crouch. Then on silent feet, he retreated back in the direction of their compound. He made it without incident, but it was the longest and most fearful walk he could ever remember, expecting to be caught and hauled back out of his boots and into the creature's crushing embrace at every carefully taken step.

He was almost there, could see the lights and hear the banter of the blokes there and smell something cooking on their stove when he heard the chunter through the night sky of an approaching chopper.

They descended the metal helicopter steps just after eight in the evening in darkness. Ruthie was the first of them to plant feet on New Hope's thin and frugal soil. She breathed in the island scents of brine and wet granite. She heard the tumble of the surf on the shoreline, which in the miasma of light rain and rising spindrift, she could not see from where they'd touched-down at a spot a hundred metres to the rear of Seamus Ballanyne's old colony dock.

She remembered the last time she'd arrived there, full of intent and fortitude. She'd rowed herself ashore, dropped in an inflatable kayak from the deck of a fishing smack by the brave, taciturn boy named Adam Cox, skippering the vessel. She'd encountered Patsy Lassiter on the beach near the Shanks' cottage ruined by grief and she'd hauled off the ground and put the pieces of him back together again. Together they'd ascended the heights and done something that had saved the lives of Phil and Edie. Though Rachel Ballantyne had actually saved the lives of Phil and Edie on that long, eventful night 18 months ago. That was the significant truth giving Ruthie what scant hope she clung onto now.

You couldn't call it a welcoming committee, because they were unpacked and roomed inside the complex when the hammering at the door came. They'd been there about an hour, about the time Helena Davenport reckoned it would take a quad bike in this clement weather to get from the workers' compound to them. She thought it safe to open up. It was dark, but it wasn't Jack Nicholson out there with his fire axe from *The Shining* and it wasn't the island's resident monster. She knew who it was and she looked forward with a thrill of affection to seeing him again.

'Steady on,' Lassiter said, as Helena threw her arms around Derek Johnson. 'Think about the damage a PDA like that does to a man of my vintage.'

But then Johnson confused things by embracing Lassiter no less ardently.

'We need some introductions here,' Edie said.

'We need some explanations too,' Fortescue said.

To Hurst, Lassiter said, 'You're packing shooter. I can see the bulge under your left armpit. I'm confident there's a plausible reason?'

'One of the two of you has seen it,' Ruthie said, 'or both of you have. You have, haven't you?'

Introductions were made. Everyone sat down. They were in Helena's suite because she was sort of their hostess. It was a different suite from the one where she'd found Greg Cody's incisor. She'd not yet noticed, in the darkness outside, that the window facing that one had been replaced. No one had wanted to berth there anyway.

Hurst told them about what he'd seen a couple of hours earlier, at dusk, from the heights overlooking the colony settlement.

'Like Grendel in Beowulf or like the Wendigo,' Fortescue said. 'Poor Georgia Tremlett was spot on.'

Johnson said, 'The only reason it hasn't attacked us in our compound is greed. It's sensed all the activity on the island, all this industry, means more people are arriving. So far as it's been able, it's resisted taking anyone because it doesn't want to jeopardize that happening.'

'So it's clever and cunning as well as big and strong.'

'We've had two unconfirmed deaths and two disappearances and they look for all the world like a probable suicide, a maritime accident and an as yet unsolved,' Johnson said.

'The only false step's been leaving the Cody trophy for Helena,' Ruthie said. 'That was showing off.'

'And allowing itself to be seen by Ricky this afternoon,' Lassiter said. 'That was careless.'

'I think you lot are vulnerable here,' Johnson said.

'Which is a bit like saying water's wet,' Edie said.

Helena said, 'Why do you think we're particularly vulnerable?'

'We're part of the infrastructure. You're superfluous. It seems to have attacked Georgia Tremlett very soon after her arrival. It will probably think it can do the same to you without really upsetting the apple cart, if you get my drift.'

'I get your drift,' Edie said.

'It's impatient,' Hurst said, 'and it's very hungry.'

'And it has two tried and tested ways of getting in here,' Helena said, glancing at the window, shivering.

'We'll move at first-light,' Lassiter said. 'It's impractical to try to do anything in darkness. We'll just be blundering.'

'And we'll be picked-off,' Helena said.

'Ever the optimist,' Edie said.

'Pots and kettles,' Helena said.

Fortescue said, 'Now-now, ladies.'

Hurst said, 'Do you actually have a plan? Please tell me you've not come all this way completely clueless about all this.'

'You tell them, Ruthie,' Edith said. 'It'll sound more plausible, coming from a Goth.'

But neither of their visitors laughed. Neither of them even cracked a smile, listening. Lassiter was reminded that Hurst had seen what he had only a couple of hours earlier. The memory would be indelible.

When Ruthie had finished, Johnson said, 'I've felt her presence on the island for weeks, Rachel Ballantyne, watching us. She's been here. She left a warning scrawled on the bathroom mirror where Helena stayed the last time she was at the complex. She told us to leave.'

'Which suggests she's on your side,' Fortescue said.

'Unless she's now just really pissed off at you for ignoring her advice,' Edith said.

'Oh, for the optimism of youth,' Helena said.

Edith said, 'The big difference between you and me, Helena, is that I've been up close and personal with Rachel Ballantyne. I've shared a cellar with her. I've had her speak to me. I've endured the sight and sound and the stench of her. She's not young, she's ancient and she's unpredictable, tricky and more dangerous than you can possibly imagine. I'm here willingly. My mouth is my way of dealing with the fear.'

'I'm sorry,' Helena said.

'Yeah, well, so am I,' Edith said.

'We're staying, by the way,' Hurst said. 'The guns might not protect us, but at least we've got them.'

Lassiter said, 'Guns plural?'

'There's a range where the guests can shoot clays,' Johnson said. 'The hardware proper's yet to arrive, but we had the one gun for a try-out back when the range was first completed. I'd forgotten about it the way you do when kit's locked away out of sight. Then I remembered it.'

'We've got two guns and plenty of ammo,' Hurst said.

'And we've got you,' Ruthie said, 'and we're grateful.'

'We should all try and get some rest,' Lassiter said, 'big day and all that.'

Something woke Felix Baxter in his penthouse flat in Manchester in the small hours. For a second he thought it might be an intruder, but his sixth-sense told him no one was sharing the space he owned with him and he owned no pets. He was the only living presence there. He was sure of it.

It was singing. It was coming from his sitting room. It was the folk song, *In My Liverpool Home*. He listened a lot to the radio housed in the Bang and Olufsen hi fi expensively situated there. Mostly he listened to talk radio. Sometimes he listened to the local station, Piccadilly Radio. Sometimes he listened to Smooth, so he was used to hearing Michael Buble and Caro Emerald, not a cappella versions of regional folk ditties. They just didn't figure on Smooth's always blandly aspirational playlist.

He got out of bed, irritated. He took his dressing gown off the hook on the bedroom door and put it on. Fear didn't really hit him until he opened the door and the coarseness of the singing became apparent. It sounded uneven and spontaneous and perversely, the very opposite of live. And then abruptly and completely, it stopped.

A figure sat stiffly in moonlight diffuse through the curtains. It sat on his sofa in a black wool coat with a double row of glimmering gilt buttons. Even seated, he could see that she'd been a tall woman in life. Her thick black hair was bobbed and her features were striking under its precise fringe. She reminded him a bit of Ruthie Gillespie, an author his son had read a lot as an adolescent, her author photo alluring on the inside cover of her books. As far as he knew, Ms. Gillespie was in good health. This woman, dully alert, was also emphatically dead.

Baxter felt frightened, but he felt something worse than fear. Wretchedness washed like poison through his guts. He clutched at his stomach and his breath came in shuddering jerks. He thought he might fall to his knees. He couldn't look at her, and he couldn't look away. Then she spoke to him.

'Better people than you'll ever be may perish because of you. If they fail, my indignity will go on. Should that likelihood occur then I promise you, you'll be seeing more of me. Your son will likely get the odd visit too.'

The sound of her voice did something loathsome to his skin, raising it in frills and curlicues of terror down his arms and across his chest and back, contouring his flesh in shock and revulsion under his dressing gown, where he shivered. His balls had contracted and shrunk, like they were trying to climb up into his body. Words formed sentences emanating out of her without the movement of her mouth, precisely shaped by lipstick. He couldn't control his breathing well enough to scream.

She stood. The movement was abrupt, her stiff tendons cracking, her lifeless energy releasing a cold, musty odour into the room. She lifted a sudden arm and touched his face with the back of her hand and he felt the ragged neglect on his cheek of her fingernails.

'This is only our introduction,' she said. 'My name in life was Lizzie Burrows.'

She dropped her arm and turned away from him and lurched out of the room, her walk the gait of someone hampered, but not properly inhibited by death.

Chapter Fifteen

At the Experience complex, they ate their Sunday morning breakfast waiting impatiently for it to get light. When it did the sky was opaque under a cold and persistent drizzle. Lassiter was mindful that the weather was due to deteriorate after midday. They were all breakfasting together, in the smaller of the two restaurants housed there. Quite an eccentric sort of breakfast; Aunt Bessie's Yorkshire puddings figured prominently under steaming puddles of Bisto gravy next to glittering piles of Bird's Eye peas in dishes improvised from freezer cabinets. As he ate, fairly heartily for a recovering alcoholic, he couldn't help but notice the looks Johnson and Hurst kept swapping.

He waited until they'd finished eating and then said, 'You two boys are up to something.'

They looked at one another. It was Johnson who answered him. He said, 'Sig Sauer didn't become the world's biggest manufacturer of handguns for no reason, Commander. That's what Ricky's carrying. I'm armed with a fuck off pump-action twelve-bore. We're pretty seriously tooled up.'

'And your point is?'

'We're thinking of a more direct approach than the one you lot have outlined. We think it holes up in the windowless church. That's where it took Georgia Tremlett. If it's there it's cornered. It's a static target.'

'Only relatively static,' Lassiter said. 'It will know the ground. And you said it's very quick.'

'The church interior's a shooting gallery, and nothing's quick enough to outrun a bullet,' Hurst said.

There was no point arguing against this. It was true so far as it went and the man clearly spoke from personal experience.

Fortescue coughed to clear his throat. He said, 'One of the theories Dr. Tremlett aired with me was that this creature didn't originate on earth. There's a strong case for saying it's an alien life form. If it is, we don't know what effect bullets will have on it, if any.'

'It's made of organic matter, wherever it comes from,' Hurst said. 'It's flesh and bone and hair. It eats and shits and breaths and it will bleed, believe me.'

'I don't think it's necessarily that simple,' Ruthie said.

'I don't either,' Edie said.

Hurst turned to Ruthie. He said, 'With respect, love, you're predisposed to believe in hocus pocus. No offence, but just look at you.'

'That thing was able to clamber up the sheer façade of this building and crack a pane of unbreakable glass. It also had the nous to disable a generator. Don't underestimate it, boys,' Helena said.

'I'm going outside for a cigarette,' Ruthie said, getting up. 'Who knows? I might cast a spell or mutter an incantation or two while I'm there. Excuse me.'

They all watched her walk out of the room.

'Not saying she isn't easy on the eye,' Hurst said.

'She's also spoken-for,' Fortescue said.

Lassiter said, 'How set on doing this are you two?'

'We discussed it on the way over here last night,' Johnson said. 'We've slept on it. We've been seriously fucked about with on the island, Helena can tell you that.'

'She has.'

'It's worth trying. I don't care whether that thing's from Mars or Pluto, it's flesh and blood. It's a bloody big target and it'll take a bullet.'

'We aim for it to take several,' Hurst said.

'When do you plan to do it?'

'I reckon it's mostly nocturnal,' Hurst said. 'Most of the deadliest predators are. If we're lucky we'll catch it asleep or at least drowsy or unawares.'

'You won't,' Helena said. She turned to Johnson, 'Don't do this, Derek.'

Johnson smiled, slightly sheepishly. He stood and said, 'What did they always used to say in those terrible '80's revenge thrillers? It's payback time.' He reached into a pocket and pulled out a short-wave radio and slid it across the table to Lassiter. He said, 'If we have any luck, I'll call it in.'

'Call it in either way,' Lassiter said.

'You've got it, Commander.'

Fortescue went outside a couple of minutes after Hurst and Johnson had left. Ruthie was pacing the cobbles of the colony's old harbour a hundred metres distant. He walked over to her. She was smoking and he could see the stamped-on butt of one she'd already smoked on the rain-slicked stone.

'Filthy habit,' she said, exhaling smoke through her nose.

'We're none of us perfect.'

'You shouldn't make excuses for me.'

'I love you,' he said.

She smiled an effortful smile. She said, 'I've got a really bad feeling about all this.'

'How did you leave it with your fan club?'

'No hard feelings,' she said. 'They got on their quad bikes and we all gave each other the thumbs-up. They're gutsy, the pair of them, incredibly so. And if we see either of them again I'll be extremely surprised. I'll also be delighted and relieved.'

'I've got a lot of faith in Patsy Lassiter,' Fortescue said.

Ruthie took a final pull on her cigarette and dropped the butt to the cobbles and ground it out under her boot. She exhaled and Fortescue observed how the smoke clung in the rain and the cold, only dispersing as if reluctantly. 'I have too,' she said. 'But what Edie said about Rachel Ballantyne last night is true. She's volatile. She's unpredictable.'

'You were the one called the council of war, Ruthie.'

'I haven't forgotten.'

'Have you changed your mind?'

'If anything happens to you, or Patsy, or Edith or now Helena Davenport, I'll be responsible. We're only here because of my stupid theory.'

'And because Shaddeh told you there isn't much time. And because he sent Lizzie Burrows to remind you of that and she'll get no rest if we don't end this and will keep on confronting you until you're driven out of your mind by it.'

'I nearly didn't tell you about what happened on Wednesday night. It makes me very selfish, doesn't it, cajoling you all into coming here.'

'You're not selfish at all. Lizzie Burrows is unendurable. I couldn't have let you come and not come with you. Patsy was coming back anyway, to keep a promise. Edie and Helena are here to help him do that. Aren't you frightened here for yourself?'

'It's on the list,' she said. 'It's just not at the top anymore.'

He closed the distance between them and hugged her. The rain was strengthening and on the thick gloss of her hair it had gathered like dew. 'Come back inside,' he said. 'You'll catch your death out here.'

They didn't approach the colony settlement on their quads. The engine noise would have given them away. They rode anti-clockwise along the coast to a point about equidistant between the Experience complex and their own compound and then parked the bikes above the tideline and went inland on foot, climbing upwards steadily, saying nothing because silence was essential and because everything about this business had already been said.

The going was heavy. The ground was getting softer and more slippery in the strengthening rain where the terrain wasn't just exposed rock. The perimeter wall of the settlement, when it came into sight, concealed what lay behind it. But that worked both ways because it also concealed their approach. With half a mile left to cover they switched off their shortwaves in case they squawked into life and delivered their quarry a warning. Then they split up, approaching their destination from points hundreds of metres apart, crouching, stealthy and careful.

There was only the one way in. Or there was, Hurst thought, unless you could vault an eight-foot wall in the effortless way he'd seen the creature do the previous evening. He found he was actually looking forward to this. Getting a shot off the previous night had been impossible at the distance. He'd doubted at first after seeing the creature that a bullet would penetrate its hide.

But at close-range the pistol he carried was a devastating weapon for its size, a slick and rapid and reliable tool of execution. He'd pump the full mag into the thing and the target was too big to miss. Johnson would do the same. His shotgun slugs were their artillery. They'd get no medals, but this was about retribution more than it was about chasing glory. He'd been pretty indifferent to Dave Carter but he'd liked Alan Newton and Greg Cody had become a close friend.

He thought of his hocus pocus crack made at the expense of the sexy Goth woman earlier in the morning. You cultivated that look and you took the flak for it, was his take on the matter. He wasn't incredulous or even cynical about the presence they called Rachel Ballantyne being on the island. New Hope had a haunted, watchful feel and he'd seen nothing human possessing the speed and scale of the quarry they were hoping to confront. It was otherworldly; but he'd put his faith in a full mag of hollow-point bullets before he'd put it in magic. Spells generally worked best in *Harry Potter* movies. Pulling a trigger was a simpler matter of cause and predictable effect.

Johnson felt better than he'd felt in weeks. He had faith in his formidable ally, faith in their firepower and was finally doing something positive after all the enervating time spent fearful and clueless on New Hope since Greg Cody's disappearance. More than that, he'd felt toyed-with on occasions. He knew that Helena Davenport had been grateful for his big and burly presence during her stay at the complex, but he'd felt humiliated even then by his helplessness to do anything practical about the ordeal they'd shared.

Now he was doing something. He was part of a decisive and efficient two-man team self-tasked with a mission that might very well set him up for life. The creature Ricky Hurst had described to him was like nothing in the known world. It wouldn't just be a trophy when they took it down, it would be a scientific sensation. There'd likely be a book deal in it and there'd certainly be a movie. He could spoil the missus rotten and guarantee the kids' financial futures. That meant a great dealt to him. Actually, it meant everything.

He'd pondered a lot on fate and destiny on the island. New Hope was the sort of bleak, isolating place that encouraged that sort of thinking. During his wireless conversations with the Commander at New Scotland Yard, he'd wondered about giving up his police career. He'd questioned the wisdom of it. There was a period after resigning when you could get back in and it hadn't yet elapsed and he'd thought about that. Now it wouldn't be necessary. Not if they succeeded when they reached the windowless church, it wouldn't.

'If it's where they think it is, it's a trap,' Lassiter said.

'Then go after them and persuade them of that,' Edie said, 'before it's too late'.

It was forty minutes after the departure of Johnson and Hurst.

'It's already too late, because they won't be deterred,' Helena said. 'It's what strike troops do. They strike. It's Hurst's background and training. You go in hard and fast and heavy and without warning.'

'Helena Davenport, military tactician,' Edith said.

Nobody responded to that.

They were all familiar with Lassiter's theory that it hid in one of the places he'd discovered during his island exile. Probably not the sepulchre to which Rachel Ballantyne had lured him, if Ruthie's supposition was true and the creature deliberately avoided her. That was one of Rachel's places and where he thought he'd most probably find her now, unless she found him first.

Lassiter thought the Being's lair was likelier the storm shelter in the heights he'd stumbled upon. It was cavernous and he'd had the impression he was the first human being to enter its granite seclusion since the time of the Kingdom of Belief. When the tempest had raged, the believers had taken refuge there, their cold and imperious leader among them. In more recent times, it had become home to something else.

This latest chapter in the New Hope saga began as it would end, with Rachel Ballantyne. They could do nothing until Lassiter tried to strike his bargain with her. Rachel was capricious and unforgiving, sometimes wicked, sometimes possessed of the snarling, deliberate evil of something only conjured at its origin to be demonic.

There was no way of knowing how she'd react. All he had was the precedent of their single prior meeting, when she'd been sad and gentle and sorry, she'd said, for his loss. He wondered had she plucked from his mind the folk songs dutifully learned after he'd been warned it was her not exactly endearing habit. He wondered how well she knew his mind generally if she was capable of roaming around in it and doing that.

Was she becoming more human, more tranquil in spirit, a softer, wiser presence than she'd originally been when she'd snarled back into life and goaded her grieving father with her antic tricks? Lassiter thought it possible that she was. It was equally possible such a supposition was no more than wishful thinking. Doctor Tremlett had suggested that her power was a profoundly out of kilter affront to nature. Could Rachel really have mellowed?

Lassiter said, 'I'm going to go to the place you found first, Phil, the cellar where they stored the whisky they distilled. You and Edie saw her there the last time, so she knows where it is. I'll wait an hour. If she doesn't come, I'll go up to the settlement and climb down into the sepulchre.' He tried not to shudder at the prospect of doing so.

Helena asked, 'While we just sit tight?'

They were in the bar. That had been Ruthie's suggestion. Bars were convivial places and this one had yet to be christened. None of them had actually cracked a bottle yet, but Helena looked to her the sort of woman who could let her hair down if the occasion prompted it. Edie was partial to the odd beer. It wasn't totally out of the question.

The décor was inflicting mixed feelings on Ruthie. The place was awash with nauticalia. There were brass ship's clocks and barometers and fishing nets and lobster pots and framed navigation charts and it was all very reminiscent of the Spyglass Inn and as such a poignant reminder of how far she was from home and the safety of her cottage and the simple joys of her daily routine. She didn't fear for herself, so much as she feared for Phil. She thought their courage made brave men vulnerable. It had probably already done for Johnson and his tough looking, lippy mate. It made her fear for Patsy, too.

Lassiter said, 'I think sitting tight the most sensible option, with Ruthie maybe nipping out for the odd cigarette break.'

'Don't be an enabler Patsy,' Ruthie said. 'Criticise me, call me a self-destructive moron.'

'There's a time for cold-turkey,' Lassiter said. 'This really isn't it.'

Ruthie smiled at that. They all did. They were feeling the tension. Everyone was wondering about the gung-ho drama at the settlement. Edie was keeping her ears alert to the triumphant roar of returning quad bikes. Phil Fortescue, not a religious man, had said a sincere prayer for the wellbeing of their comrades. Helena, pessimistic about their chances, was close to grieving already for brave, foolish Derek Johnson.

'The irony of a drunk, sitting out a vigil surrounded by casks of vintage whisky, isn't totally lost on me,' Lassiter said, pulling on his cagoule.

They each of them hugged him in turn, Helena lastly. She said, 'Come back safe.'

'I've already told you,' he said, 'I'm hard to get rid of.'

They were there. They had reached the breach in the perimeter wall, the place where the great wooden gate of which there was now no longer any trace left had once proven a mighty obstacle, oaken and iron-braced. They slipped into the gap, Hurst to the left and Johnson to the right, their weapons drawn now, their strategy to approach their destination through the buildings of the settlement separately, but to reach and enter it at the same time. They didn't need caution with the firepower they now possessed. Speed and aggression were the keys. They needed to be fast and totally emphatic, as one in what they did together.

The settlement was dismal in the chill and persistent rain. Its hovels had a sagged, defeated look. The bigger buildings were solemn, wind-scarred, close to featureless in their grim dilapidation. It was silent, no wind to croon through slate fractures and stony crevices, no birds in the vacant, porous leaden sky.

They reached the windowless church. The door was open a chink, a ribbon of darkness between wood and masonry. A smell wafted out, sour and feral. Johnson looked at Hurst, looking back at him, both of them panting now, wide-eyed, wired with adrenaline, itchy for action, craving the moment, ardent for its drama and decisiveness, desperate really to bring this weird business to its bloody conclusion.

They burst through the door, weapons cocked and raised, aware of the gloom and the stench, scouring the featureless walls in front of them and to either side, the pillar flanking the door to his right catching Derek Johnson's peripheral vision at its blurred outer extremity, there where he knew there was no pillar.

'Mother of God,' he said.

It was behind and above them. It had straddled the door and bent from the waist with its back pressed flat against the church roof. Johnson raised his gun and peered up so his eyes could confirm this and something swung with whooshing speed and a clubbing blow broadsided him and sent him hurtling into Hurst, both of them shunted fast, their heads colliding with an audible smack, the last thing he remembered a rough violation of his mouth with searing force, plucking out a tooth. Mercifully, after that, for the rest of the horror that followed, unconsciousness claimed him.

Chapter Sixteen

Ruthie outlined her alternative plan as soon as Lassiter had left them. There was no deliberate disloyalty or deceit in this. She did not think she could have deterred him from doing what he intended to in his own meticulous, deliberate way. On the face of it, his was a reasonable plan. Her approach was more intuitive. His might work, but if it didn't, there was too much at stake not to have an alternative strategy. And time was too short for that alternative to wait, the moment to attempt it was straight away.

She cleared her throat and asked for everyone's attention. She told Edie and Helena about her experience in Brightstone Forest with Shaddeh's bracelet of teeth. When she'd finished telling them, she said, 'What I'm about to tell you might just sound like my ego talking.'

'Then we'd all better make sure we're comfortably seated,' Edie said.

'Hear her out, Edith,' Helena said, 'people with inflated egos don't generally describe themselves as morons.'

'You're definitely not a moron,' Fortescue said.

'Thanks for that, Phil.'

'Get on with it,' Edith said.

Ruthie had brought her overnight bag into the bar with her. She opened it and took two items out. The first of these was a child's cotton nightdress. She unfolded it carefully. It was more than just traditional. It was positively old-fashioned, pink, with buttons up the back and bright butterflies embroidered onto its bodice at the front. It was about the right size for a small and slender 10 year-old. The second item was a silver backed bristle hairbrush.

'You're fucking joking,' Edith said.

'This child, the child still in her, has endured 200 years of cold neglect. I think she sees everything that goes on here. She asked Patsy to put her to rest. It's what she wants. He thinks he knows how to do it. I'd like to show her a bit of kindness first. I'd like her to go to her rest with a bit of dignity.'

'You're mad,' Edith said. 'I've seen her. She's terrifying.'

'I know that,' Ruthie said. 'And I need to prepare myself. She might not come, but if she does, I need to be composed enough to go through with this. I want you all to go and wait somewhere safe.'

'Nowhere here's safe,' Edie said.

'The generators are housed forty feet underground,' Helena said, ignoring her. 'I reckon that's the safest place.'

Fortescue said, 'Why you, Ruthie?'

'Shaddeh spoke to me. He wouldn't speak to both of us, he chose me. I think I'm fated to play a decisive part in what happens here. We want Rachel to do something for us, so we should show her a proper kindness for doing it. We should help her find rest just out of common compassion. We shouldn't go looking to bargain with her over that.'

Fortescue gestured at the nightgown, the hairbrush. 'Why this?'

'In her position, at the age she was, it's what I'd have liked,' Ruthie said.

Edith said, 'You've no idea what you're letting yourself in for. She's a fucking nightmare. Rachel Ballantyne's all your nightmares rolled into one. You won't get through this charade, if she shows up. And that will only provoke her.'

'Thanks for your vote of confidence, Edith.'

'You're young and all, Edie,' Helena said, 'but just now you're being a right royal pain in the arse.'

Edith began to sob at that. 'I'm scared,' she said, 'I'm sorry, Ruthie.'

Fortescue strode across to Edie and held her in his arms. He looked over her head to Ruthie. He held Ruthie's eyes and then smiled and winked at her. 'Come on, kiddo,' he said to his stepdaughter. 'Helena's going to take us somewhere safe.'

He knew it wasn't safe. And he knew Helena knew bloody well it wasn't either, because the generator had previously been tampered with. She'd told Patsy and Patsy had told him. But no one had told Edie and it was Edie who needed to feel secure. He knew, as Helena did, that nowhere here was safe.

He didn't want to leave. He wanted to stay with Ruthie and try to protect her knowing Edie was being comforted forty feet beneath the ground by Helena, a brave and proper grown-up who knew the complex like the back of her hand. But he believed fate had always played a part in their experiences there on New Hope Island and through the bracelet of teeth, it was true the sorcerer Shaddeh had chosen to speak only in the end to Ruthie.

He wanted to stay and protect her but he trusted her instinct and his intuition told him strongly that what she was doing was right. He'd seen Rachel Ballantyne and still recalled the sick feeling of dismay the short encounter then had left him with. He did not know whether Ruthie would get through this ordeal for which she'd singled herself out, but he knew what she wanted most from him just then was to trust her to try.

⚜ ⚜ ⚜

After an hour wasted in the whisky cellar, Lassiter headed for the heights and the colony settlement. He'd seen none of Johnson's people thus far and none of the maintenance crew either. He had a hunch they were sitting tight in their compound. Derek Johnson was the leader of the whole group now. They'd be nervous and feeling vulnerable and the worsening weather gave them a natural excuse to just bunker down and await his return. Lassiter was convinced by now that wait was a futile one.

He felt very differently from the way he'd felt the last time he'd been on the island. Then he'd been coping with loss, struggling with grief and trying not to become overwhelmed by despair. On a day-to-day basis he'd not felt afraid for his life. He'd thought the island a hazardous place, but had felt his life of such little value he'd been indifferent to the danger. It wasn't like that now. Meeting Helena Davenport, being with her, had changed him. Now he was afraid and he was fearful too for her. He climbed towards the colony settlement through the strengthening wind and rain in a state of heightened alertness. He was, suddenly, a man with an awful lot to lose.

He kept expecting to see a ragged figure at the edge of his vision, a forlorn little wretch whose feet didn't quite touch the ground as she moved over it, the rags she wore weirdly untouched by the downpour, her hair a chaotic halo of yellow knots, her face disquietingly incomplete. Rachel was as likely to scare you to death for a lark as she was to extend any courtesy, but he honestly felt her to be the only hope they had and was becoming anxious at the fact that she hadn't so far appeared. If she felt indifferent to their presence, it naturally followed she'd be indifferent to their fate.

He reached the settlement's perimeter wall. He walked to the breach and entered it. He had no sense, among the dripping hovels, that anything living shared the moment with him there. But he knew that this was a place that confounded the senses and betrayed reason in perverse and habitual ways. The buildings clustered around him were both haunted and cursed. This was somewhere you trusted only at your peril. He squeezed rainwater out of his eyebrows with a thumb and blinked and headed for Ballantyne's windowless church.

Lassiter pushed open the heavy door on silence and emptiness. All was still. There was a sour, secreted stink and under that, there was the coppery odour of blood. The sense of recent, murderous violence in that dark space all but screamed at him. He had no need of his dead wife's psychic gift to hear and see it. As his eyes adjusted to the gloom and he searched the floor, he saw that no scrap of physical evidence now remained to hint at what had happened there. He had the shortwave he'd been given at breakfast in his breast pocket. But he felt certain that Johnson and his ally in this hunt were beyond ever calling him on it now.

He would go to the sepulchre. There was no avoiding doing that. He'd told the others that if they didn't get this done by Sunday evening, they'd have failed. He'd concluded that the Being got stronger with every death it accomplished, every victim it devoured. Rachel was their only slim hope of defeating it, if Ruthie was right about the magic. And Lassiter thought she was. He'd great respect for Ruthie's intuition. In the past, it had been his saviour.

She'd called herself a moron but Ruthie was clever and resourceful. All of them had their qualities and he feared now none of them would survive to see the morning. Bright, unfulfilled lives would be brutally extinguished.

Even objectively, it was a genuine pity and a poignant loss. He pulled open the church door and trudged through the deluge to New Hope's secret little necropolis. Unaware of doing so, he hummed *The Recruited Collier* as he walked.

Ruthie was unaware of the presence until the tickle of decay smarted in her nostrils. When it did, she felt that the temperature of the room had dropped several degrees. It had done so without her noticing but suddenly, it felt cold. Slowly and deliberately, she turned to the source of the smell. A little girl floated a foot off the ground at the far end of the bar. Even from forty feet away, she was ragged, bedraggled, frail looking. She had sightless eyes. They were staring blindly at the nightdress. Ruthie had found a hanger for it and it hung from a shelf above the bar where glasses could be reached by bar staff taking orders as they faced their customers. Ruthie had willed this moment, sort of. She now very much wished she had helped herself to a strong and fortifying drink in preparation for it.

Except that there was no preparation adequate to it. Ruthie knew all at once that Rachel Ballantyne wasn't some revenant apparition you could rub your eyes and blink away. Rachel's presence was a malaise that had her cast all at once into a mood of wretched despondency. She was a figure in three dimensions unimpeded by gravity. She was animate without the requirement of what humans recognized without conscious thought as life.

There was all that and, above all, there was the raw fear her appearance provoked. If anything, Ruthie thought Edie Chambers had undersold the fear. She wondered how much death Rachel had inflicted in the two centuries since rudely being denied her own. She had no way of knowing. Her instinct insisted quite a lot. She sensed the unruly terror of Rachel's wrath and it made her tremble inside her clothes.

'You were here once before,' a papery voice whispered. 'You're the storyteller.'

Ruthie nodded. She was too nervous to trust herself to speak. She'd try to speak in a moment when she'd found more self-possession. Rachel Ballantyne floated and drifted before her unmoored, a shiftless, uncertain proposition. Apparently she was capricious and could be gleefully cruel. She charged the air itself there appallingly with risk. Ruthie needed a moment to compose herself in the face of this catalogue of sensory assaults. She felt at the mercy of a cyclone oddly still, at the static centre of a petrified storm.

'I would like to be told a story,' Rachel said. 'I would like that very much.'

'Would you like also to wear the nightgown?'

'That would greatly please me also, but I cannot, for I am grievous soiled,' Rachel Ballantyne said. 'I am grimy with filth, sore unworthy of such finery.'

She sounded so abjectly sad that Ruthie was lost for a response. Then she heard words spoken from behind her, clearly and strongly and shot through with sympathy.

'I'll wash your hands and feet for you if you'll permit me, Rachel. Let's go to somewhere more practical for that task. And then you can put on your new nightgown and have your hair brushed properly and hear the story Ruthie has for you.'

It was Edie. It was Edie fucking Chambers, bold and nerveless and judging from the slight smile on Rachel's smudged features and the girlish twist of pleasure at her waist, saying all the right things.

She followed them to one of the suites. Edie washed her hands and feet and Ruthie swapped her fetid rags for the new nightdress. They did most of it with averted eyes, swallowing panic and bile, fighting terror, quelling revulsion, martialing the awful pity they both felt and making that drive them to complete their tasks. And then with her role fulfilled, Edie took her bucket of putrid water and black suds floating above it and left them to continue with their unfinished business.

Rachel sat cross-legged on the suite's king-sized bed. She might have been slightly above it, her scrawny rear not quite touching the counterpane, but Ruthie spared herself that uncertain detail. She sat behind Rachel and brushed her hair, ignoring the lice that seethed on her scalp, teasing at the knots, soothing out the tangles, making smooth tresses, or attempting to, of what had been a long time brittle and dead.

She chose her story carefully. She allowed no anachronisms. It had to be a tale a girl of 10 at the end of the 18th century would understand and more importantly, enjoy. Years earlier she'd invented Princess Avalon, friend to the Goblin King and the Witch of the North, owner of a sword and sometimes wearer of armour, protector of an invisible boy present only in his shadow, rider of a magical horse that could fly. It was whimsical stuff, but Avalon was bold and spirited and her audience of one seemed to like it well enough.

'Tell me another, pray,' Rachel said at the conclusion.

'Did your father tell you tales?'

'My father had no time for mere japes. He never told me a story. He never offered me his embrace. A goodnight kiss was precious rare. I believe he loved me.'

Tough love, Ruthie thought, who didn't remotely believe in it, catching sight of Rachel's reflection in the wall-mounted mirror they faced despite her efforts not to; and noticing in so doing so that Rachel was changing, transforming. It wasn't just the honeyed sheen of her now unexpectedly luxuriant hair. It was everything. She was solid and nourished under the nightdress. The scent of her was wholesome and sweet. Her eyes were china blue and her mouth a crimson bud and there was expression on her face. She looked pretty and healthy and truly alive.

In a voice that was full and properly girlish she said, 'Tell me another story.'

This was Shaddeh's doing, Shaddeh's deathly enchantment, it had to be. Ruthie couldn't but wonder at the reason for the transformation. It wasn't to make her feel more comfortable. There was something graver and more significant to it than that. There was, she sensed, a far bigger imperative.

'Pray, another story,' Rachel said.

Ruthie had lit candles. They were scented and she'd bought them at the same time as she'd bought the nightdress and the hairbrush and she didn't think Phil would at all approve, but the scant daylight brooded wetly over the bleak vista outside and the candle flames illuminated gently. There'd been 12 Princess Avalon stories in total. Ruthie reckoned she could remember about eight of them fluently enough to recite them verbally. She cleared her throat with a cough and closed her eyes recalling and began another.

Patrick Lassiter was uncertain about what to do. It was now 4 o'clock in the afternoon, there were only a couple of hours of light left in the day and there was no sign in the sepulchre of their blighted, ambivalent little would-be saviour. He pondered on the risk of going to the storm shelter, which in his heart he believed to be the Being's lair. Was there any point? If he put himself in jeopardy, he might force Rachel Ballantyne's hand. Above all, she sought rest. He'd promised her that. No one else, he was confident, could deliver it to her.

He went there. He couldn't think what else to do. The entrance was narrow, in its cleft of stone behind the stunted bush. He thought given its size, the shape-shifter would have to squirm to get its bulk through such a narrow aperture. The thought of that made him wince with disgust.

He found his way by torchlight. Inside the great chamber, a huge spider's web had been spun, stretching from the high ceiling all the way to the floor, its rough strands the gluey thickness of a man's arm, trophies thickly clustered at its heart. There was a watch cap and a camera and an outboard propeller. There was a pistol with a bloodied grip. There was a book, Lassiter knew without examining it was Thomas Horan's journal. The web told Lassiter the creature wasn't humanoid all of the time. He inhaled air with a feral, tainted stink and wondered where to go from here. He was exhausted of ideas and soaked through and he felt bitterly defeated.

He wondered why it bothered to ape a man, when its dimensions made the impersonation so inevitably grotesque and unconvincing. All the circumstantial evidence suggested that this was a difficult trick to accomplish. It required much painstaking study, the only reason he'd survived his island sojourn. He'd still been being studied when he'd fled the place.

He figured it might be because man was the dominant species on the planet and the Being recognized and wished to gain a sort of perverse kudos from that. Like a man, then, only bigger and vastly quicker and more powerful than a man, like a savage evolutionary step beyond man, enabled not by natural selection but by occult power. Lassiter shook his head. If this theory was right, the creature mythology described as Grendel or the Wendigo manifested vanity. Vanity was always a flaw making those that possessed it vulnerable.

Maybe the Being didn't see itself as a monster at all, Lassiter mused. Maybe it was closer to the Nietzchian Superman rudely and abruptly brought to life. Smelling its departed stink in that vast and melancholy chamber, he actually thought it though more like the child-eating giants rampaging through medieval forests in folkloric stories compiled by the Brothers Grimm. Except of course, it wasn't a fairytale, he thought, seeing the trophies shiver slyly at the centre of the web. It was a nightmare. And it was real.

He was out of ideas. His leads had dried up and withered away. He was down to speculation and his last vestiges of hope. He would go back to Rachel's sepulchre on the bleak prospect of seeing her there and beseeching her to help them. He didn't honestly at that point know what else to do.

Chapter Seventeen

*I*t capered across the façade of their shelter, drawn by the light. It stole but a snatched glimpse as it slid over the lit glass and clambered up to consider for a moment on the building's roof. It squatted in the deluge and pondered, its weight and mass untroubled as it rested there by the force of the gathering gale. It had hoped the young meat, the tender cuts it craved, would be soon coming. Now it had glimpsed one, here already, yellow haired and succulent. Could it resist?

They were coming in their numbers now, foolish and blind. The time for waiting was at an end, it thought, the time for the feast was upon them. They were the feast and there would be no gristle and soft bones in the succulent flesh of the one it had just seen chattering with its dark-haired companion through the glass.

It hungered. It had discovered that the females tasted infinitely sweeter than the men. The glass in their window was no obstacle to its gathering strength. It would indulge its appetite and doing so would not stop them, they were blind and stupid and would come anyway in their numbers to be weakly consumed as was their deserved lot and humble human destiny. It would not wait. It would feast now and it would savour.

The glass imploded behind them and Ruthie turned sharply and saw huge limbs wrestling through the heavy shards and above the limbs a swollen head with livid eyes and drool hanging and looping thickly from its leering mouth.

Rachel turned her head to their intruder. She did so slowly, almost imperiously, Ruthie thought. And she saw from its expression that the creature had been unaware outside of who Rachel Ballantyne was. It knew now, though. Caution flickered like a shadow across its features. Then the grin returned. It licked its swollen upper lip with a rough, barnacled tongue, squatting because the generous dimensions of the room still obliged the creature to fold its limbs into a crouch. It didn't look cramped, she noticed, seeing the way the flesh of it rippled and roiled uneasily under horny bristles of body hair. It looked coiled.

And she heard its thoughts. They danced and capered uninvited through her mind. They were shrill with triumph. It slid the focus of its eyes to hers in thinking what it was. They were bloodshot eyes and they lustered with a savagery so ancient that the mind reeled as if with vertigo looking into them. She was aware of the awful stink of it, rough, bleak and inhuman. Ruthie fought not to piss herself in terror. Her heart stuck hammer blows against the anvil of her chest. Her scalp under her hair seemed to tingle and tighten in every follicle. She shuddered uncontrollably, struggling to remember how to breathe, crawling backwards involuntarily until the bed's headboard creaked against the hard press of her spine.

Strong enough now, it said, *strong enough to destroy the thing I've been obliged to hide from in the past. Ready to end the wait here and thus end that long indignity. And then afterwards you'll perish too. And then the waiting begins, only until your remains grow cold, for I'll savour you, madam, as carrion.*

The creature extended an arm. The reflex was piston quick. The hand on the end of the arm was a clenched club the size of a bowling ball. It stilled a foot to the side of Rachel Ballantyne who didn't react to it at all. Then it moved suddenly, with spasmodic speed, swatting her into a wall. She bounced off masonry and slumped onto the floor. Fingers the thickness of tow ropes plucked her up by her new nightdress and flung her upward to collide with the ceiling where she thudded and moaned before clattering back down to the floor again.

It toyed with her. She was a rag doll made brittle by antique bones. And the bones were breaking. Her little right leg was twisted grotesquely. Her tiny left forearm poked shattered through torn flesh. The creature dragged itself over to where she lay and hammered its fist into her face with a wet crunch of impact. It used its tongue to tease at a rip in her nightdress and tear it off her with a grunt. Rachel lay there petite and pale, blood filling her livid bruises, those of her ribs still intact, shaping a small cage under the stretched skin of emaciation.

The beast rested above her on its haunches. There wasn't the room for it to stand up straight. It put its head to one side staring at Rachel in a parodic gesture of sympathy and then it picked her up delicately between both hands as though deliberately gentle now. It folded her and raised her to its mouth and Ruthie heard the soft snap of collar-bones and spine. It unhinged its gaping, slathering jaws and Rachel disappeared as it swallowed her whole. Then it bellowed in primeval triumph and the remaining shards of the broken pane tinkled out of their sill and the walls seemed to shake with the magnitude of the sound.

I was wrong, Ruthie thought, could not have been more wrong. Catastrophically wrong, hideously mistaken about the magic's balance of power on the island. She sniffed, she was crying. She was in mortal terror and filled with self-pity too but the tears weren't for her. They were for Rachel Ballantyne, the poor, waifish, twice-dead child long cheated of life and now grotesquely perished.

Ruthie felt shipwrecked or crash-landed somewhere alien. There was nothing about this awful new world she recognized. She tried to keep still. The fresh aroma of pee and wet gush of it cooling on her thighs told her she'd pissed herself. Air shuddered in and out of her despite her efforts to remain motionless. Escape was impossible. A part of her mind was still incredulous at the fate befalling her. The creature was a nightmare made corporeal, stinking and solid, massive and inhuman, its primeval reek filling the suite's air with a rich and revolting warmth. It had destroyed Rachel Ballantyne. It had tenderized the small morsel of her meat with its cudgeling fists and then it had consumed her.

That destruction, though, appeared to have come at a cost. The creature had retreated to where it could lean back against a wall. The fingers of its great hands clutched at its torso. They danced over the coarse bristles covering its belly in a spider-leg frenzy as if seeking escape from themselves. Ruthie swallowed disgust. There was something arachnid about the creature even when it disguised itself like this. It was a shape-shifter, wasn't it? It was a living lie, an insult to nature, a corrupt, impossible sorcerer's conceit.

It fought and struggled interminably and Ruthie sat on the bed's counterpane as still as she could and watched it do so. She saw it dribble a yellowish fluid from its jaws and then heave. It heaved again. It labours, she thought, almost like some creature giving birth. She watched as something she thought akin to dread clouded its eyes. She watched as dread morphed into pain and then into the rictus mask of agony. It seemed to pucker and wilt. It moaned and shrank massively into a corner, folding its great arms and legs, seeming to diminish somehow.

And Ruthie remembered where this alien world was. She might have been shipwrecked on its desolate shore, but she knew its name. It was the Realm of Anguish and the Kingdom of Decay. It was the Land Without Light. It was Rachel Ballantyne's domain, and she had the distinct impression the creature in front of her was being obliged to learn that sorry lesson now.

The creature convulsed forward and the vomit was expelled from it in a crimson caul that thumped and then shivered and decayed on the deep, creamy pile of the suite's ruined carpet. Heat came off the caul as it shrank and withered away from a crouched shape within. The shape gained substance, hardening in growth while the creature that had voided it mewled and gasped and whimpered now.

When the figure escaping the caul came to resemble Rachel Ballantyne its growth accelerated and it sat up on the floor, limbs and torso shaping and swelling subtly to their familiar size. It was intact again; she was intact again. Ruthie saw that her clothing was tawdry and ragged and that her hair was once again dull and knotted and unkempt. The cloying stench of decay once again came off in nauseous waves from her pale, grimed skin. Her face was no longer pretty now but vaguely assembled, a child's careless recollection, a living contradiction of death stubbornly reluctant to surrender what passed for its life. Edie had called her a living nightmare. It occurred to Ruthie that their time for fairy tales had been altogether brief.

Hardly worth the bother, make-overs, she thought giddily, *they never last.* She wasn't far off hysteria. She was surprised she hadn't gone into shock or simply passed out. She'd been chosen for this, singled out for it, honoured and cursed both. *Cheers,* she thought.

The creature mewled. Rachel was ominously silent, climbing to her feet, ascending a foot into effortless space, standing now on nothing more substantial than air, floating poised before it.

'Kill it,' Ruthie said. 'Kill it, Rachel. I know that you can.'

Her voice was strange to her own ears, a guttural scrabble of urgent barks that didn't sound like her at all. It debated fear and fury in its tone, this new voice of hers. Fury was winning, though.

Rachel spoke her voice was soft, contemplative. 'It fancied it could best me. It entertained me briefly to allow it that conceit. Ha! I like sport. I've long sported. Twas my own creator gave this mean creature life. He possessed the key to the gateway it stole through into the world. That took but a fraction of the trick required in summoning me. Mine is truer magic, storyteller. Here I rightfully rule. So I lulled and sported with it.'

'Kill it.'

'Merely a game,' Rachel said.

'Kill it, please,' Ruthie said. She could smell the odour rising from where she'd soiled herself. She needed to shower and change. That would wait. It occurred to her a bit desperately that she'd altogether run out now of stories. At least, she had of the sort that little Rachel seemed to like.

Rachel laughed. It was a high, harsh sound, an expression of glee. The creature panted and bled. It had cut itself breaking the glass. It must have done and the cuts looked to Ruthie as she watched to be deepening. Cuts became rents, furrowed into savage crimson wounds ruining its bristly hide. It groaned. Some of the wounds were developing a greenly gangrenous, spoiled meat hue. Ruthie wretched.

Wind howled into the room, filling the space with cold, briny air from the darkness outside. All the candles had blown out.

She heard its voice, then, more accurately the rude clatter of its thoughts careening uninvited through her mind; *It hurts, it hurts, I hunger and hurt, I want to feast, not to bleed and perish, I am riven and dying and it hurts so. I will bargain. I will reason. I will give.*

Another, deeper, entirely implacable voice: *You have nothing to give.*

I will serve.

Silence. Then, *I have no requirement of servitude from such as you.*

'Kill it,' Ruthie said again.

'Why would I kill it, Ruthie?'

'You'd be saving lives.'

Rachel laughed again. The creature winced and flinched, a cowed monster, sickly pale, oozing blood. Rachel said, 'You're skilled at your craft, there's no denying it. Your tales have a bright spark to them and they fair diverted me. But I've a fate for this creature you'd never in a lifetime think to invent.'

Ruthie said nothing.

Rachel said, 'You'll find Mr. Lazziter at the settlement my father built. Go now. Thank Mr. Lazziter for his patience and prey tell him I'll be with him shortly. Perhaps remind him I have been patient too.'

They wrapped themselves in warm clothes and waterproofs and set off for the settlement. Ruthie brought her bag. She had more candles for the sepulchre. She didn't mention this to Phil. He'd spent his time underground teaching Helena the words of Shaddeh's incantation, learned by heart from the final pages years earlier of Thomas Horan's journal. The sorcerer had recently told Ruthie that it would no longer work and Fortescue knew that. But he'd had to do something to occupy a mind that would have been driven to distraction otherwise with worry over Ruthie. And Helena had been absorbed in learning the liturgy.

Ruthie thanked Edie for her surprise, soapy cameo.

'It was all I could think of to do,' Edie said. 'I was kind of vacillating between nervous wreck and complete bitch and I'm not really either of those, most of the time.'

It was Helena who had guessed from below ground that Rachel had arrived. The power output metres on the generator had signaled it was working harder to heat the complex. She calculated a 10 degree fall in the temperature registered by the building's thermostats on the basis of the metre readings. It was too great a plunge for the meteorological conditions on the island to have caused it.

'She thought our guest might be responsible,' Edie said, shivering.

'What you did was incredibly brave,' Ruthie said, 'and incredibly well timed. I was losing it when I heard your voice from behind me.'

Edie shook her head. She said, 'You're an easy woman to underestimate, Ruthie, and I don't mean that in a nasty way. But I think you're actually braver and smarter than the lot of us.'

They found Lassiter, when they got there, sheltering in one of the hovels with a view of the breach in the settlement wall, cold and grim-faced. Helena had brought with her flasks of coffee and chicken broth and some bread she'd thought to defrost in the morning. Ruthie told him what had occurred and he ate bread and spooned broth into himself and they all drank coffee as the rain puddled around them in the gathering gloom.

'I won't be sorry to say a last goodbye to this place,' Edie said.

'Amen to that,' Helena said.

'Your masterpiece is here,' Fortescue said.

'It is,' she said, 'but I'm not required to live in it.' She was sad about Derek Johnson, sad and angry and it showed.

'One more task to fulfill,' Lassiter said.

'A promise to keep,' Helena said, kissing his cheek, stroking the side of his face with her fingertips.

Ruthie smoked, slightly apart from the group, so as not to pollute them. She was thinking about something Rachel Ballantyne, the tormented entity that had once been Rachel Ballantyne, had said to her.

He never told me a story. He never offered me his embrace. A goodnight kiss was precious rare. I believe he loved me.

Phil came over. Gently, he said, 'Don't cry, Ruthie. It's all going to be okay.'

She sniffed. 'I'm not crying,' she said, 'it's just the rain, wetting my face.'

Lassiter led them through the narrow iron gate and down the stone steps into the sepulchre. Over their coffee, he'd told them what it was he wanted them to do. By the play of his torch beam, Ruthie took out and positioned and lit her candles. Then he switched off the torch.

Fortescue raised no objection, made no comment at all. He was a man well able to differentiate between tears and rain and the candles were quite practical down there. Their flames lit on the still, silent residents of that subterranean place resting eternally in their tattered remnants on their granite shelves.

Helena was first to become aware that she was there. Rachel didn't announce herself. Helena felt a sudden clutch of dismay grip her innards and she glanced up and saw a pale, bony figure floating fraily a couple of feet above the beaten earth of the ground in the far corner.

Lassiter saw her next. He said, 'Good evening, Rachel.'

'I trust you're here to keep your promise, Mr. Lazziter.'

There was something centuries old in the curl of the vowels and the sawdust coarseness of the voice that made gooseflesh frill on Helena's arms. She had tried to prepare mentally for this, but knew now that nothing could equip your mind for its fearful affront to the way things ought to be. Her world had lurched, out of kilter. It was all she could do to stay on her feet. She looked at Ruthie, who'd grown as pale as Rachel was. Ruthie managed a smile and winked at her.

'We're all here for that,' Lassiter said. 'We're going to sing you a lullaby and you're going to sleep.'

'I've never been sung a lullaby,' Rachel said. 'I've never slept.'

Helena couldn't look away from the little apparition's face. It was vague and ill-formed, shifting and uncertain, disconcerting because although she floated before them in space, Rachel wasn't an apparition at all. Somehow, she was real and possessed of a sort of life.

'You'll sleep tonight, Rachel,' Lassiter said. He unbuttoned his coat and shrugged it to the floor. 'But before you do,' he said, holding his beckoning arms wide, 'I'd like to give you your goodnight kiss.'

Helena gasped at the speed at which Rachel tore through space to close the distance. There was a jump-cut abruptness to it that defied physical laws. She thought Rachel would collide with Patrick with an impact that would kill him before he had time even to flinch.

But that didn't happen. When Rachel got there she stopped and paused and then clung to him and he held her in his arms and then kissed her on the cheek. 'Sleep well, darling girl,' he said, stroking the back of her head.

To Ruthie, standing beside her, Edie whispered, 'And I thought you were brave.'

But when she looked, Edie thought that Ruthie had been crying too hard to hear her.

She lay on a bier Lassiter had carved and planed and hammered together from driftwood after he'd made his promise during his island sojourn but before he'd worked out how to honour it. He was honouring it now.

They formed a circle around her, holding hands. They ignored the whiff of corruption and averted their gaze from her sightless eyes and they sang Rachel Ballantyne lullabies. Feeling and fortitude lent strength to their voices. Their shared ordeal welded them as one into harmony. Love and loyalty sweetened their tone. Together they lulled Rachel, helping her finally meet the great unpaid debt she owed sleep, and she rested. And so she was put to rest.

As death claimed her, her features resolved and clarified for just a moment into those of a pretty little girl, skin porcelain-smooth, brow unblemished, eyes closed blissfully under the curl of her long lashes. And then the skin blackened and was shed and her bones beneath were exposed and rendered themselves with age to grey ash on the bier Patrick Lassiter had built for her.

It wasn't far off midnight by the time they got back outside. The wind had dropped and the rain had stopped falling. The sky twinkled vastly with pinprick worlds of light.

Ruthie Gillespie wanted to hug Patrick Lassiter, to tell him how brave and thoughtful and compassionate and kind a man he was, but she couldn't think of words that wouldn't debase his priceless parting gift to Rachel Ballantyne's deprived spirit. Because of him, she hadn't died alone.

Because of him, she'd died at peace, contented, having known at last the simple and sublime comfort of human warmth. But Ruthie said none of this.

They walked for a while in silence.

Eventually, Phil Fortescue said, 'I can't believe it's finally over. It is, though. It's over, for all of us.'

'It's not quite over,' Ruthie said, taking his hand, swinging their arms as they walked down the slope together. 'There's a bar open at the complex and there's still time for a drink.'

'I'll second that commotion,' Edie Chambers said.

Ruthie said, 'I haven't noticed one, Helena, but does the complex have a cigarette machine?'

'I knew I'd forgotten something,' Helena Davenport said.

Chapter Eighteen

Felix Baxter stood in the light rain and gathered darkness with the scent of brine strong in his nostrils and salt air heady in his lungs. His feet were on the slicked cobbles of the Colony's old dock and his eyes were on the wood and granite edifice occupying ground higher than he did a few hundred metres inland. Helena Davenport's masterpiece, even in the prevailing absence of light, looked flawed but magnificent in its wood and granite isolation. Glass provided the flaw; or rather the flaw was imposed by an absence of glass in one of the picture windows giving on to the lightless, and therefore to Baxter unseen suite within.

He was incurious about what had become of the window. Whatever had happened there, he sensed that the missing pane was actually the least of it. His instinct was that something cataclysmic had occurred. It was over now, the cataclysmic event. He was witnessing only its aftermath. He did not yet know whether the outcome had been good for him or bad. The story continued and his part in it wasn't over. That was all he was really certain about.

His intuition told him that no living thing lurked now in the complex constructed to help fulfil the dream he'd had for this wilderness. But it wasn't empty, was it? Someone dead waited there for him. He'd recently become a believer in ghosts. He'd done so only reluctantly, but he no longer harboured any doubt about their existence. He was here because he'd been compelled to come. It was his fate and his penance both and neither could be avoided, despite the trepidation he felt at the prospect of entering first that building and then that particular room.

He wondered were the dead ever patient with the living. He doubted they were when antagonised. He thought now it didn't really do to exploit the dead by warping their true stories in pursuit of personal gain. He'd been guilty of doing that, though. He thought that the least he could do now was to be prompt for the single unearthly appointment he was there only to attend.

He'd taken a flight directly to Stornoway. He'd chartered the aircraft himself, hadn't wanted Joy or anyone else among his staff to be party to his impromptu travel plans. A great deal had changed for him following the visitation of Elizabeth Burrows to his Manchester penthouse. Humility had never been foremost among his various qualities. He'd been good at false modesty, but had never been truly humbled until his encounter with the deceased postgraduate student. Finding out who it was she'd been in life had been reasonably straightforward and he'd done that himself also. Delegating tasks had always been one of his business strengths. But Lizzie Burrows was personal and there were some things you had no real choice but to do on your own account.

At Stornoway Harbour, he'd been recommended to seek out a young fisherman named Adam Cox. Cox had achieved a degree of notoriety there. He's done so by ferrying passengers to New Hope Island aboard his smack. Baxter knew that sailors were superstitious, had remembered that fact recalling the TV series the maritime professor Philip Fortescue had fronted on the subject.

In the Stornoway Harbour bars, Baxter encountered a general reluctance to go anywhere near New Hope. A reluctance, it was suggested, only this man Cox seemed to be sometimes immune to. His most recent island passenger was a name on everyone's lips there because she was Doctor Georgia Tremlett and Dr Tremlett had apparently vanished once she'd got to her unhappy destination. And this had happened only the previous week.

'Which is precisely why I won't take you,' Adam Cox said to him, when he'd finally tracked the man down to the snug of a gloomy pub.

'How many have you had?'

'I'm not on the beer, Mister. I'm whiling away a few hours is all. The fishing's better at night. The stuff in my glass is Diet Pepsi.'

'Name your price.'

'You're not hearing me very well.'

'I'm Felix Baxter. Does that name not mean anything to you?'

'It means the New Hope Island Experience. It means deep pockets and even deeper bullshit and I'm thinking more front than Blackpool.'

Baxter laughed. Despite his dire predicament, he had to. He said, 'I'll give you a thousand pounds in cash for not much more than a couple of hours of work. Not even work, really, just diesel fuel and your time.'

'I've Doctor Tremlett on my conscience.'

'New Hope has changed.'

'New Hope will never change, Mr Baxter, as Doctor Tremlett seems to have discovered to her cost.'

'Fifteen hundred in used fifties. Come on! You won't even break sweat.'

'Oh, yes, I will.'

'So you'll take me?'

'It's your funeral.'

'That's the spirit.'

'I'm insane, doing this.'

'You've done it before. You're the man for the job.'

'I'm greedy and a fool.'

'Is your boat seaworthy?'

'Not as seaworthy as she'll be when I've spent your money on her. It's the reason I'm taking you.'

'You won't regret it.'

'Which is easy to say. Where on New Hope do you want me to put you off?'

It was the third time he'd done it, Cox told Baxter on their voyage. He talked only because he was nervous, Baxter supposed. He'd first ferried someone to New Hope Island 18 months earlier when his passenger had been the Goth children's author Ruthie Gillespie. She seemed to have made a very big impression on Cox over a relatively short period of time. She was going there, she'd explained to him, only because some friends of hers were in trouble on the island.

In other circumstances, this would have intrigued Felix Baxter. But the circumstances were what they were and he had weightier matters on his mind than Ms Gillespie's past island jaunt. And by now he knew that mystery was endemic to the place and that New Hope was somewhere good at retaining secrets it seemed not just to covet but to delight in.

I was left alone there.

He recalled Police Commander Patrick Lassiter's ambiguous statement wondering whether he'd be left alone by Lizzie Burrows; wondering would her ghastly spectre ever leave him alone in his uncertain future and the thought sent a cold shudder of fear through him that had nothing to do with the depthless void under their battered hull or even his bleak speculations on the night rendezvous to come.

'What's the matter?' Cox had said, seeing him shiver, glancing nervously out at the frothing whitecaps on water blackening with the dusk.

And Baxter had merely shrugged, thinking that fifteen hundred quid paid for a bit of trepidation on the part of his boat's pilot and that he'd rather have his steersman alert on a crossing like this than smugly complacent.

He'd said his final goodbye to Adam Cox and his inflated fee 20 minutes earlier. For the last ten, he'd stood there in the rain and simply looked upward at the complex. Now, his feet moved forward and he began the ascent to the building rumour had it would earn the talented Ms Davenport not just accolades but gongs. Even recently, that thought would have been a source to him both of pleasure and of pride. It would have thrilled through him with a ripple of vicarious achievement. But everything was relative and it was honestly something he didn't really give a toss about anymore. Everything was a matter of perspective and Felix Baxter knew that his perspective had been changed forever.

The main entrance was slightly and mightily ajar. It meant that their generator had failed and the power was off. A black mark against Ms Davenport's name, that, except he didn't really think it was, because he thought it both deliberate and nothing at all to do with bad design or mechanical failure. It meant he'd have to take the stairs to the suite with the missing window. That was okay, though. He was fit enough for that. His gym habit had been long and unbroken. He was familiar with the route because he often eschewed the lift in buildings. The stairs up to the suite were regular and even. He hadn't relished the thought of getting into the lift, if he was honest with himself. Honesty hadn't been one of his past characteristics, either, but was becoming so he knew, more and more. Events had obliged him into honesty. Truth had him cornered there.

The stairwell was slightly dank and completely dark and had a sour, subtly feral smell like an animal secretion. It put Baxter vaguely in mind of the wolf enclosure at the zoo. He could smell other fainter things under it. There was old tobacco and candle tallow and musty wool. He remembered the odour that had arisen when he'd unlocked and lifted the lid of that sea chest in the museum in Liverpool about a hundred years ago.

His throat became very dry on his ascent of the flights of steps taking him higher up and with each one he climbed, closer to his destination. He swallowed and stumbled at the same time and almost fell. He'd resisted the temptation to use the torch on his otherwise useless iPhone. It would have seemed glaringly intrusive and perhaps a provocation. His eyes were adjusting to the darkness but doing so only slowly and reluctantly. He thought this because there were sights here he didn't wish to see. He knew they would confront him anyway. It was why he was there, wasn't it?

He reached the open door of the windowless suite. There were shifting patches of starlight in the sky between flurries of night cloud he couldn't properly make out. After the gloom of the stairwell, the suite itself was quite adequately illuminated. Heavy shards of unbreakable glass glimmered broken at the foot of the windowsill. Pictures artfully hung punctuated the walls in dark rectangles. Furniture bulked and loomed, leather and canvas and polished wood, everything still, but poised to Baxter's mind, rather than properly reposeful.

Chastising thoughts clattered and reeled through his mind then randomly, unbidden. He remembered the venal words with which he'd manipulated poor Greg Cody's widow. He recalled the masked uneasiness of men who'd stayed on the island too long in his pay, afraid to confess their honest fears to him. He thought about the tavern he'd hoped to build there, tots of grog and sea shanties, the *Hope and Glory,* hopelessly and ingloriously bogus. He pondered on his long descent into corruption, *I know people who know people, Christ,* he thought, who seemed long absent from that place. Baxter wondered could you choke on self-disgust.

The tall and imposing figure of Seamus Ballantyne sat still at a desk on a straight-backed chair about eight feet from where Baxter stood. His attitude appeared stiffly reproachful. He wore sea boots and a boat cloak and a tri-corner hat made of tarred felt. Its grainy surface gleamed unevenly when he cocked his head in acknowledgement of company. The gesture was alert and not at all friendly.

There was a single peacock feather welded vertically by a smudge of wax to the crown of his hat and a lunar strangeness to his pale, pockmarked skin when light dabbed briefly at his shadowy features. He looked to be in his early 40s, in the prime of life, dead.

His voice, when it emerged from him, had the weight about it of a sledgehammer blow. His home as a sea captain had been the great 18th century northern English port city of Liverpool. But Ballantyne had been a Scot, Baxter realised, thinking, of course he had. When Seamus came to the Hebrides, he'd always been coming home. Perhaps he'd affected an English dialect as master of an English slave vessel. It might have been politic. If so, he wasn't affecting one now.

'This place ill-suits your purpose, Mr Baxter. Your scheme here amounts only to desecration. Abandon it.'

Baxter said, 'Just like that.'

'You disguise your terror with impertinent japes. Thus does weakness masquerade as strength. It's a habit ill suits any man who values dignity. Put to me the question you really came here to ask.'

'I wasn't sure you'd come.'

'Yet you know I never left.'

'That isn't quite what I meant.'

'Speak plainly, Sir.'

'I'm being haunted, Captain Ballantyne. I need to know will it ever stop.'

'Suddenly my visitor becomes a coward with the courage to admit to his fear. You're quite the paradox, Mr Baxter.'

Baxter swallowed. 'I'm a coward. And I'm afraid,' he said, 'that's the truth. I'm even more afraid, though, for my son.'

The captain chuckled. 'She's threatened to visit your son?'

'She has,' Baxter said. 'I would do anything, give everything I possess, to prevent that from happening.'

'Why, pray?'

'Because I love him.'

'More than you love yourself?'

'Yes, Captain, more than I love myself.'

'I'm to be convinced of that.'

Baxter held his arms wide. 'He's innocent of all of this. He's done nothing to offend the dead.'

'But you've offended the dead?'

'Of course I have. It's why you're here now. I've offended the living too. I've deaths on my conscience as a consequence.'

'Innocent blood on your hands?'

'Yes.'

Ballantyne was silent in response. The fugitive thought occurred to Baxter that he was merely hallucinating all of this. He was close to exhaustion and his nerves were shot and this was a stubbornly barren place in the night's empty seclusion. But he could smell palm oil and hemp rope and salt pork. He could smell canvas sheets drying in some spectral breeze and the tang of brass polish and barrelled rum and knew that this was all of it the odour of the sea as it had been aboard a ship in an era now long vanished from the world.

As these smells grew familiar to him, there was the warm hint under them of exotic spices he knew was the scent of the captain's cruel and sunlit voyages to the coast of Africa. And under that there was a base note of sweet decay he thought might be the whiff of disease rising from a slave hold.

And there was the figure in front of him; the grim, solid presence darkly toying with an hourglass on the desk at which he sat, flipping it impatiently as if harrying time itself.

And there was the voice. There was that gravel-charged bark of command that made Baxter flinch when it emanated from the captain's throat and chest, summoned impossibly from lungs long bloodless and cold. He wasn't at all imagining that, he knew.

Finally, Ballantyne said to him, 'The sorcerer has forgiven me my sins against him. Perhaps everything now is a consequence of that, because I've since forgiven him. My own beloved daughter is at long last at rest. This latter cause for joy inflicts on me a great debt of gratitude. I owe that to the scholar of the sea and his companion with the decorated skin. I owe it to your architect and the scholar's stepdaughter. Most grievously I owe it to an officer of the law, a man of prodigious courage and surpassing kindness.'

Baxter thought he could identify in his mind the people to whom the captain referred. That Helena Davenport was among them didn't even rouse his curiosity. All he cared about was that they had apparently succeeded in what they'd attempted together to do. It might even mean his haunting was now at an end. He hadn't been haunted for all that long but present company accepted he'd already had quite enough, in his life, of ghosts.

'I'm pleased for you,' he said. 'I'm pleased for Rachel too.'

'In saying which, you sound sincere, Sir. So in return for your good wishes, I shall tell you something eternally true. You reap only what you sow, Mr Baxter. In this place, on this stony ground, yours is a harvest of scorn.'

'Is there nothing I can do?'

Ballantyne chuckled again. It was an awful sound. He raised a finger and pointed, which was worse. A blood-coloured ruby embellished the ring worn below the first knuckle of the pointing finger and the movement of lifting his arm released ancient odours from the corrupt flesh rank under his clothes.

'The sorcerer has seen fit to leave in peace the poor spirit who took his bracelet of teeth from my sea chest. In consequence, she has departed your life. She will never now afflict the life of your son. You need no longer be fearful on his behalf. So I'd say you too owe a mighty debt of gratitude.'

'How do I repay it?'

'You leave this artful folly of a building and you never return to it. You gather those of your crew that survive where they presently cower in your camp at the southerly point of my island. You equip your sturdiest boat and you cast off and sail directly for the mainland. Do not tarry. Do not risk a single backward glance. Go now.'

My island.

'And you?'

'The party to whom I'm indebted will shortly arrive here. They plan the modest celebration to which their act of mercy entitles them. I would not subject them to the sight and sound and stink of what I became. Instead I will seek an end to myself, believing I will find it now.'

'There's no light.'

'On the contrary, this evening's events have proven there is always light, Mr Baxter.'

'I meant here, in this building. For their celebration.'

'A circumstance your architect can alter, albeit only temporarily.'

'I see.'

'It's my sincere wish you've seen everything you need to. There's no hope for you, Sir, if you have not.'

No hope on New Hope.

Baxter didn't consider that he needed any time to think matters through. It wasn't the moment for debate or even hesitation. He looked swiftly about him and then drew in a deep breath. He said a silent farewell to Seamus Ballantyne with something between a nod and a bow, more reverential this, than merely courteous. He felt profound relief and a tinge of regret but none of the loss he'd expected. He turned and walked out of the suite and away from the complex and into the rain without once looking back, a man reprieved and blessed, born again and headed he hoped and believed for some welcome kind of betterment, already in him vastly overdue.

Phil Fortescue and Ruthie Gillespie visited Liverpool a full fortnight after departing New Hope for what she suspected both of them hoped would be the final time. They'd again spent a few days in Southport, playing the antique amusement machines at the end of the pier and window-shopping along Lord Street, having arrived in Phil's babe-magnet Fiat coupe with him this time instead of her at the wheel. They'd strolled through the Wayfarer's Arcade and eaten an unseasonal ice cream on Nevill Street and toured the galleries of the Atkinson. Ruthie was impressed by the paintings purchased in the past by the town's discerning public servants. Phil told her he was too.

Ruthie revisited the Guest House at lunchtime on their first full day. And she bought the same meal she'd ordered on her last attempt to eat there. And she ate it unmolested, calmly sipping between mouthfuls at a modestly sized glass of Chablis. The surface of the drink only shivered slightly from the tremor in the hand gripping the stem of her wine glass when she lifted it from the table to her lips. She ate and drank almost sure that she would do so unhindered by the rude presence suddenly of someone undead, disconcerting in their decades-long distress at what they'd become. And that's what duly happened.

It wasn't enough, though, she didn't think. She thought that as a couple, certainty eluded them. She thought they appeared relaxed to one another rather than fraught or careworn but were neither of them really tranquil or serene or truly happy. The doubts lingered. She knew the island loomed at the back of their minds, brooding as blackly as the clouds of a gathering storm. So they travelled to Liverpool, where Phil said they would find out for sure whether a fate they equally detested now had at last finished with either or with both of them.

'Why did we come to Southport?' Ruthie asked, getting into the Fiat's passenger seat.

'So we could go to Liverpool,' Fortescue said.

'Because we have to put the bracelet back,' Ruthie said, closing her door on herself with a clunk of finality.

'That's only the half of it,' he said.

She didn't know what he meant in saying that. She didn't ask. She'd find out, she was sure but felt in no particular hurry to do so. She felt raw and almost wounded. She'd experienced too much. They both had. Their recent ordeal had wearied them, to Ruthie's tired mind and it wasn't over yet she knew, as the car ate the miles on the short journey to Liverpool and she watched the flat, verdant fields slip by on their route without another word passing between them.

It was raining when they got to Liverpool. They parked the car and walked the distance through drizzle to the Maritime Museum. The cloth bag containing the bracelet of teeth was in Fortescue's right hand. She walked on his left side. She did not take his left hand in hers, as it was her habit to do when carefree, to swing their arms together as they walked. Doing so in her present mood would have felt to her counterfeit.

'It's like the end of something,' she said.

'That's because it is the end of something, love.'

They passed a derelict cinema building, white paint peeling off plaster like some scrofulous disease; smashed lozenges of glass around a once grand, now padlocked main entrance door, Deco accents pointless in their geometric precision, a poster in a tarnished frame catching Ruthie's eye as they walked by.

The poster showed a little girl. She was very pretty in a period dress and buckled shoes and a bonnet tied with a red ribbon in a bow under her chin. She held a small bunch of flowers, white petals blossoming between both hands. She was frowning slightly, which struck a discordant note with Ruthie as she thought there'd better have been a bright smile to light up that lovely face. But it was only a glimpse, no more than a fleeting impression and then behind them.

They were there.

Ruthie shivered. She looked at the ornate, pillared façade of the building before them knowing that for the man standing beside her this was where it had all begun seven years earlier.

'I need a cigarette,' she said. 'I'll have one while you go in and get us through the formalities.'

'The formalities were done over the phone. You know that. You're just going to stand here on the cobbles, smoking in the rain?'

She blinked up at the grey sky. She said, 'The last time I did that they were the cobbles of Seamus Ballantyne's dock on the island. It was a fortnight ago and you told me you loved me.'

'Well, it was only the truth.'

'Is it still the truth?'

'I think so.'

'I'm scared, Phil,' she said, taking her cigarettes and Bic lighter from the pocket of her coat.

'We both are,' he said. He winked at her and smiled and then walked into the museum's vestibule. Ruthie smoked listening to the seagulls clamouring above, aware of the cobbles rain slicked and slippery under her feet, wondering why the little girl on the film poster had looked familiar and then as she flicked away her butt and turned to enter the museum, knowing why it was.

The room, when they'd descended the three flights of stairs that led down to it, seemed very cramped to Ruthie with two of them occupying it. She was quite used to nautical props. The Spyglass Inn back in Ventnor was full of the brass lustre of old ocean-going artefacts and that was her local pub, she'd spent a lot of time there.

The difference was that the fog bells and brass ship's clocks and bronze propellers and such in the Spyglass were only there for decoration and to lend the pub's interior an atmosphere fitting to its name. Here by contrast the objects were important of themselves. There were furled battle colours and vicious looking pikes she thought probably for fending off boarding parties. There was a pyramid of piled iron canon balls. There was a side-drum that looked as though it might have been used by a boy in a scarlet uniform to beat the marines aboard to quarters on a man of war in the time of Nelson and Trafalgar.

Phil would have been able to tell her about the true history and significance of the drum, about its provenance. He'd have been able to tell her about the specifics of everything there if she but asked. She didn't ask, though. She just stared at Seamus Ballantyne's sea chest, his initials picked out on the oak curvature of its lid, less than innocently reposed against the wall in the spot furthest from the door.

Was it less than innocent?

Ballantyne had been the master of a cruel trade. But it became barbaric only really in retrospect, in what Phil would term a revisionist perspective. At the time it was considered normal and even respectable and it was the abolitionists who'd been regarded as out of the ordinary. Judged on the values of their own harsh period, Wilberforce and his crew had been no more than a minority of vocal cranks rebelling against established convention.

He'd become truly cruel later though, had Ballantyne. When his New Hope Kingdom of Belief began to be consumed, he'd turned to the human sacrifice he'd witnessed on his voyages to Africa in a desperate bid to appease their destroyer, or to strike some kind of occult bargain. That was the story, anyway. No one living knew the specifics, but that had been the bleak and bloody purpose of the windowless church.

'It's different,' Phil said to her.

'What is?'

'Everything is.'

'You're talking in riddles,' she said.

'No, I'm not. The atmosphere's changed.'

'I wouldn't know, Phil,' she said, 'I've never been here before.'

He turned and looked at her. He glanced down at the cloth bag he was carrying, but that hung motionless and mercifully silent and still from the fingers of his right hand. He looked at her again. He said, 'Even the air in here, before, always sort of impended, Ruthie. It's hard to put into words, but it was like some unspoken threat hung over you. It was oppressive. It was horribly oppressive. Unless I'm wrong and you can feel it, that's gone.'

'It's just sort of musty and claustrophobic, down here,' Ruthie said. 'I think you should open the chest.'

'Showtime?' he said.

'I bloody well hope not.'

His free hand groped in his pocket and came out with the key. He squatted before the chest gesturing for her to squat beside him. She did so. She was aware that her breath had become shallower. She thought that her pulse had become more rapid than was usual. Her mouth was dry. It was completely quiet down there and entirely still and quite gloomy under the one dim yellow overhead light. Heating pipes gurgling suddenly somewhere startled her and she almost grabbed Phil's arm as her mind rationalised the unexpected sound. But she didn't.

Phil turned the key in the lock and raised the chest lid. She was aware that this had been an ordeal for him when he'd had to do it in the past, working here as Keeper of Maritime Artefacts, completing a routine inventory of the contents of Ballantyne's sea chest, enduring the uncomfortable sense of being watched until almost overcome by a feeling of terror he'd described as closer to instinct than any more subtle sort of foreboding.

Was he feeling something similar now? It didn't appear from his expression as though he was. His features were set, but all she could see in his eyes was a calm determination to get this done. It was different, now. He'd just said that himself. Everything was different.

The chest lid yawed open with a long, languorous creek of its elderly hinges. Phil dropped the bag containing the bracelet of teeth into it. It seemed to slither down with a sibilant hiss to rest at the bottom of the chest's heaped contents. Just teeth, she thought, tinkling innocently on their silver chain.

Evening sunlight flashed then through Ruthie's mind. She clenched her fists and closed her eyes and memories of a summer day at dusk embraced her warmly in the luminescent light at the edge of the sea. She was outside the Spice Island pub on Portsmouth Harbour 18 months earlier and was seeing Phil in the flesh for the first time. Water lapped gently in her ears. Around her there was laughter and the careless chink of drinking glasses. She could smell sun cream and a splash of spilled beer drying on a wooden tabletop.

He sat staring out at the Solent Forts, at their bulk, ominous and indistinct in heat shimmer, *his features hewn into handsomeness by imponderable loss,* she remembered thinking then, Seamus Ballantyne's pocket watch ticking in his bag to remind him of the fortitude needed to live on enduring the cruel loss of his wife. Ruthie hadn't known that about him then. She hadn't known until later when he took it out and explained that to her as the watch ticked determinedly on the table between them.

It wasn't ticking now.

The chest lid had opened on silence. The watch was there, Ballantyne's Breguet half concealed in a fold of boat cloak, its blued fingers still against the flawless white enamel of its face, its maker's name etched between the 10 and the 2 of its circle of Roman numerals.

'It stopped at a quarter to twelve,' Ruthie said aloud. 'Could have been just before midday, but wasn't. It stopped at night, just as we finished singing to Rachel, at the precise moment she went to sleep, just as we put his daughter finally to rest.' It was impossible to say this for certain, Ruthie knew. But she was equally certain it was true. Her personal history over recent years had left her with no belief any longer at all really in coincidence.

She looked at Phil, who stared unblinking at the watch. He'd made no move to pick it up and examine it further. He'd just pushed the concealing fold of boat cloak back to reveal its face fully. He stared. And Ruthie thought she knew what he was thinking and it hurt her terribly but she couldn't find it in herself to end his reverie with a touch or with further words. So she said nothing. Instead she stood and took a retreating step and waited for him to return to the present. And eventually he did, closing its lid, locking the chest, his eyes still fixed on nothing any longer there.

Or living, Ruthie thought.

You were thinking that if only you could turn back time then you would. You were thinking about your dead wife and how much you loved her. How much you still love her. Oh, Phil. You were thinking about how short and precious were those lost days and it's nothing to do with me because it all ended before we began but it haunts you still and I saw that when I saw Ballantyne's stopped watch and watched you remembering. And wishing too, which is the worst part. It's no one's fault, but it's no good, Phil, because if you live in the past, then of course we have no future.

When they got back outside again, Ruthie thought the strengthening rain only appropriate. She made no move to take Phil's hand in hers. They walked silently, side-by-side. When they passed the derelict cinema, the poster in the tarnished frame was blank. Between the pavement they walked on and the road, a small bouquet of white blossoms lay trailing its lost petals in the gutter.

Love F.G. Cottam?
Join the Readers' Club

Get your next F.G. Cottam thriller for FREE

If you sign up today, this is what you'll get:

1. A Cottam exclusive; his brand new novella, *The Going and the Rise*
2. Details of Cottam's new novels and the opportunity to get copies in advance of publication
3. The chance to win exclusive prizes in regular competitions.

Interested? It takes less than a minute to sign up. You can get *The Going and the Rise* by visiting www.fgcottam.com

Manufactured by Amazon.ca
Bolton, ON